RISKING HER HEART

RISKING HER HEART

A CONTEMPORARY ROMANCE NOVEL

ROCHELLE KATZMAN

Book Antiqua font used with permission from Microsoft.

ISBN: 978-1-63161-031-8

Published by TCK Publishing

www.TCKPublishing.com

Get discounts and special deals on books at

www.TCKPublishing.com/Bookdeals

Sign up for Rochelle's newsletter to stay tuned on her latest releases and updates:

www.RochelleKatzman.com/free

CONTENTS

1

LIVVIE'S HAND TREMBLED as she held her raffle ticket. They had been calling out winners for the last hour, but so far, she hadn't won. Hopefully, it'd stay that way. She hated these events, as they seemed to bring out the worst in her. And nothing could be worse than the day she'd had.

Today, she had been fired. She had to keep repeating that in her head for it to sink in, and so far, it hadn't. Writing for *Raven's Edge* had been the only sane thing she had in her life, and now it was gone. Like all of her ex boyfriends.

If it was up to her, she'd give her raffle ticket to Carly and then run out of the catering hall as fast as she could. If Livvie hadn't promised her best friend that she would attend this event months ago, she would have cancelled. But this was for the autistic school for children that Carly worked for, and Livvie wanted to support her best friend.

She glanced around the room at all the men wearing tuxedos, and the women in long black dresses like the one she wore. She wondered which husbands were cheating on their wives. If she could guess, she'd say most of them. Rather like the producers at the meeting this morning, especially William Krasner, the executive producer of the show. How many times had he asked her a question and then subtly touched her boob? So many times, she couldn't count. Each time he had said it was an accident. But that wasn't true. The décor in William's office gave the illusion everything was perfect. As she sat in the black leather chair, clutching her small severance package in her sweaty hands, her eyes scanned the bamboo flooring and the expensive artwork on the newly painted beige walls.

What she'd found most disturbing about William's office were the pictures sitting on his glass table next to the beige leather couch: one large photograph of his two children with him and his wife dressed in matching white t-shirts and jeans, and an older picture of his wife in her wedding dress. The office made it seem as if William was a successful, happily married man. But rumors were flying around the set that he was cheating on his wife. He had even tried with Livvie. Luckily, she still had morals and turned him down flat. She never wanted to be the other woman. Every rich man she had ever known who held some type of power cheated because they could. They got away with it because no one dared to cross them.

"Stop looking so miserable, or your face is going to stay that way," Carly said as Livvie rolled her eyes. "Besides, I think your number is going to be called soon. I can feel it."

And that was why Livvie was trembling. She hated hearing her number called, as with it came a momentary sense of panic because she'd have to run up to the front of the room while her table cheered, all attention on her.

Carly nudged her in the arm. "Just pretend you're happy. For me. I needed you to come here. The school needed you. If I wasn't an employee, I'd have bought a raffle ticket, but I'm not allowed. And if it weren't for this school, I wouldn't have any money to go to the clubs or go shopping with you. You owe this school."

"I don't shop anymore," Livvie responded. She was paid well writing for *Raven's Edge*, but living in Los Angeles was expensive. Her savings account wasn't large. Coming here tonight had been expensive, especially with forking out $100 for a raffle ticket.

"You're doing a good deed, Livvie. And if the universe sees you doing a good deed, maybe it will help you out," Carly said in a stern tone.

"Maybe," she whispered under her breath. If only life worked that way. Her entire existence was a struggle. Most people either had career issues or love-life issues, but as of today, Livvie had both.

Carly grabbed her arm, which was already bruised from when she had nudged it.

"I have a feeling you're going to win the next one. Every woman in this room will die from envy."

Livvie squinted as she looked at the front of the room to see what the next raffle prize was. And then she stopped breathing. She didn't want to win that one. She would be far happier if she won the prize after that—a basket filled with lottery tickets.

Frantically, she scanned the catering hall for a place to hide. But she was stuck in an enormous-sized room with marble floors, crystal chandeliers, and an endless number of tables. She felt as if she couldn't breathe.

The presenter resumed speaking.

"The next raffle prize is a one-week stay at Morganthal Winery owned by Mr. Drake Morganthal. He will personally give the lucky winner a tour of his vineyard, and you'll have the opportunity to taste many of his highly acclaimed wines."

Carly grabbed her arm again and spoke in a loud whisper. "Could you imagine spending a full week at Drake Morganthal's house? You'd definitely have to find his bedroom and then sneak out of your room at night and surprise him." Carly laughed. She really was breathtakingly beautiful. When she laughed, her entire face lit up. She and Livvie looked the exact opposite, and she seemed to attract men wherever they went. Even tonight, Carly was wearing a short, hot-pink silk dress with little spaghetti straps. It accentuated her long blonde hair, pale skin, and blue eyes. Livvie was wearing a long, strapless black dress, which matched her long dark hair. They both had ivory skin and blue eyes of different shades. Carly's were sky blue while Livvie's were darker.

"This has proven to be the most popular raffle prize offered. In fact, this was the first year we had to turn people away at the door because of fire regulations. Mainly women, from what I've heard."

Everyone in the room laughed at the presenter's words, which jarred Livvie out of her thoughts and back to reality. Drake Morganthal was gorgeous, successful, and powerful—a deadly combination in her eyes. Models, actresses, and every other female on this planet drooled either all over him or all over his picture. From what she'd read, he used to work on Wall Street, making millions or probably billions, and then he bought a winery in Napa. He was well known, rich, and sexy as hell. And these were the reasons she hoped not to win. Because she had recently decided to no longer live in an illusion. She had taken off her rose-colored glasses, stepped on them, and threw them away. Those types of men couldn't be trusted, and she *had* to stay away from them. She had no intention of staying away from *all* men, only alpha-males. Her new dream man was humble, quiet, and treated her like a queen.

"The winner is ticket 89976."

Apparently, the universe had a great sense of humor.

2

TWO MONTHS LATER, Livvie arrived at Drake Morganthal's house, which was more like a castle, actually. She stood in the entrance hall, her suitcase by her side as she looked around in awe. From the pictures on the Internet, she expected his home to look beautiful, but in person it was surreal. A security guard had let her in after making sure she was truly Olivia Collins, the lucky raffle winner. She was definitely the raffle winner. The lucky part remained to be seen.

A bald man in a dark suit, who introduced himself as Mr. Birkshire, had welcomed her to the winery and told her to wait in the entrance hall, and he'd go find Mr. Morganthal.

Livvie wondered if he was talking about the owner, *Drake* Morganthal. Last night, she'd made a bet with Carly regarding whether he would be here this week, and if he was, if he'd even give her the time of day. Livvie had bet that he'd either not be here, or he wouldn't give five minutes of his time to some random raffle winner. Carly said that he would not only be here, but the minute he saw how pretty Livvie was, he'd personally show her a great week. Livvie adamantly disagreed.

"I'm sorry, Ms. Collins. Mr. Morganthal was delayed but should be here in a moment. Is there anything you'd like to drink while you wait?" Mr. Birkshire asked.

Livvie smiled. "Nope, I'm good. Thank you." This whole thing reminded her of how she felt when she was sitting in a dentist's office, waiting for her name to be called. She couldn't understand why she felt so unnerved. Even if she was meeting one of the most eligible bachelors in the world, it wasn't as if she'd be spending time with him this week.

Besides, today she was turning over a new leaf and taking back control of her life. She was tired of having a man dictate her every move for her, whether it was the producers at *Raven's Edge*, her ex-boyfriend, Zach, who had cheated, or her first love, Liam, who had done a number on her. For the last few months, she'd been mourning over all of them. Every minute of every day her heart ached. It had taken her months to get back to herself after Zach. For one solid year, she had allowed Zach to call the shots in their relationship. She worked around his schedule to see him, she ate where he wanted to eat, and she never argued when he'd cancelled plans at the last minute. She'd been so scared of having another failed relationship; she'd lost herself.

As of now, she'd decided the ache in her heart had to stop, and she refused to fill it with another unhealthy relationship. She had painfully learned her lessons, and she had no interest in repeating them. She deserved to be with a man who respected her enough to commit and who loved her inside and out, regardless of her flaws.

Carly told Livvie the best way to start fresh was to go on vacation. Since she still didn't have another writing job, she'd opted for the free trip. The raffle prize included airfare, car rental, and a one-week, all-inclusive stay at Morganthal Winery.

Staying at Drake Morganthal's home was not exactly the best way to start her new life when she'd sworn off arrogant men. Her next boyfriend must be the opposite of arrogant. The moment she detected even a drop of conceit, he would be out of her life forever.

While she waited, she continued to look around. The entrance hall looked like one you'd see in a fancy house magazine. The floors were shiny, dark wood, and the walls were a rich shade of beige. About twenty feet away were the fanciest set of stairs she had ever seen. The staircase curved dramatically, leading to a bridge at the top with a wooden banister elegantly tying it all together. A magnificent black chandelier with candles hung from the gigantic cathedral ceiling. There were no pictures on the walls, but candelabras were everywhere. In front of the stairs stood a round, mahogany wood table with an enormous, square, glass vase containing all sorts of flowers. She didn't know a lot about flowers, but she did spot pink ginger in there. On the far wall, facing her, were windows overlooking the vineyard and rolling hills for as far as her eyes could see. Drake Morganthal had exquisite taste.

Last night, she hadn't been able to help herself. Carly and she had obsessively Googled him. At thirty-three years old, not only was he the hottest man, ever, but also extremely successful. One minute he was on the news, giving financial advice, and the next, he was appearing on billboards promoting his winery. When he wasn't working, he usually had a famous model or hot actress on his arm. The paparazzi went crazy over him. His winery had only been around for four years, but it was already extremely popular and profitable. He had made billions on Wall Street and had suddenly quit and started Morganthal Winery after working one summer in a vineyard in France.

Desperately needing fresh air, Livvie ran to the front door and opened it. Inhaling Napa deep into her lungs felt good. This was the reason she agreed to come here. She needed to get out of Los Angeles, breathe the fresh air in Napa, and enjoy being in nature. These things were important for her to fully heal, so she could find Mr. Right, and stop dating arrogant assholes.

"Ah, there you are, Ms. Collins. I'm so sorry to keep you waiting. It's been a crazy morning."

At the sound of the deep, masculine voice, Livvie's first instinct was to run. *Everything will be okay*, she kept telling herself. If she didn't feel comfortable staying here, she could leave. She wasn't trapped. As she gathered her courage, she gripped the door tighter.

"Oh, no, I hope you're not leaving already," the man said.

Livvie took one last deep breath of the Napa air then turned around. But the site awaiting her at the top of the grand staircase was nothing she could have prepared herself for. Drake Morganthal was gorgeous. No wonder he was known to date only famous models or actress.

"I wasn't leaving. I was only breathing in the fresh Napa air. It's cleaner than it is in Los Angeles." Livvie said the first thing that came to mind, and she expected a funny comeback line. Cocky men always had funny comeback lines. It wasn't fair to think this man was cocky. For all she knew, he was the nicest man in the world. But usually, in her experience, good-looking men who never committed to a woman acted cocky.

But Drake Morganthal didn't have a funny comeback line. In fact, he had no line at all. He stood there staring at her, and although she couldn't see his eyes, as he was at the top of the stairs, she could feel his gaze on her, and it was making her feel self-conscious. Maybe it was her outfit. Carly told her to wear something that made her look presentable, in case she saw Drake. But Livvie hadn't listened. Not that she didn't look presentable... But she was wearing her blue tank top with a pink butterfly on it and her skinny jeans. At least she'd flat-ironed her long, dark hair before she left for the airport that morning.

"You're Olivia Collins? The raffle winner?" Drake asked.

Livvie swallowed hard. "I am," she said. "Did I come on the wrong week?" She had no idea why he looked surprised to see her.

Drake slowly walked down the stairs, not breaking eye contact with her. The closer he got to her the better she could see his thick, dark hair and piercing green eyes.

"You came the right week. Sorry, I guess I'm a little thrown."

"Don't worry. I throw people off all the time." She didn't, but it was the best she could come up with, especially since he was standing close to her. And he looked so tall…definitely six foot something.

Drake stepped even closer. Livvie's heartbeat sped up. Was he making a move? They'd just met. But all he did was push the front door closed over her head behind her.

"I'm Drake Morganthal." He held out his hand, obviously expecting her to take it.

"You already know my name, but please, call me Livvie. Everyone does. Even the people who I throw off." She took Drake's hand but immediately tried to pull back. His grip was strong, but the skin-to-skin contact shook her. His touch felt oddly intimate. How crazy was that? She'd just met the man.

Drake laughed under his breath, while shaking his head. "You have a good sense of humor. We need that around here."

He was still holding her hand, but after another moment, he loosened his grip, and she was able to pull away.

"Well, then I'll try to be as funny as I can this week." She smiled wide.

Drake inhaled sharply, taking a step away from her and running his hands through his thick, dark hair. Did her smile scare him? Was it too much?

Drake cleared his throat. "I'm glad to hear it," he said. "And welcome to my winery. Do you have any questions?"

"Are you going to be here all week?" As handsome as he was, she was hoping he would have somewhere else to go. She felt so on edge around him. Plus, she really wanted to win the bet she'd made with Carly.

Drake chuckled. "Since this is my house, yes. Does that present a problem?"

"What? Oh, no. I was just curious." It did, but she couldn't tell him that.

Drake took another small step back. Did he feel as uncomfortable as she did?

"I'm sorry," he said. "My mind is a little preoccupied. Congratulations on winning the raffle."

"Thank you. Someone had to win it."

"I'm glad it was you."

"You are?" Livvie asked. Maybe he was good at giving lines.

"Yes, a slimy old man could have won," he said.

"Or an ax-murderer," Livvie added.

Drake laughed. "Yea, that would have been bad."

"So I could see why you're relieved it was me." She smiled at him again.

The laughter she saw in his eyes changed.

"That and many other reasons," he said, his tone suddenly serious.

"I could still be an ax-murderer. Have you felt how heavy my suitcase is? I could have an ax and other devices packed in there." Livvie knew she was rambling about nothing, but she was trying to find her center. Being around this man was making her feel so unbalanced.

Drake smiled, and it made him look even sexier. She hoped she'd survive this week.

"I haven't picked it up, but I'll remember to lock my door at night."

He didn't lock his door at night? Carly had told her that if he was here, Livvie should sneak into his room at night and get under his covers naked. She had to bite her bottom lip to keep from laughing.

"Smart man," she said.

"You're a breath of fresh air, Olivia."

He didn't want to call her Livvie.

"And I like fresh air, Mr. Morganthal."

"Shit," he said under his breath. "My manners seem to be nonexistent with you. Please, call me Drake."

"Okay, Drake." Hearing his name on her tongue felt strange. She'd said it a thousand times to Carly, but saying it to him was a different story.

His eyes became super intense. "Tomorrow morning, I'll take you around my vineyard. You're old enough to drink wine?"

"Are you serious? I'm twenty-nine."

"You look young."

"I use a good moisturizer."

Drake laughed and shook his head. "I guess I should have asked if you liked wine?"

"It's fine."

"Fine as in good, or fine as in okay?"

"Fine as in fine."

Drake laughed and shook his head again. "I'll teach you to like wine."

She didn't want him to teach her anything. After this encounter, she wanted him to be busy at work and forgetting she even existed. This man was a charmer. A dangerous charmer.

"You don't have to, but thank you. I'm sure you're super busy. I'll make sure I stay out of your hair." She'd almost said "sexy hair," but she'd resisted the urge. Barely...

"I'll make time for you."

Livvie sighed. Great. Now she was in trouble. "Thank you," she said.

"Come, I'll show you to your room. Mr. Birkshire will bring up your luggage later."

Livvie followed him up the stairs and down a long hallway. Walking beside him like this felt strange. She felt there was an expectation when a woman walked with a man, especially with a man she'd just met. She'd have to be charming and make small-talk. There was an intimacy about walking side by side, even if there was no hand holding, which, of course, there wasn't. But she wasn't making small-talk or being charming. They were both silent. And it felt natural.

Drake held the door for her, which led to another hallway. He was acting like a gentleman. A charming, good-looking gentleman...and one who wasn't known for making a commitment. Bad combination in her eyes.

Maybe she should leave now, but she didn't want to. Especially when he opened the second-to-last door in the hallway.

Livvie gasped. "It's beautiful. Is this my room?"

Drake chuckled. "For the week, it is."

Livvie thought he emphasized "week," which made sense. That was probably longer than most of his relationships had lasted.

Livvie walked farther into the room as she took it all in. Three of the walls were painted a very pale pink, and it looked as if an artist had painted beautiful white roses on them. Floor-to-ceiling windows covered the wall across from her, allowing a view that overlooked the vineyard and the mountains. She felt as if she was standing on a cloud with the magical view in front of her. The room had a big white couch. Throw pillows covered in a pink-and-white rose-patterned fabric were lined up across the seat. In fact, all the furniture in the room was white, and on the night table stood a vase filled with real pink and white roses. She looked at Drake over her shoulder.

"Thank you," she whispered.

She walked toward the enormous windows overlooking the vineyard. Before she drove up the hill to come here, she'd parked at the side of Main Street and had gotten out of her rental car to get her first glimpse of Morganthal Winery. She had gazed up at the breathtaking, fairytale-like white castle, and she'd felt hopeful, excited even. She must have spent thirty minutes standing there staring like that, but she didn't care. Even if Drake Morganthal himself saw her, it wouldn't have mattered.

She felt Drake come up from behind her. Gently, he moved her hair away, uncovering her eyes. The action started her.

"Sorry, I had to do that. I wanted to look into your eyes and see what you see when you look at my vineyard."

Talk about feeling thrown off. "It's beautiful," she answered honestly. "It's perfect. Exactly what I needed."

"And what do you need?" he asked softly.

"A week of freedom."

"I'll personally make sure you have the week you've envisioned," he said, touching her hair gently again.

It was driving her crazy. His nearness alone made her body pulse and her cheeks flush. And his touch added to the heady excitement, like an electric force going from his hand to her hair. Not being able to help herself, she subtly moved into his hand that was caressing her. And then she recalled she'd only just met him.

"I envisioned a week alone, walking through your vineyard," she said, her voice breathless.

"We'll see about that," he said, before stepping away. "Mr. Birkshire will come at seven o'clock and take you to the dining room for dinner. I'll see you then." He walked away, but when he reached the door, he turned.

"Don't worry if you don't like wine. I'll think of other things to do to occupy your time. And I can be *very* creative." Then he turned back around and left Livvie standing there dumbfounded.

And in an instant, a fear of Livvie's came true. Another man in her life had uttered the last word, and he was sleeping right next door.

3

AT SEVEN O'CLOCK on the dot, Mr. Birkshire knocked on her bedroom door. With her luggage and purse having been delivered to her room immediately after her arrival, Livvie had time to rummage through it and pick something to wear for dinner. First, she had to decide what look to go for. What does an unemployed writer wear to dinner at Drake Morganthal's house, with Drake Morganthal himself? She contemplated for some time, and she almost called Carly. Almost. She wasn't ready to hear the familiar sound of her best friend's voice for two reasons. One, she was worried she would burst into tears, and two, she knew Carly would make a bigger deal than necessary about being near Drake Morganthal for the week. And it wasn't such a big deal. Well, it *was* because it was a once-in-a-lifetime experience, yet it *wasn't* for the same reason.

After spending what felt like an endless amount of time in thought, Livvie chose an off-the-shoulder, black cocktail dress that stopped just above her knee.

Sexy but not over the top. She could have chosen something less sexy, but she felt Drake expected her to wear a dress. Not that she needed to impress him or anything, but she was also wearing the dress for herself, as it gave her more confidence. When she'd packed, she hadn't been sure what she would need, but luckily, she had brought a little of everything. Once she'd finished dressing, she slipped on her high-heeled black sandals and then opened her door to a serious-faced Mr. Birkshire. Did Drake pay him not to smile?

"Good evening, Miss Collins. Drake is awaiting your presence in the main dining room. Please, follow me."

"Thank you."

Livvie inhaled, feeling as if she was taking her last breath, and followed him down the long hallway until they reached the grand staircase. She imagined what it might feel like if she lived here and walked down these steps every day.

Once in the entrance hall, he led her through an enormous room filled with oversized couches, a large, marble bar, and full-length windows overlooking the vineyard. She liked how all the floors throughout the house were a dark shade of wood with rugs to give it a comfortable feel.

The dining room was also beautiful. Again, windows overlooked the vineyard. The walls were the same shade of green as the outside hills and the vines themselves. There was a long, dark wooden table—the exact one Livvie had seen in a movie. More candelabras decorated the walls, and the white candles had been lit for ambiance. But the most magnificent sight was the dark-haired, extremely tall, green-eyed man standing perfectly straight in a black suit that clung to his body as if it was made for him. And with all of his money, it probably had been. Livvie's nerves increased, and her body trembled.

"Cold, Olivia?" Drake smirked and motioned for her to walk farther into the room.

He jarred Livvie out of her thoughts, and she turned to thank Mr. Birkshire for walking her here when she noticed he was gone. She had been so engrossed in analyzing Drake's appearance that she hadn't even heard him leave.

Drake had asked her a question, but she didn't think it required an answer, so she took a deep breath and gracefully walked toward the handsome man who was holding her captive with his eyes.

"Why so formal?" she asked once she reached him.

Drake raised his eyebrow, looking as sexy as hell.

"The suit or calling you by your full first name?"

Livvie couldn't help but smile. "Both," she said.

Drake didn't answer. Instead, he gently put his hand on Livvie's arm, but the feeling his touch invoked inside her felt anything but gentle. Once again, his flesh against hers made her feel as if she was on fire...intense and crazy. Livvie looked into Drake's eyes as if he could explain why she reacted to him that way. His gaze seemed distracted.

Unfortunately, it seemed as if he was able to un-distract himself pretty quickly. Regaining his composure far easier than she did, Drake pulled out a chair for her, which was right next to his. The feeling of panic overwhelmed her. She gripped the back of the chair, fearing she would faint.

"Is there a problem?" Drake looked concerned.

"No one else is joining us?" Livvie tried to mask her panic.

Drake shook his head. "No, does that bother you?"

Yes, it bothered her. She wasn't exactly disappointed; "uneasy" would be a far more accurate description. Panic stricken, more like it. When she'd won the raffle ticket, she had imagined herself eating at a table filled with tourists or his employees who worked in his vineyards. Not just with him…alone.

"No," she whispered, which was a direct lie, and she despised lying. Trying to avoid further eye contact, she sat down.

Drake remained standing but moved closer to the back of Livvie's chair. Goosebumps erupted on her back, causing her heartbeat to speed up. She felt so unnerved with him behind her; she wished he would sit down. Instead, he leaned over and whispered in her ear.

"I didn't take you for a liar."

Livvie didn't move a muscle for two reasons. First, his breath tickled her cheek and felt amazing. Second, Livvie just happened to be inhaling as he'd bent down, and she got a good whiff of him. *Oh my goodness*. He smelled of cedar and a trace of what she'd imagined was his vines. His scent was intoxicating and masculine. Carly once told her that if a woman liked the way a man smelled, she was finished. Livvie hoped her best friend was wrong.

She had no idea how to respond. How did he know she was lying? They had only met a little while ago. Drake straightened and then sat down in his chair. At last, she could breathe again!

"I wasn't lying." *Another lie.*

Luckily, Drake seemed to have ignored her.

Mr. Birkshire appeared and placed two square white plates in front of Drake and her. Two men followed and placed the sterling silverware down. Each man was dressed impeccably in a dark suit. One of them looked at Livvie and smiled. He placed a napkin on her lap and smoothed it out for her in an almost sensual way.

Okay, that felt uncomfortable.

"That's enough, Andrew. She's more than capable of straightening the napkin on her lap," Drake said in the most authoritative tone she'd ever heard.

Andrew's eyes widened, and then he immediately exited the room, followed by everyone else.

"Thank you," Livvie said.

Drake looked up at Livvie and half smiled. "For what?"

"For coming to my rescue. I felt a little uncomfortable." Livvie smiled back.

"You don't need a man coming to your rescue."

Livvie's smile faded. Drake's words hit a little too close to home. She'd always thought she did need a man. That was how she had been raised. But since Zach had hurt her, she had decided she was okay on her own. He was right. She didn't need a man to come to her rescue.

"Thank you," she responded.

"But you're still more comfortable lying than telling the truth."

Mr. Birkshire and the others returned to the room and placed a wineglass and a water glass in front of each of them. Livvie was relieved. She wasn't a liar. She had just refused to tell him her deepest, darkest feelings. She had only just met the man, after all.

Mr. Birkshire poured red wine into Drake's glass. Drake swirled it, smelled it, and then tasted it. It was the sexiest thing Livvie had ever seen. She had watched pretentious men and women taste wine that way before, but the way Drake closed his eyes and sniffed it seemed like a passionate act. He was revering it, treasuring it, almost making love to it.

All sorts of images sprang to Livvie's mind, such as how his long fingers would feel against her body. He was touching the glass gently yet firmly at the same time. Is that how he touched his women? How he would touch her? When his lips tasted the wine, he savored it. Is that how he acted when he kissed a woman or went down on her? Livvie blushed and immediately stopped her dangerous train of thought. Drake, on the other hand, opened his eyes and stared directly at her. She was sure he knew what she was thinking. Without breaking his stare, he spoke.

"Perfect. Thank you, Mr. Birkshire."

Mr. Birkshire nodded and then left the room. Andrew placed salad plates in front of them both, and the no-name employee placed salad from a large bowl onto their plates. The second they turned around to leave, Livvie became nervous. There was no way she could avoid the lying issue. She sighed as they closed the door. But she needed to be an adult and deal with this head on.

"I don't lie," she said the minute they left.

Drake raised his eyebrow. "But you do avoid the truth. You'd rather avoid telling others how you really feel."

"And what do you think the truth is?" She hated it when men thought they knew her better than she knew herself. It infuriated her.

Drake began eating his salad but remained focused on her. Then he dropped his fork onto his plate and sat back in his chair. Livvie picked up her fork but stopped before she loaded it with lettuce.

"If we're going to survive the next week together, Olivia, I need you to be honest with me. I don't want you thinking of me as the Drake Morganthal you've read about." Drake ran his hands through his hair. "Fuck, I don't even think of myself as *that* Drake Morganthal."

"What do you want from me?" Livvie replied, although what she really meant was: *What do you expect from me?* Because men always expected something from her. All she ever wanted was to be herself with a man and for him to accept that. But she always had to be who they wanted her to be. Not anymore. Those days were done. If her next boyfriend didn't love her for who she was, then screw him.

Drake inhaled and then spoke in such a serious tone that left Livvie feeling as if she was being hypnotized.

"I want you to be honest with me about how you're feeling. Communicate with me. I understand you're here because you won the raffle, but I'd also like your opinion on some of my wines. You're not a big wine drinker, so your opinion and ideas will be fresher, not clouded, more innocent."

Of course, this is all about his precious wines. Maybe if she weren't a raffle winner but some gorgeous model or actress, he would want her to be honest for different reasons.

"I like wine," Livvie responded honestly. "I don't enjoy the feeling of not being in control."

Drake smiled softly. "We have that in common then."

Livvie swallowed hard. "You like being in control?" *Of course he likes being in control.*

Drake picked up his fork and resumed eating but paused and looked intensely into her eyes. "I don't like it, Olivia. I need it. I demand it."

Drake delved into his salad, and Livvie joined him. Her appetite was non-existent, but eating gave her something to do besides staring into Drake's intoxicating eyes. After a few minutes of silence, it became awkward.

"You told me your family doesn't live here, but do some of your friends?" *Or a girlfriend?*

Unfortunately, he looked up at her again, his eyes even more intense.

"No, and I have no girlfriend. Nor do I plan on getting one. I have no interest in that type of relationship."

Livvie inhaled. He seemed good at reading her mind. Not that he needed to explain to her in detail that he was commitment phobic. She wasn't asking him about his dating life. But they were spending an entire week together, and if they were going to be eating alone like this, she needed to make sure she wasn't acting inappropriately or saying anything wrong. Like touching his arm as she had earlier. The sparks that had gone off inside her were not something she would want to repeat if he had a girlfriend. Even though it was completely innocent.

But she could sense in Drake's changed demeanor that her prying into his personal life pissed him off. She wouldn't care if he had a girlfriend. Well, that was another lie. She would care, but not for the reasons he thought. Zach had cheated on her with his assistant, and she never wanted to be the woman with a man who had a girlfriend—or a wife, for that matter.

"You don't need to be composed around me," Drake said softly.

"Is that why you're mad at me?"

"Why would you think I'm mad at you?"

They had both completely stopped eating.

"Because I asked you a personal question."

Drake pushed his chair closer to the table and to Livvie. He then took a big sip of wine and motioned for Livvie to do the same. She listened, and as the delicious wine touched her tongue she felt calmer.

"I don't mind the personal questions. I expect them. You're as curious about me as I am about you," he told her.

Livvie took another sip of the wine.

"But I'd like you to remove the walls around you that you're holding on to so tightly. Remove the baggage." Drake took a sip of wine.

"So I can give you an honest and innocent opinion of your wines?" Livvie asked with a hint of sarcasm.

Drake held the glass in his hand and looked at her. "No, so we can have a more enjoyable week together."

Mr. Birkshire and the others appeared again. They quickly cleared the table and placed lobster tails and mashed potatoes in front of them then left. She was convinced they felt the rising tension in the room.

They ate in silence. Livvie wasn't that hungry, but the lobster tail tasted decadent.

"You know," Drake said while pushing his plate away. "When I was approached with the idea of allowing a random raffle winner to stay at my home for one full week, I hated the idea."

Livvie put down her fork and pushed her plate away as well.

"I kept thinking some stranger would win who would grate on my nerves. Someone who was so in awe of my fame or someone afraid of it. Worse still, I thought I'd get someone who would manipulate and figure out a way for me to benefit their life according to their needs."

Livvie swallowed and looked away.

"But I agreed to the raffle idea, anyway."

"Why?" she asked, glancing back at him.

"Because it was for a charity very dear to me, and except for some bottles of expensive wine that would mean nothing to most people, I had nothing else of value to offer. I value this charity very much. It was also for a school, and they didn't think raffling bottles of wines was appropriate. I guess I could have written them a check, but they needed more prizes."

Livvie looked away again. He was up to something. In her experience, men never revealed their feelings without a good reason. Somehow, she knew she was tied into the reason.

"So imagine my surprise when you walked through the door," Drake continued. "And not only because of your exquisite beauty."

A twinkle appeared in Drake's eyes, and he continued talking. "You see, Olivia, after meeting you, I realized you don't fit into any of those categories."

"I don't?" Livvie asked.

Drake leaned back in his chair. "No, you don't grate on my nerves. You're not thinking of ways I can benefit you. You're not in awe of my fame, and you're not afraid of it, either." Drake paused. "But you are afraid of me."

"I'm not," Livvie said.

"Shhhhhh…you are." Drake paused again. "You see, Olivia—"

"Please, call me Livvie."

"You see, Olivia."

Livvie rolled her eyes, and Drake ignored her.

"The woman who ordered a red rental car, the woman who parked on Main Street and looked up at my castle was a courageous, spontaneous woman who was taking a risk by coming here but was very much up for the challenge."

Great, thought Livvie. She should have known a man such as Drake Morganthal would have cameras everywhere.

She also had a strong feeling she wouldn't like what he said next. And when Drake grabbed her hand, which she hadn't noticed was clenched in a tight fist, she felt as if she wanted to run. But she couldn't. Drake opened her tight fingers and in slow circles with his thumb caressed her palm. Then he continued speaking in an almost trancelike way.

"But the woman who looked into my eyes for the first time in her life, and the woman who showed up at my dinner table wasn't afraid of my fame. Instead, she was afraid of me, as a man."

Livvie began to speak, but he instantly cut her off.

"Please, let me finish."

It took everything for her not to tell him to fuck off. But she couldn't with his thumb making hypnotizing circles on her palm.

"And as a man, imagine my surprise when I saw how beautiful you are. Imagine my surprise when I looked into your alluring blue eyes for the first time, and it took all my willpower to look away. Imagine my surprise when your touch in the guest bedroom set me on edge, making me want to throw you onto the bed and fuck you right there and then. Forget about the handshake. I never knew a handshake could feel so sensual. And imagine my surprise when I watched you sip your wine, and I felt jealous that the wineglass felt your lips before I did."

Stunned that they were sharing similar thoughts and fantasies, Livvie tried to move her hand away, but Drake wouldn't let her. Her heart was beating wildly, but this time it had nothing to do with anxiety. Instead, her body felt as if it was on high alert. Her nipples hardened under her dress, and she had to squeeze her thighs together, afraid of making his dining room chair wet.

"So you see, we have a problem, Olivia."

"We do?" Livvie whispered. She knew what her problem was. She needed to stay away from him.

"Yes, we do." Drake continued torturing her with his hand massage. "I want you to be the woman I saw approaching my house. The woman who's craving freedom and adventure."

Livvie licked her bottom lip. She didn't mean to, but she was so engrossed in his words. And so thrown off kilter by how well he could read her. No man had ever managed that. No man had ever cared enough.

"What do you suggest?" Livvie whispered again, as her mind was warning her of danger.

Drake softly smiled. "I'm glad you asked." He paused. "As a man, I want to help you find that adventure. Help you find the freedom you so badly crave. So I have two ideas."

Livvie swallowed, her entire body pulsing.

"My first idea, which is my preference, is that I fuck you every day and every night for the next week. I'll make sure you come multiple times, every time. I'll make sure you're completely satisfied, and you'll have the week you crave. But at the end of the week, we'll be done. I don't do long-term, committed relationships. And you must know this up front. But I guarantee you'll have one of the best weeks of your life if not *the* best week."

Livvie could smell her arousal. She prayed Drake couldn't smell it, too. "Or?"

Drake was no longer smiling. "Or you could know how badly I want you. How badly I want to do all of these dark and dirty things to you." Drake paused again. "But I won't touch you, other than occasionally on your arm or hand. The type of touch a friend would give you. I'll show you around my vineyard, eat with you, and spend time with you, again as friends would do. And I want you to find freedom in that. Freedom to know I want you as a man wants a beautiful woman, but I give you my word I won't act on my desires. You're safe with me, Olivia, to let go. To be the woman who's inside you."

Livvie looked Drake deep in his eyes to see if he was being sincere. And from what she could see, he was. What would it be like to be with a man who had no intention of touching her sexually, all the while, knowing he wanted her? He was right. There was a certain freedom to that. And the fact he was willing to give her this meant something. At the same time, could she go a full week without touching him? Knowing that this beautiful man could do all these kinky things to her, which she craved. Things that would make her feel free but in a different way. Things he had probably done to tons of women before her.

Before she could make up her mind Drake released her hand. Mr. Birkshire entered with Andrew, and they cleared the table and looked at Drake expectantly.

"Dessert, Olivia?"

Drake raised an eyebrow, and Livvie knew he was demanding she make a choice. He hadn't given her much time to analyze his proposition. But the other men being in the room made her think clearer. Drake had no intention of going further with her than this week. And she was sure her heart could not take it.

"No, thank you." She made her choice, and there was no going back now. She liked the feel of his hand massage, but there was no way she would go further. Drake as a friend was one thing. Drake as a lover was another. Not only was she through with alpha-men, there was no way in hell she'd be with one who was also a commitment-phobe. No, thank you.

Drake looked at Mr. Birkshire and nodded. The other men left the room, leaving Drake and her alone once again. He stood, and Livvie stood with him.

"I still have work to do. May I walk you back to your room, or do you remember the way?"

"I know the way," she said.

Drake nodded, and together they walked toward the door on the other end of the dining room. When they reached it, Drake grabbed Livvie and threw her against the wall. With one hand he grabbed both of hers and placed them above her head, so she was unable to move. And with the other he reached under her dress and touched her crotch on the outside of her panties.

Livvie's clit began to pulse, as his hand remained firmly against her most intimate area.

"And as a man, I wanted to make sure the first woman who has rejected me was as affected by him as he was by her." Swiftly, Drake moved her panties aside and thrust two fingers inside her.

Livvie couldn't help but moan. He suddenly stopped, instantly removed his fingers, and released her hands.

"As I suspected, you're dripping wet, Olivia."

Drake looked into her eyes, and Livvie knew he was giving her another opportunity to change her mind. Of course, she'd love if he fucked her, but it was wrong, unless he proved otherwise.

He leaned in toward her and inhaled.

"Vanilla, how appropriate," Drake whispered in her ear and then straightened up. He looked at her for a moment, nodded, and then he opened the door and left.

She could have followed him as that was the direction of the stairs, but she didn't. She needed to compose herself first. This may have been the first time Drake had been rejected, but it was also the first time she hadn't given in to a man. And even though her body was screaming at her that she had made the wrong choice, she was convinced this was the start of a very interesting week.

LIVVIE HAD SET her alarm for four-thirty the next morning, making sure she had time for a shower before meeting Drake in his vineyard. At least she assumed she was meeting Drake in his vineyard. When she had arrived at her room the night before, there had been a note under her door from Mr. Birkshire, informing her to be ready by 5:30 a.m. for a vineyard tour. But after choosing Plan B instead of Plan A, she might not be meeting Drake after all.

Last night had been complete torture. No matter how she looked at it, if she slept with him, she'd never hear from him again after this week, and if she denied herself and didn't sleep with him, she still wouldn't hear from him after this week. Both thoughts depressed her terribly. She obsessed over her decision until three in the morning. She had never tossed and turned so much in her entire life.

What made the situation even worse was that she kept listening for Drake to open his bedroom door. She desperately wanted to call Carly, but Livvie was afraid Carly would tell her that she had made the wrong decision. Because in the grand picture of Livvie's life, did it really matter? One way or the other, after this week, he'd be out of her life for good.

She also regretted leaving her vibrator at home. He had gotten her all worked up and then…nothing. When she heard him finally open his bedroom door at around 2:00 a.m., she succumbed to using her finger. She came instantly, thinking about everything that could have happened but didn't.

Livvie sighed as she closed her eyes and allowed the hot water from the shower to drip down her body. The water felt good, but Drake's tongue would have felt much better. Livvie immediately opened her eyes. Where had that thought come from? She couldn't think that way. It would only lead to her destruction, and hadn't men already done enough damage? As much as she wanted to let go and have fun with Drake, she couldn't. Her heart couldn't take any more. And Drake was obviously a player and a charmer.

The shower wasn't helping like she'd hoped it would. Quickly, she washed her hair and body and turned off the water. And as she stepped out of the shower and grabbed one of the enormous, fluffy white towels, she realized what she really feared. What if Drake acted all weird when she saw him? What if he no longer had any intention of seeing her and had one of his employees give her a tour? Men usually acted all weird when they were rejected, and according to Drake, she was the first woman who had ever rejected him. She wished she had that kind of luck when it came to men.

Holding the towel close to her heart, she sighed. She loved the feel of the cozy cotton against her skin. She would definitely have to ask Mr. Birkshire where they had bought them. The bathroom was beautiful, too. She loved all the white marble, and the crystal chandelier was gorgeous. Maybe if she took a picture, she could try to design this look as closely as possible in her own home. First, though, she needed to find another job, so she could afford it.

With her towel fully wrapped around her, she opened the bathroom door and was about to walk out when she noticed a sticky post on the door. She read it quickly before holding it to her chest as if the note was sacred. Drake must have come into her room while she was in the shower. She could have sworn she had locked the door last night, but since this was his house, he must have the key. Still, she was surprised he had entered the room without her knowing.

With trembling fingers Livvie reread the note. It was instructions on how to find him in his vineyard. He said there was a path outside that she needed to follow.

Looking through her sundresses for the millionth time, she decided on her white one, a cotton dress with short sleeves and a low V in the front, showing some cleavage but not too much. It made her C-cup boobs look a little bigger. But she hoped she wasn't playing with fire. After last night, she didn't want him to think she had changed her mind and wanted to go with Plan A. She did, but having sex with him wasn't coming from a place of intelligence, and Livvie prided herself on being intelligent. The back of the dress had a large black bow, which she quickly tied. Not wanting to be late, she slid on her white sandals and left the room.

Following his instructions, she found the cobblestone path, which led directly to him. And when she spotted him examining some grapes on the vines, she froze. Luckily, he hadn't seen her yet, so she could observe him without his knowledge. Livvie was grateful she had these few minutes to stop and stare. Her eyes were more than content, taking in how gorgeous he was in his tight jeans and white polo shirt. His jeans weren't too tight; they fit perfectly. Even though he looked casual, he still exuded strength and power. She always went for intelligent and ambitious men, but like Drake, they lacked in other ways that mattered. She just had to make sure she didn't get close enough to smell him.

"Are you going to stand there all day staring at me, beautiful?" Drake looked up from what he was doing and smiled.

She smiled back, relieved he didn't seem angry with her. He looked her up and down, making her feel like the most alluring woman in the world. Then he smiled at her again. She wanted him with every fiber of her being, even though he had devastated her last night by demanding she make a choice. Why wasn't he willing to compromise? Livvie knew the answer, but it was hard to admit it to herself. Men such as Drake had money and power. They didn't think they needed to bend. That was the difference between the two of them. She would have compromised. She would have thought of a way that worked for them both. Isn't that what mature individuals did if they were clearly attracted to each other? But Drake didn't compromise. And neither did Zach, for that matter.

"Hi, beautiful."

Drake continued to smile, causing Livvie's heart to thud.

"So you can call me beautiful, but you can't kiss me good morning? On the cheek, of course." Livvie said.

Drake's smile faded.

"Oh, I can kiss you, but I won't, especially on the cheek."

They both stood there in a staring contest, and the sudden tension between them increased.

Drake inhaled. "Come, I'll show you my vineyard."

With the sun slowly rising, Drake walked over to Livvie and grabbed her hand. She guessed that holding hands was allowed. But feeling his hand in hers again jarred her. The feeling of his bare skin against hers was almost too much. She didn't experience the electric-like shock feeling she'd felt yesterday. Instead, various sexual images came to mind.

Be careful, Livvie. You're treading on dangerous ground.

As they continued to walk, he slowed their pace and began to explain the vines to her.

"So I'm hopeful that this year will produce the best wines yet. The weather has been a little dry, but the temperature has been perfect." Drake's enthusiasm was contagious.

Livvie found herself hoping this year would produce the best wines yet, too. This was the year she had met him. Years to come, when she was out of his life, she'd go to the liquor store and see the year on a bottle, and it would be a little secret between her and the bottle of wine.

Much of what Drake was telling her she already knew from reading Google obsessively before she had arrived, but hearing Drake's version was nice. He spoke clearly, precisely, and passionately. He truly loved his vineyard, and she was a little jealous of it. He had a long-term, committed relationship with his grapes, and he wouldn't get rid of them at the end of the week. It was absurd to think such a thing. But her frustration over Drake giving the two of them an expiration date truly pissed her off.

"It took me a long time to find this piece of land, Olivia." Drake stopped walking when they reached a part of his vineyard that overlooked the hills.

Livvie was about to correct him and ask him to call her Livvie, but she stopped herself. At first, she wasn't thrilled when he called her Olivia. It reminded her of when she used to get in trouble as a child, but when he called her that, it made her feel special, and she liked that, a lot.

"What made you choose it?" she asked instead.

Drake looked out over his land as if he cherished it. And once again, Livvie felt a small pang of jealousy.

"Everyone thinks I worked on Wall Street, and then one day, I woke up and decided to throw all of that away and buy a vineyard."

"Well, Google did sort of imply that," Livvie said while smiling sweetly.

Her statement was enough to cause Drake to remove his focus from his vineyard and look directly at her. And when Livvie's eyes met his, her heart fluttered.

"And how would you know that?"

"I Googled your vineyard before I came."

Drake raised his eyebrow. "You did, huh? If you read most of the articles, they said how dedicated I am to my vineyard, but when we met, you seemed surprised to see me."

Livvie bit her bottom lip. "I didn't think you'd be here, I guess," she said, shrugging one shoulder.

"Where did you think I'd be?"

Again, Livvie shrugged. "Anywhere but here?"

"Olivia, where did you think I'd be?"

Livvie swallowed hard. "On your private yacht with some actress or model."

Drake laughed. "First of all, I don't own a private yacht. I could if I wanted to, but boats never did anything for me. And second, why would I be with some actress or model when I could be here with my little raffle winner? When I could be with you, Olivia?"

The laughter stopped, and Drake became serious. He looked at her with those penetrating eyes again. Tension surrounded them once again, but this time the tension was definitely sexual.

"I'm sorry. I guess I judged you."

Drake grabbed both of her shoulders. "Olivia, don't judge me again. I could understand if a so-called actress or model did. In fact, I'd expect it. But not from you. I don't want you judging me." Drake shook her lightly.

"Why?" Livvie whispered.

Drake paused but remained holding her. "I don't know," he said softly, then he released her arms and walked farther into his vineyard.

He hadn't grabbed her hand, and Livvie missed his touch. She couldn't understand why he was so upset. With the two choices he'd given her last night, how could she not judge? He was a strange man.

Livvie had to practically run to keep up with him. He was tall with incredibly long legs. And she was only five foot three. So she did the only thing she knew to do. *She* grabbed *his* hand. He didn't push her away. Instead, he gripped her hand tighter and slowed down. The tension eased off of him, and she felt more than relieved.

"So what made you choose this land? You didn't finish telling me." Livvie asked.

"When I first started working on Wall Street, I had this client who liked fine wines. Whenever he wanted to talk business, he'd make me fly here to Napa to meet him. At first, I found it a nuisance, but as the visits became more frequent, I started to fall in love with Napa. I think it had more to do with the fact that I was tired of living in Manhattan. I never had any privacy in New York. Everyone always seemed to want something from me, and since almost everyone I knew lived in New York, I couldn't avoid anyone. But here I could be private. I could be myself, and no one seemed to expect anything from me."

Livvie could relate to that. It was the exact type of relationship she wanted with a man.

When they passed a picnic table, Drake released Livvie's hand and sat down. She felt uncomfortable standing, so she sat opposite him with the table between them. She wished the table wasn't there, and they could sit closer. Drake seemed different amongst his vines than he had at dinner last night. She liked this Drake better. He was real and down-to-earth. She could only imagine what he'd been like when he lived in New York City. *Probably an arrogant asshole,* she thought. But that wasn't fair of her. Maybe he put a wall around him to protect himself. She had a wall like that, too. Maybe it came in a different form, but it was still a wall.

"I understand why you like it here," Livvie said, trying to fill the silence.

"Do you like it here?" Drake looked directly into Livvie's eyes as if her answer was important.

"I do." Livvie paused and smiled at him. "It's beautiful and peaceful." She briefly closed her eyes and inhaled the fresh, Napa air deep into her lungs, savoring the feeling. "And I feel alive here."

When she opened her eyes, Drake was still staring at her, as if she was someone special. She believed she was special, too, even though she was going through a difficult time.

"So you didn't finish telling me why you chose this particular piece of land?"

Drake broke eye contact and looked at his vineyard. "As I was saying, I came here more frequently. Well, not here, but to Napa. The more I came here, the more exhausted I felt. New York was really taking its toll. My client noticed. I remember him sitting down with me and asking me what I really wanted to do with my life. The first thing that came out of my mouth was that I wanted to own my own vineyard and make my own wines. I've always liked wine. No, let me correct that; I always appreciated wines, but the idea of creating something from the earth in the most serene place on Earth seemed very attractive to me. And it felt natural. That's when my friend told me about a large piece of land he owned. He paid me a fortune to invest his money over the years, but I'd never heard of this land. He told me he bought it when he graduated from college but never knew what to do with it. He was a successful real estate developer in the area, but he was burned out in the same way I was burned out in New York." Drake paused and glanced back at his castle. Livvie followed his gaze and saw workers tending to his vines. Every so often, one of them would wave at Drake, and he would wave back. It made Livvie's heart flutter, and for some reason it brought tears to her eyes.

"So what happened?" Livvie asked.

He cleared his throat and glanced back at her then continued to ogle his land.

"My friend brought me to see this place. It was empty, of course, and there was no house here, but I instantly fell in love with it. So my friend made a deal with me. He said this land was very important to him. He used to come here and think for hours on end. But he knew this land deserved more than one man sitting alone thinking on it. So he told me what he came up with. Basically, he said he'd sell it to me, inexpensively, on one condition. I'd have to give him a job for the rest of his life. He wanted to change his life, as well, and he believed I could create something special here. He had no interest in owning a vineyard, but since he was knowledgeable about wines he said he'd help me in any way he could." Drake paused.

"What did you do? I mean, I know you bought it, but what happened?"

"I agreed. I bought it first, then I left Wall Street and worked for four months on the toughest but most profitable vineyard in Burgundy, France."

"And that was all the training you needed?"

He laughed. "No, I needed a lot more than that, but the man who gave me this land helped me a lot." He paused as if debating whether to continue. "And he still does. I'd be lost without him." He winked at Livvie. "And you know him, as a matter of fact."

"I do?" His wink had made her feel all sorts of crazy things.

"Yes, you do."

"Well, who is it?" Livvie playfully hit his arm.

"Mr. Birkshire."

"Mr. Birkshire?" Livvie was so surprised that she leaned back without thinking. She had forgotten she was sitting on a bench, and she lost her balance and fell all the way onto her ass, landing in the dirt. She had never felt more mortified in her life.

"Olivia Collins, what am I going to do with you?" Drake stood over Livvie with his hands on his hips. He bent down and grabbed her arm to help her up but then stopped. Instead, he lay down next to her on his side, facing her.

"You know, many women have thrown themselves at me over the years, but I've never had a woman throw herself down on my beloved vineyard."

"Drake!" Livvie playfully punched him in the arm again.

"Are you hurt?" Drake asked.

"No, I don't think so." She laughed.

Drake lifted up her right leg and moved it. Then he did the same with her left leg.

"What are you doing?" She stopped laughing as Drake's touch was bringing back darker images as it had earlier.

He looked at her with a twinkle in his eye, still turning her leg in different directions.

"Making sure my little random raffle winner isn't hurt."

He took off her sandal and moved her ankle in circles. Then he pushed his thumb into her ankle and farther up her foot. Moving back and forth. Then his other hand joined in the deep massage. His fingers were firm, and his touch started to feel sensual. She clenched her vagina, and the muscles in her pelvic region contracted.

"Your random raffle winner isn't hurt," she said while holding back a moan.

Drake didn't respond. He laid her foot gently on the ground and then took off her other sandal and resumed his torture. Livvie closed her eyes. Having her feet rubbed was one of her favorite things. When she was employed and she would get a pedicure, she used to pay them extra to massage her feet longer. But this felt different. When Drake stopped touching her feet and moved his hand higher to her calf and then above her knee, she opened her eyes.

"Drake. You told me you wouldn't touch me."

"But you could be hurt. I'm making sure you're okay. Isn't that what a good host is supposed to do?"

"No. And it was my fault, so I promise I won't sue you," she said jokingly.

But as Drake moved farther up her thigh, Livvie's pelvis raised on its own. And that's when she knew she was in trouble. She quickly sat up and moved his hands away. She didn't want to make a big deal about this, especially since she was having the best morning of her entire life, but she knew if she allowed this to continue, soon, she would no longer be wearing her sundress. Livvie laughed, but the sound came out as more of a giggle. Carly giggled like that whenever she was around some guy she had a crush on. Livvie had always hated that sound. But it did get Drake to stop touching her. She lay back down and peered up at him. He seemed to be deep in contemplation. If only she could read his mind.

"It seems my little random raffle winner loves my vineyard as much as I do, and she can't seem to get enough of what I own." Drake interlaced one of his hands with hers and moved to her side. With his other hand he grabbed a handful of dirt and dropped it between his fingers on her legs. The feeling of the dirt over her naked legs caused Livvie's heartbeat to escalate.

"Do you need to feel my vineyard on your body?" Drake picked up more dirt, but this time he let it slip through his fingers onto her neck. Livvie felt the pulse in her neck increase as well as the pulse in her clitoris.

"Do you need to feel me so badly that the only way you think you can, is by feeling something I own all over your body?"

Livvie swallowed hard as she looked directly in his lust-filled eyes. Her body felt as if it was on fire.

He picked up more dirt and dropped it on the lower part of the V on her sundress, where her cleavage was showing. Technically, he wasn't breaking any rules because he wasn't touching her, even if it felt as if he was. It was driving Livvie crazy. As the dirt hit her cleavage her nipples hardened, and Drake was staring at them.

He picked up more dirt and allowed it to fall on her thigh, right where her dress ended. She opened her legs slightly, wanting something she knew she shouldn't have.

"Drake," Livvie pleaded, even though this was starting to feel wrong.

Drake continued the torture. "You're afraid of me, Olivia. You're afraid of how you'd feel if I touched you, if I caressed you like my small part of the earth is doing."

When he poured the dirt on her other thigh, Livvie's pelvis raised, along with the alarm in her head.

"Drake," she whispered again. "This feels so good, but after our discussion last night should we be doing this?"

Drake stopped what he was doing and stood. "No, Olivia, I gave you my word I wouldn't touch you in places that only a lover would touch. But I didn't say I'd make it easy." He looked over at the workers. "I'll see you back at the house." Without another word he left Livvie and walked toward the workers who were calling his name.

Livvie closed her eyes and took a deep breath. Her body was still pulsing from the touch of his dirt on her naked skin. At least her dress remained on. His dirt felt so sensual on her body, she couldn't imagine how she'd feel if he actually touched her. Well, that wasn't true. She could imagine; she just didn't think it was a good idea.

Livvie grabbed onto the bench and slowly stood. She wasn't hurt, but she was a little embarrassed. She brushed the dirt off her body the best she could. What would the workers think if they saw her like this? Knowing there was nothing she could do, she ran her hands through her long hair and raised her chin a little higher. And as she walked through his vineyard and passed him and the workers, she pretended not to notice them. But she did, and as their eyes followed her she knew they thought she had fucked their boss. However, the only eyes she cared about were those that belonged to the man she couldn't have. She had to stay strong, because her heart couldn't take another unhappy ending. The task should be easy, considering the man could be overbearing and unbending. Unfortunately, she'd also learned that there was a side to him that wasn't arrogant. A side to him that was humble and kind.

5

THE WALK BACK to her room was dreadful. It had been nice, spending the morning with Drake, especially as she could be completely herself around him. She didn't have to pretend to be someone else as she had done so frequently in the past with men. Zach had wanted her to be all Hollywood, so that's who she was when she spent time with him. And her first love, Liam, had wanted her to be the perfect girlfriend and eventually his perfect wife who would say the right things and always make him shine. She'd hated all of it.

Her parents had raised her to be a wife, but she didn't blame them. Livvie graduated from an Ivy League university, and she loved to write, but her main goal in life was to get married. When things with Liam went sour, she'd decided to move to Los Angeles, yet still, that voice inside her head said she needed to find a man. So she'd dated this guy Jared, who meant nothing to her. And then she'd met Zach, who cheated on her, so once again, she'd become

Livvie, and she wanted it to stay that way. However, she was terrified. Drake was trying hard to charm her. And he'd made himself very clear about the fact that he wouldn't make her choice easy for her.

Livvie opened her bedroom door and ran to her bathroom. She took off her dirty dress and turned her shower on full blast. She closed her eyes and allowed the water to soothe her. What would happen next? She hoped she wouldn't succumb to Drake's charm, and she'd stay true to herself. It had taken her months to become Livvie again after breaking up with Zach, and she had no intention of ever being anyone else in order to please a man. No man was worth it, including Drake Morganthal.

She wasn't opposed to marriage. In fact, she wanted to marry, eventually. She just didn't want to be someone who she was not.

Once clean, Livvie pulled on the white terry cloth bathrobe hanging on the back of the bathroom door. She still felt edgy after the hot shower. The only way she'd feel better was if she called Carly, the only person in the entire world who understood her.

Barefoot, Livvie found her purse and rummaged through it to find her cellphone. Taking a deep breath, she sat on her bed and turned it on. Carly would likely be so mad at her. Livvie was supposed to call when she arrived, but then she'd met Drake, and she hadn't been ready to explain everything. But now it was crucial. How would she stay here for another six days if she felt so torn?

Her phone lit up, indicating that it was switched on. She waited to see how many unanswered messages she had received. There were four voice messages and three texts from Carly, plus one call from her mom. Livvie was infuriated to see ten voicemails and fifteen texts from Zach. Each text was in caps, screaming at her for failing to return his calls.

Asshole. He would have to wait.

The text that intrigued her most was from her old producer's assistant, Liz. Her job was to assist the producer, but she was also in charge of communicating with everyone involved in the television show. And she had apparently never taken Livvie's name off her contact list because she still received updates on the show.

Most of the updates were negative, usually informing everyone that the show would soon be cancelled because of poor ratings, but this text started with two words: *Great News!*

With a trembling hand, she clicked on the message and began to read.

Great News Cast and Staff! Thanks to the new writers, this month's ratings are sky high. The producers and the network are super pleased. Everyone keep up the great work! XO, Liz

Livvie read the text repeatedly. When they had first notified her that she was being fired, she had called her parents and started crying, which was so unlike her. Livvie had never been one to cry, especially in front of other people. Her parents had told her not to take it personally because she wasn't the only one to be fired. That was true, as five other writers were also fired, and they were all told that the company was bringing in a brand new writing staff to shake things up on the show.

Nevertheless, all the other writers who'd been fired had immediately found new jobs, with other television shows. Everyone except Livvie. Her agent had sent her resume and writing samples to all the same shows, and they had all rejected her. Lately, even her agent had stopped pushing for her. The last time they'd spoken, her agent had said they would try again in a few months. But Livvie was giving up all hope.

The only thing she loved doing was writing, which had helped her to be financially independent and successful. But now she was spending all the money in her savings account, and it was passing through her hands like water. Los Angeles was a super expensive place to live, but that's where most of the writing jobs were located.

Her phone vibrated in her hand. She glanced down and saw that Carly was calling. Inhaling deeply, Livvie pressed *decline*. There was no way she could talk to her best friend now. If she heard Carly's voice, Livvie would burst into tears. She felt like such a failure. She was becoming obsessed with a famous playboy who only went for celebrities. And the one thing she loved more than anything in the world, she had failed at. The Drake Morganthals in the world didn't matter, nor did his beautiful castle or vineyard. In fact, nothing mattered. Her parents had trained her to be a good wife. But Livvie had trained herself to be a writer. She always wrote, and now *Raven's Edge* was doing better than ever—without her. Were her exes all doing better without her, too?

Livvie closed her eyes and ran her hands through her wet hair. If she stayed in her room any longer, she would cry, and she didn't want her eyes to become all puffy. With her luck Mr. Birkshire or

Drake would knock on her door. She desperately needed to go outside and breathe in the fresh air.

Since she had barely unpacked, Livvie opened her suitcase and grabbed her favorite pair of jeans and her green, ribbed tank top. She wasn't in the mood to put on a pretty sundress or wear something sexy; she just wanted to wear something that made her feel like herself. And this was always her go-to comfy outfit. If she ran into Drake and he judged her for it, then so be it. She didn't need to prove herself to anyone, especially a commitment-phobe like him. Besides, she would do everything to avoid him. Her hair was still wet from the shower, and she felt like shit. She squeezed any remaining water from her hair and threw on her black sandals. Then she applied some light-pink lip-gloss and ran out of her room in a hurry.

Livvie ran so hard that the second she inhaled the fresh outdoor air she started to cough. She bent over and rested her hands on her knees to catch her breath. She wasn't out of shape. She did yoga four times a week and went to the gym three days. But internally, she felt unhinged, as if she was being continuously punched in the stomach and trying to fight the pain.

Finally, she calmed her breathing and looked around. She'd exited the castle through a different back door than the one she had used earlier. Right now, avoiding Drake was her priority. He only wanted to sleep with her. Then, once he got her, she'd be left feeling empty. No way would she let a man do that to her again.

Livvie walked through the vineyard but in the opposite direction from the one she'd taken that morning. She felt a lot better, being out in the open air. She needed this. Nature always made her happier, which was why she had agreed to come on this vacation. That and the fact that her winning ticket assured her of free room and board and a plane ticket paid for by Morganthal Winery.

Livvie found a vacant bench by the side of the castle. She sat down and looked all around. It was so pretty here. Drake had told her earlier that Mr. Birkshire would come here and think. He thought there was something special about this land. Maybe if she sat here long enough, she'd feel it, too. Inhaling the fresh air, she allowed it to seep into her lungs. She hoped that maybe, somehow, her soul would be fed. Maybe she'd feel alive again. She missed that feeling. Writing made her feel alive.

She'd felt alive and happy when she first went to college. And then she'd met Liam and had fallen in love. When she met him, he was in the prelaw program, and then he went to law school. Livvie thought he was probably working for his dad's firm by now. That had always been his vision. And she thought she'd go on to get her Masters of Fine Arts in creative writing, but she hadn't done so. When Liam cheated on her, she'd run to Los Angeles. She'd felt grateful when the producers had hired her to write for *Raven's Edge*. And then Zach appeared in her life, and she felt as if her dreams were coming true without Liam, which meant so much to her. And now look at her.

Livvie closed her eyes, leaned back on the bench, and extended her legs straight out. She clasped her hands and laid them against her stomach. She wasn't a pretty sight, but she didn't care. She was tired of being someone she didn't want to be. All she wanted to do was write. That's when she truly felt at peace. Maybe she'd feel a similar peace this week at Morganthal Winery. But not if she continued to feel so screwed up over Drake.

"Excuse me, Ms. Collins?"

Livvie opened her eyes and practically jumped off the bench. It was Andrew from last night, although he seemed different than when she'd met him at dinner. He was wearing jeans and a blue polo shirt to match his clear-blue eyes. The short sleeves highlighted his bulging arm muscles. His blond hair looked messier, but she loved that he wore it a little on the long side. He looked really good.

"Ms. Collins, I'm sorry to disturb you, but I'm checking to see if you need anything?"

"No, you're not disturbing me at all. I'm good. I don't need anything, but thanks for asking. I was inside and needed some fresh air." Livvie smiled at him simply because he was adorable.

When he returned her smile, her breath caught in her throat. Drake was super handsome, but Andrew was adorable. And she could bet he'd be open to having a real relationship. Not that she was thinking that way, but she was sure he wouldn't have made her choose between a Plan A and a Plan B. And he wasn't an arrogant alpha-male.

Sliding over slightly, Livvie made room for him to sit down. He seemed nice and harmless. Maybe some small talk would make her forget her problems.

"Yeah, I like coming to this bench to think, too. It's kind of away from it all but close enough to the castle that if you have to use the bathroom or get something to drink, you can run back in."

"Do you want to take a seat?"

Andrew ran his hands through his hair, making it look even messier and sexier. He smiled and sat so close to her that their knees were slightly touching. For a split second, Livvie felt a twinge of guilt. If Drake saw them, he might not be happy, but then again, he wasn't offering her anything but sex.

"So how long have you worked here?"

Andrew turned toward her and licked his lips. But it was his eyes that intrigued her. He looked at her as if he wanted to devour her, but his gaze lacked the dominance and intensity of Drake's.

"I've worked here for the last two years. I don't only serve Mr. Morganthal his meals, you know. I also help take care of the vines." Andrew licked his lips again.

Livvie did not find the action sexy at all, but she'd bet that was his intention.

"And I go to college. I'm in the seven-year school plan versus the four-year plan. Did you go to college?"

"Yes."

Livvie glanced down at Andrew's hand that was inching toward her knee.

"Were you on the seven-year plan?" He leaned in closer to her.

"No, I was on the four-year plan. But seven years would have been nice."

Livvie smiled, and he moved even closer. Was he going to kiss her? Did she want him to? And why was it that with him she would have contemplated a one-night stand, but with Drake it was out of the question?

Because Drake can hurt me, she thought. And Andrew couldn't. Because she didn't feel intense passion with him. She didn't feel anything with him. And she wished she didn't feel anything for Drake, either.

Andrew leaned in even closer, fully ready to go in for the kill, but Livvie felt undecided if she'd let him. She stared at his lips, hoping they would give her the answer, when she felt a presence behind her. In fact, it was more than a presence; it was a force.

"What the hell is going on?" Drake said sternly.

Livvie turned her head as she felt her entire face growing warm, and Andrew jumped off the bench. So much for him coming to her rescue.

"Andrew and I were just talking." Livvie smiled sweetly, trying to ease the tension oozing off Drake, but the dark intensity in his eyes told her it hadn't worked.

"So you lie to me again." Drake spoke in an authoritative tone.

Livvie swallowed hard.

"Sorry, Mr. Morganthal. I was on break and seeing if Ms. Collins wanted anything." Andrew stuttered some of his words. "I'm going back to work now." He turned around to leave.

"Andrew, I haven't dismissed you yet."

Andrew turned back around. His face was pale, and his hands were trembling. He quickly put them in his pockets. "Sorry, Mr. Morganthal."

"Consider this your first and last warning. If I ever catch you flirting with—or worse, *touching*—Ms. Collins again, I'll personally escort you off my vineyard and make sure you never get a job in the entire Napa area again. Do you understand?"

"Drake!" Livvie said.

But it was no use. Drake continued staring at Andrew as if he had committed some horrific crime, and Andrew's face became even paler.

"I understand, Mr. Morganthal," Andrew said softly.

"Good. I'm glad we had this chat." Drake paused. "You're excused now, Andrew. Go back to work."

"Yes, sir. Sorry, sir." Andrew instantly turned and then practically ran away.

"That was harsh," Livvie said. And she meant it. How dare he treat Andrew that way! He wasn't doing anything wrong.

Drake grinded his teeth as he spoke. "Don't tell me how to treat my employees."

"I'm not telling you how to treat your employees; I'm telling you how wrongly you treated *one* employee." Livvie stood and ran her hands through her hair. There went her idea that she'd find some peace outside and not run into Drake. Livvie groaned.

"Frustrated, Olivia?" Drake raised an eyebrow.

"You could say that."

"I'm more than willing to help you with that." Drake raked his eyes down her body.

How dare he, thought Livvie. "I want more than a fuck and run," she said.

Drake smiled, but it didn't reach his eyes. In fact, it made his eyes look even more dangerous.

"And you're demanding this after only knowing me for twenty-four hours?"

Livvie bit her bottom lip. This wasn't going how she planned, because she hadn't planned. What had happened to the Drake from this morning? The charmer? She'd liked him, a lot.

"No, I'm not demanding anything at all," Livvie whispered. She closed her eyes, desperately wanting to forget this confrontation.

"Do you want him?"

Livvie opened her eyes and scrunched her forehead. "Who?"

Drake stepped closer to her. "Don't lie to me. You know exactly who I'm talking about."

She wasn't lying. She was honestly confused, but she knew whom he meant. It had just taken her a moment. "No," she whispered again.

Drake stepped closer.

"Then why were you allowing him to kiss you?" He stepped even closer.

"I didn't. I wasn't." She felt flustered with him so close.

"Olivia, do not lie to me," he demanded.

Out of nowhere, Drake grabbed her and smashed his lips against hers. He pushed his tongue into her mouth, forcing her to open for him. And once his tongue was where he wanted it to be, he slowed down, moving his lips sensually on hers. Livvie moaned and followed his lead. Dominant men had kissed her before, but nothing could compare to this. *This* kiss felt like heaven. His lips one moment felt smooth, and then rough, like the man himself. Livvie had never been into the tongue thing, but he made it feel natural, like two new lovers exploring each other. Drake moved even closer to her, pressed his entire body against her. She threw her arms around his neck and ran her hands through his thick, dark hair. She had been dying to do this since the day they met.

And then it hit her. She had only met him yesterday. And today she was kissing him as if she couldn't get enough of him. And she couldn't. That scared the life out of her. At the end of this week, he would want nothing from her, and she wanted more for herself. She needed to write again. Without her writing, she wasn't grounded. She wasn't centered. She was off balance. Writing centered her. Writing made her feel whole.

But Drake was the one who inevitably broke the kiss.

"Olivia, where did you go?"

Livvie looked into his eyes, which were filled with concern, and that was her undoing. Tears instantly welled up in her eyes, and she tried desperately to swallow them down, but she couldn't stop them. One was already sliding down her cheek.

"Olivia, I made you cry." He looked panicked.

He grabbed Livvie and sat her down on the bench. She held onto her arms.

"No, Drake, it's not you."

Shock appeared in his eyes. "You're giving me a line? Not only are you the first woman to reject me, but you're the first woman to give me *that* line." Drake paused and ran his hands through his hair. "I'm sorry, Olivia. I blew it. I touched you intimately, and I gave you my word I wouldn't. If you want to leave, I understand. I'll buy you a plane ticket to anywhere you want to go. You could have a one-week vacation like the raffle ticket promised. Hell, I'll even fly you to most expensive hotel in Hawaii.

I'm sorry. I'm normally not like this. I don't know what the hell has gotten into me."

Livvie placed her hands gently on his cheeks. "Drake, stop. I enjoyed the kiss."

"But I promised you I wouldn't touch you intimately." Drake looked intensely at her.

"But it happened. And we didn't fuck. We just kissed."

He was studying her. She felt as if he was trying to read her soul, which both unnerved her and made her feel even more vulnerable.

"What's wrong, Olivia?" he asked in a way that made her feel as if she mattered. "Olivia, I may want you more than I've ever wanted another woman in my entire life, but I also want to get to know you."

"Why?" she whispered.

Drake held her face as if she was a precious doll. "From the moment I saw you parked below my castle, I wanted you. The way you looked up at my home, it felt as if you were a woman who had been stuck inside the box of life for so long, and for the first time, you were able to breathe. My camera picked up your essence perfectly. You're beautiful, Olivia. I've been with many beautiful women. Your beauty is natural. You don't need all the heavy makeup or plastic surgery. There's not an ounce of fakeness inside or outside of you. But there's also a deep sadness about you."

Livvie felt another tear roll down her cheek. She tried to swallow them back.

"Please, don't hold back tears on my account. You've been holding them back for so long. For too long." Drake scanned her face. "What has life done to you, Olivia Collins?"

Livvie tried to pull away, but he only held her chin tighter, forcing her to look at him directly in the eye.

"Compared to other people's lives, it's really nothing." There was no need for him to feel sorry for her. The text from Liz had thrown her off. That's all it was, and she would get past this.

"Let me be the judge of that."

Livvie didn't want to tell Drake about the text. At the same time, she didn't want to keep it inside. She wanted to talk about it.

"I was working as a writer for a television show. *Raven's Edge?*" Livvie looked into Drake's eyes to see if he recognized it.

He nodded. Of course he did. Everyone had.

"Continue," Drake ordered.

"And the lead actress quit, which I'm sure you know."

"No. I've never seen the show."

"Well, once she quit she was replaced by another actress, Missy Wade?"

Drake shook his head. *Good,* thought Livvie. He didn't know her. Livvie would have been devastated if he'd slept with her.

"And Missy was terrible, so the ratings went down big-time. Then the producers called me in with five other writers and blamed the lowered ratings on us."

"But it wasn't your fault."

Livvie took a deep breath. "I thought that, too, until I checked my messages on my cellphone before I came out here." Livvie paused.

"And?" Drake asked.

"I got a text from an assistant from the show who's in charge of contacting everyone when she has news. She had never taken me off the contact list, I guess. Anyway, her text said that the producers and the network were super happy because their ratings went up. And they thanked the new writers for it."

"Oh, Olivia, I'm sorry." Drake grabbed her cheeks with both of his hands.

Tears flowed down Livvie's face. "But that's not why I'm so upset. I mean, that's part of it, but the real reason is that I feel lost without writing. I don't feel like myself. It's not that I feel as if I'm so good at it or anything, it's just that when I write, I feel free. My soul feels alive. And without writing, I feel dead inside."

"When you write you feel alive, like the hopeful woman who was looking at my castle in awe."

Livvie nodded, but the idea that Drake had been staring at her when she first saw his home down on Main Street was a little unnerving. That moment had been meant for her alone. It felt as if Drake had invaded her privacy. She wasn't ready for that. But what he said next surprised her.

"I know what it feels like to be dead inside."

"You do?" she asked.

Drake nodded. "When I was working on Wall Street and made a ridiculous amount of money, none of that mattered, because I felt so empty."

Livvie swallowed. "And that's why you bought this place?"

"Yes, but buying the land was only a start. Then I needed to build the perfect house that would feed my soul."

"And did it work?"

Drake smiled. "Somewhat, more than when I was a slave to Wall Street." Drake paused. "But then I met you. And between dinner last night and our walk through the vineyard this morning, I feel fully alive for the first time in a long while."

Livvie eyes widened. "But you've only known me for twenty-four hours."

"Yes."

"And you're only offering me this week."

"Yes."

"Why?"

"Because that's all I can take. You're afraid of never writing again, but I'm afraid of committing to a woman. Relationships don't last, Olivia. Once the fighting begins, it's over."

"I thought you weren't afraid of anything."

"No, you *assume* I'm not afraid of anything. But if you stop putting me in a category and look at me as a regular man, you would see I have fears like anyone else."

Drake was right. It was easier to put him in the category of an arrogant alpha-male. Since Zach, she'd been training herself to stay away from them. If Drake were a humble man, he would be harder to resist. Livvie glanced away from Drake and brushed the remaining wetness from her face. Pursuing Drake was still a waste of time. She wished she didn't want him so badly. And now that she had gotten a taste of his lips, she craved him like mad.

Livvie exhaled loudly as she stood. "I think I'm going to go back to my room and lie down." She started to walk away.

"Wait." He grabbed her arm to stop her. "If the only way you feel alive is to write, then write."

Livvie turned and looked at him. "But I need to make money, Drake."

"I know, but maybe that's the problem. You're so worried about finding a writing job that you stopped doing what you love." He paused. "I'm sure you wrote as a child even though you weren't getting paid."

"But I still need to make money."

He looked at her with those gorgeous emerald-green eyes. "I understand, but if you start to write from your heart, it'll lead to something. Olivia, when I bought this land from Mr. Birkshire, I knew I wanted to create a vineyard. But I had no idea if I'd make great wines that I could make a profit on or really bad wines and this place would become more of a hobby. I was well aware there was a chance I'd have to go back to Wall Street."

"But weren't you already a billionaire?" Livvie was convinced he didn't understand her after all.

Drake ran his hands through his hair. "Yes, but I'm not one of those men who could quit his job on Wall Street and then have nothing to do all day but spend his money. I need a life purpose, Olivia. I find that even wealthy men with families who quit their day job have too much time on their hands. Maybe they have too much time to think. I don't know. All I know is that they end up being really selfish and self-centered."

Livvie rolled her eyes.

"You think I'm arrogant, Olivia. And you're right, I am. But I try hard not to be selfish. Just because I don't want a long-term relationship with a woman doesn't make me selfish. Being stuck in one relationship for the rest of my life holds no interest to me. Period."

"That's harsh."

"Maybe." Drake shrugged.

Livvie started to walk away when she realized that for the first time in her life, she could have the last word with a man, so she turned toward Drake again.

"Oh, and Drake?"

"Yes?"

"Writing isn't the only activity that makes me feel alive." She smiled as innocently as she could and then turned and walked away again.

The look on Drake's face had been priceless. But somehow, she knew he'd still get his way.

"Oh, and Olivia?"

She grinded her teeth and turned.

"Write," he said with a huge twinkle in his eye.

Livvie groaned and then continued to walk away. She heard his laughter all the way back to the door of the castle.

But what bothered her the most was the fact that he was right. She should be sitting her ass down to write. She should also be doing a lot of other things, too, including staying away from Drake Morganthal.

BY THE TIME Livvie had reached her room she was fuming. Why was it that men always had to have the last word? Plopping herself onto her bed, she closed her eyes and counted to ten. What the fuck had just happened? One minute she had been feeling sorry for herself, and the next, Andrew had tried to make a move on her. But would she have let him? If Drake hadn't busted them, would she have kissed Andrew? Livvie sighed. No, she wouldn't have. Andrew was adorable, but he didn't excite her. Drake, on the other hand, was an entirely different story. When Drake kissed her, she felt as if she was in the middle of an earthquake, tornado, and tsunami, all at the same time. That kiss… Livvie inhaled. She had never felt the earth shattering when she had kissed a guy before. In fact, she had never enjoyed kissing, period. Either guys didn't know what to do with their tongues, or their lips were too gentle. Something always turned her off. But Drake's kiss was the opposite.

Livvie drifted to sleep until she heard a knock at her door. She bolted out of bed, secretly hoping it was Drake wanting to kiss her again. And that maybe he had been as affected by the kiss as she had been. But as she moved closer to the door, she thought he probably hadn't been affected by it at all. After all, he was used to making out with famous women who kissed for a living in movies.

"Who is it?" Livvie yelled when she reached her door.

"It's Mr. Birkshire, Ms. Collins."

Why was everyone so formal around here? And what was his first name? She'd have to remember to ask Drake. She opened the door to find Mr. Birkshire standing in the corridor with his arms clasped behind his back.

"Hey, Mr. Birkshire. Is everything okay?" She had no idea why she had asked him that except that for a split second she thought maybe Drake was throwing her out of his house. Maybe he had bought her a plane ticket to Hawaii as he had mentioned.

"Of course, I was just checking to see how you're enjoying your stay so far?"

"Um, it's been interesting." Livvie smiled.

"Interesting is good in life sometimes and very much needed."

Mr. Birkshire paused, and Livvie shifted her feet a little.

"Do you want to come in?" Livvie asked.

Mr. Birkshire unclasped his hands and presented her with a wrapped package.

"No, thank you. I also came here to give you this."

Livvie looked at the present and then back at him. "What is it?" She didn't think her winning raffle ticket included a gift.

"It's from Mr. Morganthal. He wanted me to give this to you immediately."

With trembling hands, Livvie took the gift. It felt way too heavy to be a plane ticket. Livvie felt relieved and confused at the same time.

"Why?"

"Open it and find out."

She held the gift in her hands as if it was a treasure. It was wrapped in purple wrapping paper with a big lavender bow. How did he know her favorite color was purple? Hands shaking, Livvie opened the package. She could have thanked Mr. Birkshire and sent him on his way, but she needed him here. The package was taped pretty well, but she didn't want to rip the paper. Even though it was silly, she wanted to save it forever.

When she finally had the package unwrapped, Livvie stared at a brown leather-bound journal with her name on the bottom in gold. She opened the journal, and on the first page, Drake had written her a note in black ink.

May this journal be filled with your beautiful words. Write until your heart's content. ~ Drake

Tears welled up in Livvie's eyes, but she held them back. "He gave me a journal," she said softly.

Mr. Birkshire nodded. "Yes, he's one of the most thoughtful human beings I know."

"He is?" Livvie asked. Drake and Mr. Birkshire had been friends for a long time. Livvie wanted him to tell her everything he knew about Drake.

"The journal obviously didn't break his bank account, but he knew you needed it as your survival tool."

"Did he tell you why?" Livvie asked.

"He doesn't need to. If he believes someone needs something, he'll do everything in his power to give it to that person."

"I just saw him maybe an hour ago."

"He must have known how badly you needed this."

Livvie swallowed and hugged the journal to her chest. "Drake had told me that you sold him this land."

"I did, and I'd do it again," he said.

"You believe in him," Livvie stated.

Mr. Birkshire nodded. "He has proved himself many times."

Livvie was dying to ask him how, and her eagerness for answers must have shown on her face.

"Do you know the charity you attended where you won the raffle?" he asked.

"Yes, it's for an autistic school." Carly had worked there for years.

"Mr. Morganthal was jogging through town about nine months ago and ran into an autistic boy and his father. The father was trying to get his son to do some form of physical activity. The boy took to Mr. Morganthal, and the father was more than pleased. Mr. Morganthal said he would jog with them if it'd help. So they met every day for a few weeks. But the boy needed serious help, and his dad couldn't afford to send him to a decent school. Mr. Morganthal started doing research and found the school where you bought the ticket. But they were filled to capacity. And it didn't matter that he would have paid them in cash for the remainder of the boy's schooling. Then he found out they were hosting a charity. The one you attended. He offered them his best wines, but they didn't want to promote drinking. So they came up with the idea for the winner to stay at his vineyard for a week. And if Mr. Morganthal agreed, then they would allow the boy to attend the school."

"And I won," Livvie whispered.

"I'm assuming you've gotten to know Mr. Morganthal a bit over the last twenty-four hours. Do you think he's the type of man who'd readily open his home to a stranger?"

"No," Livvie said.

"Exactly, but as that was the only way to get the boy into that school, he agreed."

Livvie swallowed back her tears.

"And then, Ms. Collins, he took it a step further. Knowing that the family wasn't wealthy, he paid for their move to Los Angeles and bought them a house right near the school." Mr. Birkshire paused. "You look surprised."

Livvie nodded.

"And that's just one of many stories about his generosity and thoughtfulness."

"Then why won't he consider entering into a committed relationship? Why is he so afraid?" Livvie blurted out and then bit her lip.

Mr. Birkshire opened his mouth and then shut it. She was worried he wouldn't tell her why, and she really needed to hear it from the one person who seemed to know him.

"I won't tell you all the details of his life. Only he can tell you. But I feel you should know that his parents got divorced when he was ten years old."

"And that scarred him?" Livvie knew of many people who had grown up in divorced homes, and they weren't all messed up in relationships. It seemed as if Drake had been more affected than most. But who was she to judge?

"It did," Mr. Birkshire responded. "But it was more than that. Mr. Morganthal watched his mom suffer from a broken heart. The actual divorce didn't damage him as much as watching his mom become sadder and sadder throughout her marriage. She didn't physically die, but in a way, what happened to her was just as bad."

"And he fears that." Livvie didn't need to ask that as a question. She knew it was the truth.

Mr. Birkshire nodded, confirming what she thought.

"And he doesn't want to put anyone through that."

That makes sense, thought Livvie. Mr. Birkshire turned as if he was going to leave but then pivoted back around.

"I almost forgot to tell you; Mr. Morganthal has a business dinner in town, and he won't be home. Would you like me to send your dinner to your room?"

Livvie's heart delved into her stomach. "Yes, please," she said softly.

Mr. Birkshire turned again, but Livvie had one more question for him.

"Mr. Birkshire?"

He turned. "Yes, Ms. Collins."

"Will you please call me Livvie?"

Mr. Birkshire paused. "Only when you've earned it."

Livvie wasn't sure what he meant, but she knew he wouldn't explain. "Then thank you for bringing the journal to me." She forced a smile.

Mr. Birkshire turned and left her room. Livvie closed the door. Still holding on to the journal for dear life, she leaned against the door and slid to the floor.

"Who are you, Drake Morganthal?"

LIVVIE SAT ON her bed cross-legged and scrolled through her empty journal. Although she had read Drake's message a million times, it was time to deal with the rest of it. Both her and her journal were empty. How funny and ironic. It was up to her to fill the journal and to fill herself with happiness. And this leather-bound object would help her heart become content once again.

It was interesting that Drake had bought her a journal and not a laptop. But she was well aware of why he had chosen a journal versus a laptop, and it had nothing to do with money. He knew Livvie would be more inspired to write with a journal. And as a little girl, that was how she had learned to write. How fitting that he had chosen to bring her back to her beginnings, to simpler times. Drake had given her the most precious of gifts. He had given her back her dream. And right this second she was holding her lost dream in her trembling hands.

Livvie picked up the purple wrapping paper she'd thrown on the floor and noticed a pen taped inside. She laughed. It was a Tiffany pen, her favorite. When she was fifteen years old, she'd asked her parents to buy her a Tiffany pen for her birthday. At that age, she was writing like crazy, and she wanted a special pen to go along with her dream. She remembered in detail the euphoric feeling she had when she'd picked up the pen for the first time and wrote in her notebook. This leather-bound journal would help her feel whole again. It was the missing piece to her puzzle. And it had nothing to do with a man except for the person who bought it for her.

This feeling she was experiencing had been missing every day when she'd wrote for *Raven's Edge*; a feeling she hadn't felt in years. Her epiphany made her feel incredibly sad but free at the same time.

Now more than ever, she knew what she needed to do. She closed her eyes and squeezed them shut exactly as she had as a little girl. Within seconds, different story ideas came to her, like magic. But one story stood out more than the others. Then she slowly opened her eyes and turned to the first page of her new journal.

Haley drove down the paved road as if she had been there a million times. She hadn't and couldn't understand why she felt as if she'd lived there before. She wanted and needed this to be the perfect week. Not only because she finally had a vacation — one she needed badly. But also because this place...this beautiful, majestic place...made her feel as if she'd come home. The wood cabin sat against the clear blue lake, reminding her of the lake house she had once visited with her family. The wind blew the trees gracefully around the house, as if they were dancing a ballet. Haley stopped her car, opened the door, and ran out with her hands in the air, doing a dance of her own. Maybe hers wasn't as graceful as that of the trees, but it was her version of a freedom dance. She was free for one week of her life, free from problems, worries and bills arriving in the mail.

Livvie put down her pen as an, "*Ah-ha*" moment struck her, which felt overwhelming. The description she'd just written fit how she'd felt when she'd first seen Drake's house — as if she had come home. Oddly, she hadn't felt as if she really had a home — not since she had left her parents' house to go to college. But the idea she felt at home here was somewhat terrifying, because she was experiencing an illusion. This wasn't any more "home" than her house in Los Angeles. She had been here only one day, and yet she already felt a strong connection. She felt safe here. And after this week, she'd never return. She'd be back in Los Angeles with the exact opposite feeling.

Livvie continued writing, and by nightfall, Mr. Birkshire dropped dinner by her door — salmon with fresh asparagus and roasted potatoes. It was just as delicious as yesterday's dinner, except Drake wasn't with her tonight, and she felt the loss.

After she ate, she wrote a while longer and then tried to sleep. But she found herself tossing and turning, straining to hear if Drake had returned. Where had he been all afternoon and evening? Maybe he had gone somewhere else to get laid because she had turned him down. The idea made her feel sick. But finally, at two o'clock in the morning, she heard him outside his bedroom door.

She was dying to thank him for the journal, so without analyzing and obsessing over her decision, she got out of bed. She was wearing one of her favorite pajama sets—a blue silk tank top that matched her eyes and blue silk shorts. She heard him open his bedroom door, so she quickly ran to her own door and opened it.

With his hand on his doorknob Drake turned and looked at her, but she could tell he had been drinking. She couldn't smell the cedar and his vines; all she could smell was alcohol. Livvie cringed inside.

"Yes?" He looked at her as if he wanted to eat her, and then he raised an eyebrow.

"I just wanted to properly thank you for the journal and the pen." Livvie smiled up at him, but as he had been drinking, she guessed her timing was bad.

"Then thank me properly."

He looked her up and down, making her instantly wet and aware of how little clothes she was wearing. She felt her clit pulse, so she immediately clenched her vagina, hoping to stop the feeling. She knew what Drake was like when he was sober; what was he like when he was drunk?

Not feeling comfortable enough to look him directly in the eye, Livvie looked down at her bare feet. Thank goodness she had gotten a pedicure before coming here.

Drake chuckled and opened his door. "Olivia, if you'd like to thank me properly, then thank me properly. Make up your mind." He paused and looked as if he wanted to devour her. "But coming out of your room, for whatever reason, at two o'clock in the morning in the sexiest pajama outfit I've ever seen, knowing how badly I want to fuck you, whether I'm sober or drunk, was a really bad idea."

And then Drake shut his door in Livvie's face. She guessed she deserved that. What had she been thinking, coming out here at this time of night—or rather morning? That was just it. She hadn't been thinking. She'd needed to see Drake as she had missed him at dinner, and she felt a strange separation anxiety. That was a bad sign, especially because she came here to heal from men. *Nice going, Livvie.*

Her frustration grew even worse when she heard Drake's shower turn on. She forced herself to walk back into her room, close her door, climb into bed, and throw the covers over her head.

A few minutes later, she heard a knock on her door. Hoping it was Drake, she jumped out of bed and opened it.

"Here, put this around you." Drake handed her a large blue blanket, which she secured around her. "Good. Now I can look at you without thinking dirty thoughts. Come with me." Drake held out his hand, expecting Livvie to grab it.

"Are you drunk?" As much as she enjoyed his company, if he was drunk, she'd rather stay away.

"I was buzzed, but the shower sobered me up," he said. "I wouldn't be with you if I was drunk. I want you when I'm sober. Being around you when I'm drunk would be pure torture."

"You want me that much?"

"Yes, now come on." Drake's hand was still extended.

Livvie took it, even though she felt slightly uneasy. He was fully dressed in jeans and a sweatshirt. If he was drunk he probably would have shown up in a towel after his shower.

"I swear, I'm not drunk. And I promise I won't touch you," he said, before leading her out her bedroom door.

She believed him. In fact, his promise made her feel safe. She kept one hand around the blanket as she walked with him down the hall. He released her hand for only a second to open a door, before grabbing it again. Together, they climbed a small, winding staircase. At the top of the stairs was another door. Drake opened it, and Livvie gasped.

"It's beautiful, Drake."

They were on his roof. The view was breathtaking. Since it was still dark out, she could see millions of stars. Even the mountains had little lights coming from houses that were nestled in the trees. It looked magical. It looked surreal. It looked perfect. She felt Drake's eyes on her, so she turned toward him.

"You're beautiful, Olivia."

He squeezed her hand and she squeezed back. Then he led her a little farther down to where there was a large couch. He sat down, and she followed, their hands still clasped.

"I like to come up here at night. I never get sick of seeing the stars. All those years I lived in New York I never saw a single one. The bright city lights made it impossible. But here you see thousands."

Livvie got more comfortable, pulling her legs up and tucking them under her and tightening the blanket around her. No small feat, considering she was still holding Drake's hand, but she didn't want to let him go.

"I've only seen stars in Los Angeles when I've gone hiking in the mountains."

"You went hiking at night? Was it safe?" Drake asked, concern etched all over his gorgeous face.

She laughed and shivered slightly. "Yes, I'd go with a bunch of women. It's totally safe."

"Come here." Drake released her hand, so he could scoot Livvie closer. Then he put his arm around her. "You'll feel warmer now."

Livvie loved snuggling up against him. Neither Zach nor Liam liked to cuddle. It always bothered her. She was a very affectionate person.

"Thank you," she said softly. "I feel warmer already."

Drake tightened his arm. "I'm sorry I didn't bring a bottle of wine."

"I don't need wine. I just like being next to you." Livvie bit her bottom lip. "I'm sorry. I shouldn't have said that."

Using his free hand, Drake raised her chin. "I like it, too. I enjoy your company very much." He paused. "You were right to say no to me, even though no woman ever has. I wanted to sleep with you before I got to know you. That was wrong, and you deserve better. I'm not saying I don't want to sleep with you now, but I'm respecting your wishes."

She smiled softly. "Thank you. You're not easy to resist."

He chuckled. "I'm glad to hear that. I'm not a perfect man, Olivia. I wish I didn't have these commitment issues. If I didn't, I would pursue you like crazy."

Livvie looked into his eyes, seeing the pain reflected in their depths. "What happened to make you so dead-set against committing to one woman?"

"I watched my mom go through hell. I was young, and I couldn't do anything to make her feel better," he said. "I know I should be over it by now, but it's etched in my sub-conscious."

Livvie touched his face gently. "Have you seen a therapist?"

"Yes, years ago. But I still haven't been able to commit. And now, I no longer want to."

She looked down at the blanket. "Do you think you'll ever change your mind?"

"There are moments when I want to change my mind. Like when I met you."

Livvie's heart beat faster. She was leaning against Drake. She was sure he could feel it.

"That's something at least." She didn't want to look at him.

"Olivia, look at me," he said in his demanding tone.

She raised her eyes. "I'm looking."

Drake smiled. "We may not have a future, and we may never see each other past this week, but I promise you, I will remember every moment we're together."

"But I've only known you for a short period of time." Livvie had never felt so confused in her life. She was snuggling with an alpha-male who couldn't or wouldn't commit to one woman, but who seemed vulnerable, soft, and warm at the same time.

Drake sighed. "I've been telling myself the same thing, and I don't have an answer."

Livvie leaned closer and rested her head against his shoulder. "I forgot to thank you for the journal. That was the reason I came out of my room earlier."

Drake chuckled again. "It wasn't because you wanted to fuck me?"

Livvie laughed, even though her eyes started to feel heavy. "No, I want to be with you, but I'm scared."

He kissed the top of her head. "I know. Let's fall asleep outside for a bit. Then I'll take us back down."

Livvie couldn't argue. She was already half asleep. This was the safest she'd felt in a long time, maybe ever.

Drake bent down and whispered in her ear. "I'm respecting your wishes, but eventually, I will have you. I always get what I want." He held her tighter.

Livvie was too sleepy to respond. Besides, maybe Drake was right, but she wouldn't give in without a fight.

WHEN LIVVIE HEARD her alarm go off, she groaned. Absolutely exhausted, she got out of bed and showered. The only thing that drove her in her sleepy state was the thought that she'd be spending time with Drake in his vineyard this morning.

Last night had felt like a dream. She had fallen asleep in Drake's arms. Sometime later, he'd picked her up, dropped her off in her bedroom, and then he went to his. But not before he kissed her on the forehead. She hoped today would be as magical. She was worried Drake would have reverted to his old, arrogant self again.

She debated what to wear a thousand times. Finally, she dressed in her floral, off-the-shoulder, short-sleeved, silk blouse, which hugged her hips. Then she put on her skinny jeans and black sandals. She would have preferred to wear her comfy jeans from yesterday, but these jeans looked better on her. She wasn't sure how Drake would respond to her this morning after last night.

When she walked down the grand staircase, she ran into Mr. Birkshire cleaning the candelabras. Is there anything he didn't do?

"Hey, Mr. Birkshire." Livvie smiled.

He continued dusting but glanced toward her without smiling.

"Good morning, Ms. Collins."

He resumed cleaning, and Livvie had to stop herself from running down the rest of the stairs and out into the vineyard. She couldn't wait to see Drake. Did that make her pathetic?

She took the exact path she had taken yesterday according to Drake's instructions, but she didn't see him anywhere. She looked at her watch. She'd found him here at this exact same time the day before.

*Hmm...*where could he be? There were men working in the fields, but when she asked them where Drake was, they only smiled. Then she saw Andrew, and she ran toward him, hoping he would know, but when he saw her coming, he walked the other way, pretending he hadn't noticed her.

Feeling she had no other option, she walked back into the house. Surely, Mr. Birkshire would know. Luckily, she found him exactly where she'd left him, cleaning the candelabras.

"Hey, Mr. Birkshire?"

As he had done earlier, he continued dusting but glanced her way. "Yes, Ms. Collins?"

"Have you seen Drake?"

This time he didn't even look at her. "Mr. Morganthal should still be resting. This isn't his morning to work in his vineyard."

Resting? Livvie scrunched her forehead. "I thought he worked in his vineyard every morning?"

She felt defeated. She could have slept late like Drake.

"No. Every Monday afternoon and evening, he has wine tastings in the area. It's important for him to know what's selling and how the different wines taste. It usually runs late into the evening, so he sleeps in on Tuesdays."

"Oh." Livvie looked down. She didn't want to tell him she'd been with Drake after he'd gotten home last night. At the same time, she wondered why Drake hadn't told her he slept in on Tuesdays? "I guess I'll go back to sleep then, too."

Mr. Birkshire looked down at Livvie as she started climbing up the stairs.

"Why do you look so unhappy?"

Livvie stopped climbing. "I thought I was supposed to go out into the vineyards every morning," she said.

"You are. There are others who can show you the ropes, you know."

"But no one out there gave me the time of day." Livvie sighed dramatically and resumed walking up the stairs.

"Let me get someone to show you around." Mr. Birkshire wiped his hands on a cloth from his pocket.

In a strange way, Livvie thought he was testing her. She didn't want just *anyone* to show her around. She wanted Drake.

"That's okay, Mr. Birkshire. I'll go to my room and get some sleep. Sorry for disrupting you."

Mr. Birkshire nodded and resumed dusting. Livvie noticed he'd dust a spot and then stop, and then dust a spot and stop. She was so mesmerized watching him that she stopped climbing the stairs.

"Leave your baggage at the door, Ms. Collins."

Mr. Birkshire continued dusting. He didn't look at Livvie when he spoke, and yet she knew what he was trying to say.

"I can only leave my baggage at the door if I know for sure that it's safe to do so." She had felt safe last night, but in broad daylight reality hit her. She couldn't be with Drake.

"Nothing in life that feeds the soul is safe, Ms. Collins. Nothing is a guarantee. And the biggest risks in life to take are always the most dangerous. But would you rather carry your heavy baggage around wherever you go, or leave it at the door, and start to live freely again?"

Livvie swallowed and then continued on her way. Mr. Birkshire wasn't looking at her anyway — on purpose, she supposed. She was surprised he'd spoken so directly, and she felt as if he was kind of scolding her, the way a concerned dad would. And he was right. But with all of Drake's issues, was this the right situation to release her baggage? She honestly didn't know.

Livvie did go back to sleep. She was so exhausted; she didn't even take off her clothes. When she returned to her room, she'd been tempted to call Carly back, but Livvie wasn't in the mood to confess her feelings for Drake. She had only known him for three days. Maybe all this was nothing more than a brief attraction? What woman wouldn't be attracted to Drake Morganthal? But deep down inside, she knew that wasn't true. This wasn't just an attraction because she had experienced brief glimpses of who he really was. He was thoughtful, generous, and passionate. Google had never revealed any of that.

She was awakened by a knock on her door. She wasn't surprised, as she doubted they would allow the lucky raffle winner to hide in her room all day. She ran her hands through her hair, making sure she looked decent, and then opened her door.

Her heart delved into her stomach when she saw it was Mr. Birkshire.

"I came here to tell you that Mr. Morganthal requests your presence in the dining room for some scone tasting."

The second Livvie heard "scone," her stomach growled loudly.

"Sorry," Livvie said. She wasn't one of those people who pretended that their stomach hadn't just made a mortifying sound. She would rather just acknowledge it and move on. "So why scones?" She questioned him in an effort to stop her heart from beating wildly at the idea Drake had *requested her presence.* There was something incredibly sexy about that. When this week was over, she would definitely be *requesting* Carly's presence to help her get out of her severe depression.

"He's hiring a new baker, and he'd like your opinion."

Wow! Not only was Drake *requesting her presence,* but he would also like her opinion.

"Will I be eating cake, too?" Livvie loved scones, but she would never turn down cake.

Mr. Birkshire looked extremely frustrated. She had never seen that look on his face before. If she could get him to be frustrated, maybe, eventually, she could get him to crack a smile.

"Perhaps. Good day, Ms. Collins." Without a second glance he closed her door.

Livvie shrugged and did the only thing she could think of to do. She opened her bedroom door and walked to the dining room. After all, Mr. Morganthal had *requested her presence.*

LIVVIE DIDN'T END up walking to the dining room, she more like ran there, but who could blame her? Scrumptious treats were awaiting her, and one of them came in the form of a tall and handsome, green-eyed man, who had been so sweet to her last night. Plus, if this baker were anything like the other baker Drake had, she would be leaving here at least ten pounds heavier than when she arrived. The thought depressed her, but not as much as denying herself scones and possibly cake. When she reached the dining room door, she slowed her steps, reluctant to appear too eager. Not only did she crave sugar, but also she craved the man sitting at the head of the table with his mouth full and his hands filled with delectable treats. How she would love to be the delectable treat in his hands. The thought alone turned her on.

"Ah, I see you've come," Drake said with his mouth full.

She felt a huge butterfly in her stomach. Could Drake sense her secret yearning? There was no way he could know just from sitting at the other end of the room. But hearing him say "come" made her think of only that. Forcing her mind to shift gears and reminding herself why she was standing in his dining room was not an easy task.

"I could never turn down scones." Livvie smiled widely. She had been smiling a lot lately. But Drake wasn't the only reason she was smiling. No matter how turned-on she felt scones also excited her. The thought of them alone made her mouth water. Great, now she was wet in two places! Livvie started to laugh at the thought.

"What's so funny?" Drake asked still with his mouth full.

Needing to think of a way to get out of answering his awkward question, she slowly walked over and sat next to him in the exact spot where she had sat at dinner the other night. It felt strangely natural to be near him. She remembered when she had first sat here, she had been nervous beyond belief. Now, rather than feeling nervous, she felt over the moon to be spending time alone with him.

"You won't tell me what's funny?" Drake had a twinkle in his eye and scone crumbs all over his chin.

She would love to lick them off him. "I was just thinking about how much I love scones." Livvie had no choice but to give him a half-truth. She wondered if the day would come when she didn't feel the need to lie to this man. Maybe if she listened to Mr. Birkshire and left her baggage at the door, she could start to trust Drake.

"That's what made you laugh?" Drake looked at her with doubt in his eyes and instantly stopped chewing.

No, thought Livvie. "Yes, my mom used to make fun of me when I was a little girl. She'd tell me that no matter what was going on in my life, I'd never say no when it came to eating something with sugar."

She missed how simple her life had been when she was a child. Back then she hadn't had to deal with losing her job and being unemployed. Drake grabbed her hand from under the table and squeezed it, causing what felt like an electric current shooting through her body again.

"It's both happy and sad, remembering our childhood."

Livvie swallowed hard. She wished she had thought of another reason why she had laughed.

"Thank you," Livvie whispered.

"Thank you?"

"Yes, for being so kind." And she meant it. He had given her the journal yesterday, and Mr. Birkshire had told her how he helped the autistic boy. And he took her up to the roof at two o'clock in the morning. He was full of surprises. Who knew what other kind deeds he had done?

This time Drake laughed. "No one has ever said I'm kind." He smiled warmly at her. "I think I know how to be more than kind."

He wiggled his eyebrows up and down, making Livvie laugh.

"By giving me a scone?" Livvie tried to sound as flirty as possible. When it came to the art of flirting, she was awful. Carly had told her to give up flirting altogether and just be herself.

"Oh, I'll do more than *give* you a scone." His eyes changed from humor to intense lust. Drake reached over to a large plate of scones and took a moment, examining each one, as if wanting to make certain he chose the perfect specimen.

"Ah," Drake said as he finally picked one. He gently broke it apart with his fingers and once again turned toward her.

Realizing he was about to feed her the scone himself, she held her breath, her stomach doing summersaults. She was beyond turned on already, and she wasn't sure what she wanted to taste more — his delectable fingers or the delicious scone.

"Open up, princess."

Livvie would have opened her mouth no matter what, but his use of the term of endearment made her feel as if she would have done absolutely anything he wanted. Women were never too old to be called princess. At least that's how Livvie felt. And as she sat up straighter to take the scone into her mouth, her nipples hardened. Why her nipples would harden from a simple term of endearment, she would never understand, but they did. And now not only was she experiencing the feeling of his fingers touching her lips and the burst of mouthwatering sugar hitting her tongue, but her nipples wanted to get involved, too. She acknowledged them by giving them some attention. She moved forward slightly, so they brushed Drake's arm as he fed her a chocolate chip scone. When her nipples made contact, she moaned. Luckily, Drake thought her moan was as a result of tasting the scone. Or at least she hoped that was the case. And he laughed. Not a full out laugh, but a soft, seductive laugh that caused even more havoc between her thighs.

Something had shifted between them when they were on the rooftop. She wanted it to continue. Her fear was Drake becoming arrogant toward her again.

"Another?"

Livvie smiled as she finished swallowing the scone.

As he broke off another piece, she instinctively opened her mouth once again. The sugar, chocolate, and the fact that he was feeding her was driving her crazy. With both hands, she grabbed onto his arm, desperately trying to center herself again. Once the rest of the scone had been placed in her mouth, he brushed his thumb along her lips. She wondered if he still considered this not intimately touching.

And she was determined to emphasize the point. The second Livvie swallowed, she circled her tongue around his thumb and moved it back and forth, tasting him. How she wished it was his cock and not his thumb, but she had chosen Plan B. She looked into his gorgeous eyes, and she could read the intensity in them, mirroring hers.

"Olivia, if you keep this up, I'll be feeding you more than just scones. And I'm trying desperately to keep my word with you." Drake paused. "You did come down here for scones. Am I correct?"

"Well..." Livvie said as flirtatiously as she could. What was she doing? She was playing with fire; that's what she was doing. "I also came down for some cake."

Drake laughed. Livvie loved that sound, and the fact she had caused it made her feel all mushy inside.

He pecked her on the lips and then shouted Mr. Birkshire's name.

The man appeared through a side door. "You called, sir?"

"Yes, my lady requests cake. Please have the new baker bring in a piece. A very large piece, Mr. Birkshire."

Mr. Birkshire nodded and then left the room. When they were once again alone, Livvie grabbed the sides of Drake's face.

"Thank you," she whispered. She wasn't used to a man trying to please her. Usually, she was the one trying to please them. And it felt odd. Good, but odd. Especially coming from a man who never wanted a committed relationship.

To make matters worse, Drake kissed her on the lips in response to her thanking him. A kiss that was far from a peck. He inserted his tongue into her mouth as if he deserved to be there. Her tongue automatically joined his, and they connected in the way that the rest of her body was dying to do. He ran his hands through her hair, and she didn't even care that his fingers were covered with crumbs and sugar. It felt more natural, being messy. Livvie mirrored his actions and ran her hands through his hair. Instinctively, they both moved closer, while tugging at each other's hair as their lips performed a dance of ecstasy.

The kiss would have lasted forever, but Mr. Birkshire cleared his throat. She was super mortified, and her face grew hot. She hated it when her face gave away her emotions. Drake, on the other hand, was cool as usual. He stopped kissing her and nodded at Mr. Birkshire, as if kissing a woman in the dining room with scone crumbs all over his hands was the norm around there. And maybe it was, to Drake. Maybe Mr. Birkshire had seen this hundreds of times. The thought made Livvie cringe inwardly.

When the cake appeared a second later, Livvie wasn't sure if it was such a good idea for Drake to feed her again. She wanted him badly. And feeding her food directly from his fingers wasn't making resisting him any easier. Luckily for her, Mr. Birkshire stayed in the room.

"Mr. Morganthal, I also have news."

Drake didn't seem at all happy with him still being there. "Yes?" he said quickly.

"Your mother will be joining your lunch party tomorrow as well."

Drake sighed loudly. "Why?"

"She implied on the telephone that she hasn't seen you in a while. I figured the easiest way for you to deal with her would be at lunch with others."

Drake nodded. "I don't like it, but you're right. Thank you."

Mr. Birkshire nodded and left the room. Drake handed Livvie a fork, and together they dove into the vanilla buttercream cake with tiny pieces of chocolate in the center. It tasted divine, but after finding out about his mom's impending visit, Livvie felt uncomfortable.

"So what kind of lunch are you having tomorrow?" she asked after she had swallowed a big bite of cake.

"It's a lunch with some of my loyal customers. They're flying in from the East Coast."

"Just for lunch?" Livvie asked.

"No, they have business in San Francisco, I believe, so they're stopping here first."

Drake resumed eating the cake, and Livvie felt too awkward to ask more questions. She was dying to know if she was invited, but she couldn't ask. After all, she was only his raffle winner. Although, she felt like they were becoming good friends. To avoid asking the question, Livvie shoved a mouthful of cake into her mouth.

Unconsciously, she moaned. From the look on Drake's face, she guessed he had never heard a woman moan while eating cake. Livvie stared back at him as if she had been caught taking a cookie from the jar. She wanted him to think she was a sophisticated adult like the women he was used to, but unfortunately, her cake obsession gave away that she was really a little girl inside a woman's body. Livvie inhaled deeply and continued eating the cake, still moaning at odd moments.

Mr. Birkshire appeared once again, as if he sensed Drake needing him. They had the oddest relationship.

"Yes?" Mr. Birkshire asked.

"If Olivia's recent display is any indication of how good this new baker is, please hire him immediately, and tell him to make the exact same cake for tomorrow."

Livvie felt her cheeks flush, while Drake looked at her with a twinkle in his eye and an "I want to fuck you" smile on his face.

"Yes, sir." Without batting an eyelid Mr. Birkshire nodded and left the room, once again leaving them alone.

"As much as I'd love nothing more than to stay and watch you eat this cake, I must prepare for tomorrow," said Drake.

Feeling as if she had outstayed her welcome, Livvie grabbed her napkin and dabbed the sides of her mouth as gracefully as she could. She felt like she had buttercream all over her face. But Drake grabbed her hand as she was in the middle of dabbing herself.

"Please finish the cake without me. Watching you eat this was a huge turn-on. I'd like to picture you finishing it while I'm working away."

Livvie's heart beat faster as his fingers grazed her chin. She stuck her tongue down toward his fingers and began licking them. They still tasted like the scones he'd fed her. She licked them thoroughly, enjoying the taste and feel of him. She gazed into his eyes. She would have been perfectly happy, keeping her eyes closed, but his eyes kept on changing. First he appeared shocked, but then his gaze filled with an intense desire. Judging by the look on his face, he didn't want her to stop, so she continued licking even faster, wanting to give him a performance to think about while he worked. She licked in circles, making sure she touched every part of his fingers while holding his gaze the entire time. Then he looked at her as if she was the most ravishing woman he had ever seen. His eyes grew in intensity, and he clenched his jaw as if it was taking every bit of control he had not to throw her down on the dining room table.

Then reality crept in. What was she doing? Playing with fire. That's what she was doing. With much reluctance Livvie stopped licking and released his fingers. She grabbed the glass of water and began gulping it down, trying desperately to get his taste out of her mouth. Not that she wanted to. She adored his taste, but she had to look out for her fragile heart. There was no way she could sleep with Drake. It would feel as if she were throwing all the work she'd done on herself in the last few months right into the garbage.

When she looked up at Drake, his eyes were filled with anger.

"Does my taste repulse you?" Drake wasn't yelling, necessarily, more like speaking quietly with a force that would scare anyone.

"No, not all." Livvie spoke softly, but only because she felt guilty for almost crossing the line.

"Then why did you stop?" Drake's tone had not changed.

"I didn't want to stop," Livvie said quietly.

"Then what's the problem?" Drake asked.

Livvie inhaled. She needed to be honest with him. He was honest with her on the rooftop. "I'm afraid to sleep with you, and I'm afraid not to sleep with you."

"Why are you so afraid?"

"Because you gave us an expiration date," Livvie blurted out.

Drake looked at her as if she was one of those emotional, crazy types of women Carly and Livvie always swore they'd never become.

"Olivia, you would have slept with Andrew for one night and been completely okay with never seeing him again."

Okay, he has me there, thought Livvie. And the fact he knew that didn't make her feel any better.

"But my heart wasn't involved with Andrew. And with you it is. What happened to the Drake I spoke with on the rooftop? He told me I deserved more," Livvie said.

"We already crossed the line. My dick may not be inside you, but the line was crossed." He groaned. "Be careful, Olivia. This week cost you one hundred dollars—the price of the raffle ticket. I wouldn't want it to also cost you your heart."

He threw his napkin onto the table and stormed out of the dining room, leaving Livvie alone. She looked at the piece of cake Drake had wanted her to finish without him. Not only was her appetite ruined, she also wanted to throw the cake against the wall. However, it wasn't the cake that had caused this. Clearly, Drake and she both had issues. He had told her exactly who he was on the rooftop. Should she leave? Livvie considered it for a brief moment. No, that was a cowardly thing to do, and Olivia Collins may be a lot of things, but she was no coward. Drake would have to throw her out, and so far, he hadn't. That gave her at least a little hope. But Carly had once told Livvie that when it came to men, feeling hopeful could be dangerous.

10

LIVVIE AWOKE BRIGHT and early to her alarm
again. She wasn't sure if Drake would be outside
working the vineyard this morning, but she felt as if
they needed to clear the air. She also knew his mom
and some of his customers were coming for lunch,
and he hadn't invited her, so it was unclear whether
she'd get a chance to see him today at all.

After the cake episode, Livvie had spent the
remainder of the day and evening writing in her
room. Mr. Birkshire had left her dinner again by her
door. She was grateful that he, at least, had thought
about her. She felt so exhausted that she had fallen
asleep quickly after eating and had no idea what
time Drake made it to his bedroom. Maybe she had
frustrated him so much yesterday that he went out to
find a willing woman to fuck. She was sure that
wouldn't be hard for him. Any woman but her
would be more than eager to have sex with him,
even if he directly told them it would only be once.
Maybe Mr. Birkshire was right, and she should have

left her baggage by the door, but that didn't seem right, either. How was she supposed to let loose if he wasn't willing to compromise? Besides, she wasn't asking to be with him forever. All she wanted to know was that they would stay in touch and see what happened. Was that too much to ask?

Livvie rose from her bed and ran to the window, hoping to spot Drake in his vineyard. She scanned the length of the vineyard and then remembered to look toward the path he had instructed her to take the other day. And she found him. He must have been kneeling by his grapes because he slowly rose from the ground as if he was a God. He looked like one, anyway. Tall and regal as he looked up at the sun, perhaps gauging how the weather would affect his grapes for the day. She couldn't see exactly what he was wearing from her bedroom window, but she noticed his beautiful arm muscles and his hot-as-hell body. She wanted him so badly. Once she left here, she would only see him on the cover of magazines, in articles about his winery, and maybe even on the news.

Livvie inhaled deeply and leaned her head against the window. She adored him after only a few days, and there wasn't anything she could do about it. Olivia Collins, an Ivy League school graduate and unemployed television writer had fallen for a man she'd only known for a few days. And there was no way she could protect her heart. And what was the point anyway? She tried to make intelligent choices, but her heart seemed to lead the way, and she hoped everything would be okay.

It wasn't even about his looks. She was getting to know Drake on the inside, and she liked him.

As hard as it was, Livvie stepped away from her window and opened her closet, having finally unpacked. She decided to wear her blue sundress, which matched her eyes. This dress always made her feel good, with thin straps and a low neck that showed her cleavage. It made her chest look bigger and her hips smaller. She grabbed her white, flat sandals, ready to begin the day. With one more glance out the window, she picked up her journal from her night table and then headed out the door.

Livvie crept down the stairs, unsure what mood she'd find Drake in when she finally met up with him. When her ex-boyfriends were in a bad mood, they would usually ignore her or act mean. Maybe he wasn't like other men when it came to moods. She knew he wasn't like other men in general, except for the commitment phobic part. Unfortunately, there were a lot of those out there. Drake confessed to having a real fear of commitment. She wished she could change that.

When she reached the bottom of the stairs, she gripped the banister, as if she might draw some strength from it, find the courage she so desperately needed. She wanted Drake to realize what he'd miss when she left. And the only way to do that was to be her true self—strong, brave, and fearless. She had to remind herself that she was no longer the naïve woman she was when she was engaged to Liam, or the angry woman she was when she got fired and Zach cheated on her.

Feeling in control once again, Livvie raised her chin a little higher and approached the back doors that led to the vineyard. The vision that awaited her caused her to suddenly stop. Looking out the window, Livvie saw a woman who appeared older than Drake giving him a hug. Livvie studied the woman's face and her beautiful features. As her hair was the same dark shade as Drake's, and they shared the same color emerald eyes, Livvie assumed this was his mother, who had seemingly arrived super early. Livvie had hoped to have at least a few more hours alone with Drake before his mother and his other guests arrived. With only a few days remaining, every moment felt precious.

Maybe this would be better, though. Maybe not being alone with him would stop her from wanting to devour him every chance she got. She had been walking around with wetness between her thighs for days now. Clearly, she needed to calm herself down.

Pushing those thoughts aside, Livvie inhaled deeply and opened the French door. In the back of her mind, she thought they may want some mother-son time, but his mother must have seen Livvie standing inside the door, so there was nothing she could do but face the introductions. His mother was the last person she would want to meet. After all, any mother can recognize a female lusting after her son. Talk about awkward.

The second Livvie stepped outside, Drake and his mom stopped talking, which made Livvie feel as if she had made a grave mistake. What was she thinking? She was only a raffle winner. She had no right to assume Drake would want to introduce her to his mother. Plus, she hadn't been officially invited to join them all at lunch. Maybe Mr. Birkshire and Drake had intended for her to eat by herself in her room.

Drake pinned her with his gaze and didn't look away, and despite the presence of his mother, he raked his eyes up and down her body, pausing for a moment in his perusal of her when his gaze hit upon the general area of her hips and breasts.

Staring back at him, Livvie felt as if she was being sucked into a vortex. Her body reacted to him very differently than her mind. She could control her mind, but her body felt entirely different.

"Drake, are you going to introduce me to this lovely young lady, or are you both going to continue staring at each other?"

There's nothing like another woman telling it like it is, thought Livvie. She'd always appreciated a woman who didn't hesitate to speak her mind. She only hoped his mom was a lot less intimidating than her son.

"Yes, *Mother,* I was about to; I'm just surprised to see my little raffle winner out here so early in the morning," Drake said while grinding his teeth.

Livvie guessed he was still mad about yesterday. If she were just a "little raffle winner," why would he even care?

Livvie stuck her hand out for his mom to shake. "Hi, you must be Drake's mom. I'm Olivia, but please call me Livvie."

Drake's mom grabbed her hand tightly and returned her smile. Livvie had an urge to run into her arms and cry like a baby, but instead, she inhaled and held back her unshed tears.

"Please call me Veronica." She placed both her hands around Livvie's and squeezed. The action made Livvie feel oddly safe and comforted.

"So you're the raffle winner?" Veronica asked with a twinkle in her eye. Up close, the woman was beautiful, just like her son.

"Yes, I'm the lucky raffle winner," Livvie said a little too sarcastically.

Veronica squeezed her hand once more. Livvie held Veronica's hands for strength in the same way she had held on to the banister earlier.

"You know, honey, when I heard that my son was allowing a stranger to stay at his sacred castle for the week, I was surprised. But Drake has a good heart, and he'd do whatever it takes for a stranger to have the best care possible."

"Mother!" Drake was still grinding his teeth.

"And to find out that this lucky raffle winner is a woman as beautiful as you are makes me believe that once again the universe knows better than I do." Veronica was beaming from ear to ear.

"What do you mean?" Livvie asked.

"Fate, my dear." Drake's mom grabbed Livvie by her face and kissed her on both cheeks.

"Enough, Mom, you're scaring away my little raffle winner, and apparently, she scares easily."

Livvie glared at Drake. How dare he bring up their issues at a time like this? And she wasn't easy to scare. Far from it. But he had told her yesterday to guard her heart, and she was sticking to it, regardless of how wet her panties were when she was around him.

"Sexual tension. I love it. This is going to be a fabulous day, after all. I'm glad I arrived early to watch the fireworks." Veronica clapped her hands.

Livvie, on the other hand, felt awful. Forget about the next three days; how would she survive today?

"Sweetie, what's that in your hand?" Veronica asked.

Livvie had completely forgotten that she was holding her journal. "Oh, I thought I'd come out here this morning and write." She hoped Veronica wouldn't ask more about her writing. She didn't feel comfortable telling her that she'd been fired from *Raven's Edge*.

"I gave her that journal," Drake added, sounding cocky.

"How lovely, dear."

"She's writing a novel, Mother. She's quite a talented writer."

Livvie immediately looked up at him. "Thank you, Drake, but how did you know?"

"I know everything that goes on at my winery."

"What he meant to say, sweetie, was that he knows everything that goes on with you. Now if you two lovebirds don't mind, I'm going to take a brief nap before the rest of your guests arrive. Don't worry, Drake, I'll be leaving after lunch, so you can spend the evening with your little raffle winner."

Veronica winked at Livvie, which caused Livvie's cheeks to flush. She hoped they didn't look too red.

"Stop embarrassing her, Mother."

"Don't worry, darling. She's a strong one." Veronica kissed Drake on the cheek and then gave Livvie a hug before stepping back inside the castle without another word.

Alone with Drake, Livvie wasn't sure how to act.

"Thank you for the journal again and for coming to my rescue." She smiled at him, unsure of how else to behave. A man had never come to her rescue before, and she had no idea how to handle it.

"You already thanked me for the journal, although not as I would have liked," Drake said with a twinkle in his eyes. "Olivia, you have nothing to feel ashamed about for being laid off."

"I was fired." Livvie's heart sped up, but not because she'd been fired.

"You were laid off. The producers weren't attacking your talent as a writer. They were just frustrated over the lower ratings, and they blamed it on you. They were wrong, and they're the ones who should be embarrassed. Not you."

Livvie swallowed hard. "Thank you. I needed that." Tears welled up in her eyes.

Drake must have noticed—he seemed to notice everything about her—and he instantly grabbed her in his big, strong arms and held her tightly. Tears began to flow. She didn't want them to. When it came to this man, she was constantly breaking her own rules. She had never cried openly in front of a man. It made her too vulnerable. Yet she was crying in front of Drake, and he didn't seem to care. If anything, he was trying to be there for her. Any other man would give her an excuse and leave. Those types of experiences had caused her to become harder, less trustful, and more introverted.

She grabbed Drake even tighter. This was what she had wanted when she had held on to his mom and the banister earlier. This was the strength she craved, and she found it in Drake Morganthal's arms.

When he started to caress her hair it was almost her undoing. Almost. But she couldn't stay vulnerable like this forever. He wasn't her boyfriend.

Livvie inhaled deeply and luckily stopped her tears from continuing to flow. She knew what she had to do. She just didn't want to do it. Instead of grabbing him even tighter, she stepped away and rubbed the remaining tears from her eyes. She could do this. There was no choice. No way would she be one of his many women, but that is exactly what she would be if she stayed a moment longer in his arms.

"Thank you," Livvie said softly.

Drake ran his hands through his gorgeous, thick hair, something she had done a few days ago when they had kissed and had been dying to do again ever since.

"What are you thanking me for now?" Drake sighed. "Stop thanking me altogether. You're obviously not used to a man being nice to you. And with my track record I don't want to be the one man who changes your opinion of my entire gender." Drake ran his hands through his hair once more and then walked right past her and into his house, slamming the door.

Livvie ran her hands up and down the journal and then held it close to her heart. She closed her eyes and inhaled the Napa air. She hoped to get strength from her journal in the same way she'd drawn strength from Drake's embrace. With the journal close to her heart she did find some strength.

"And another thing!"

Drake came back out and slammed the door again, scaring Livvie half to death. She opened her eyes and jumped back.

"If you continue to wear that sundress for the entire day, I'm not guaranteeing that I can hold my end of the bargain."

Drake looked her up and down then grabbed her from the back of her head and smashed his lips onto hers. He didn't devour her mouth the way he had the first time he'd kissed her. Instead, he held his lips tightly against hers. Hard. She thought he would release his strong hold, but when she tried to pull away, he only tightened his grip on her. She was forced to breathe through her nose. This wasn't a passionate kiss, and it didn't invoke those feelings from her either. This was more of a power play. Drake was used to being in control, and she, Olivia Collins, the little raffle winner, had thrown off Drake Morganthal, the powerful winery owner and one of the wealthiest bachelors in the entire world.

Finally, Drake stepped away. Livvie barely had time to catch her breath before he walked back into his house and once again slammed the door. Livvie's last thought before she followed him was that she hoped she was making the right decision by staying. Judging by the way Drake had just kissed her, all deals were off. Her heart wanted this, but her mind was still fighting. Right now, Livvie had no idea which one would win.

LIVVIE STORMED BACK into the house and slammed the door behind her. It was time she gave him a piece of her mind. But when she walked into the entrance hall, she couldn't find him. In fact, she could no longer even hear his footsteps. Where had he gone?

Livvie sighed and looked around the entrance hall and the living room.

"Looking for my son?"

Livvie jumped and glanced around for Drake's mom.

"I'm up here, darling," Veronica said as she walked down the grand staircase.

In the last ten minutes, both Drake and his mom had scared the life out of her.

"Hi, Veronica." Livvie smiled at her. It wasn't his mom's fault that her son was so frustrating.

Veronica walked up to Livvie, placed both hands on her arms, and gently squeezed them, making Livvie calm down.

"I know my son can be the most frustrating man, but please be patient with him." Veronica paused. "I think he's rather fond of you."

"I think he's rather fond of himself," Livvie blurted out. She wasn't surprised that his mom believed Drake was fond of her. She was more surprised that his mom used the word *fond*. Why was it that both he and his mother spoke so properly? Almost as if they were from England.

"What's troubling you, sweetie?"

Wow. She was good. Intuitive as hell. Livvie wasn't sure if she should be honest about her thoughts at the moment. She didn't want to offend the woman. She liked Veronica, and Livvie wanted the older woman to like her, too. After all, she was Drake's mom, so making a good impression was important. But Livvie had a feeling that honesty was the best way to go with Veronica.

"Please don't be offended when I ask you this." Livvie started talking, but Veronica cut her off.

"Why is it that when someone asks me not to be offended, I instantly get offended. Out with it, my dear."

Great, she was already upsetting his mom, and they had only been speaking for what, two seconds?

"Okay, I'm sorry. You're right. Why is it that both you and Drake speak as if you're from England, but you're not really from England?"

Veronica laughed. "Darling, we are from England."

"You are?"

"Well, sort of. I grew up in Connecticut, but I met Drake's father and fell madly in love. He's from England. When I married him, I had to move there because that's where he had a job. So I moved there, had Drake, and when Drake was ten, I missed Connecticut so much that I told his father I was taking Drake back there. Drake's father was furious, as he couldn't leave England because of his job. And that was the problem. Drake's father worked all the time. I realized my marriage was somewhat of an illusion. I rarely saw him. My heart felt like it was shattered into a million pieces. With my family far away, the only reason I got out of bed in the morning was for Drake. Some days even that was difficult. So I left and took Drake with me. His father filed for divorce and then missed Drake so much that a year later he sold his company, made millions, and moved to Connecticut, too."

"Did you get back together?"

"No, I don't think he ever forgave me for leaving and taking Drake, and I wanted to be with an American at that point. He ended up moving back to England."

"Did you remarry?" This conversation was a little awkward, but since Drake's mom was opening up, Livvie didn't want to ruin the moment. Drake had opened up to her last night, but it was important to get his mother's point of view.

"I never wanted to remarry. I have many lovers and one in particular that I fell in love with, but I like my freedom. I think that's what attracted me to Drake's father. The fact that he lived in England made me feel as if I was free, but then that feeling wore off, and I missed home. We argued about it a lot." Veronica paused. "Drake used to hear us arguing, and he hated it. He couldn't understand it. He used to tell me that even though his father and I are married, we were also friends, and friends shouldn't argue. To be honest, those were the only arguments we ever had. There was no bitter divorce. My heart suffered the most. After all, he was my first love. To this day, we are still friends. But from what some of his ex-girlfriends have told me, the moment they have an argument with Drake, he ends it."

"Really? Veronica, arguing is a part of life. There's nothing wrong with it."

Veronica sighed. "I know that, and you know that, but Drake doesn't argue with anyone. He hears what they have to say, and then he makes a decision accordingly, and he never looks back. That's one of the reasons he thrives so well in business."

Livvie had a sudden thought. "But he argues with me."

"Oh, yes?"

"Yes, and he hasn't kicked me out of his house. Then again, I'm leaving in a few days. We've always had an expiration date."

Veronica smiled and gently touched Livvie's cheek. "No." Veronica shook her head. "I knew he liked you. You're different from all the women I've seen him with."

"Tell me about it." Livvie rolled her eyes.

"You're beautiful, Livvie. What I meant was that you aren't fake like the rest of them. I don't find women with fake boobs and plastic surgery beautiful. You have long, dark, beautiful hair, exquisite blue eyes, and the perfect petite body. Plus, you wear little makeup."

Livvie blushed from head to toe. How embarrassing to be getting a critique by Drake's mother.

"Thank you," Livvie said softly.

"You glow, Livvie. You're genuine and honest, through and through. And you wear your emotions on your sleeve, which is very refreshing, my dear. Plus, it gives Drake a chance to be Drake. He will know how to help you when you need it, and he'll know how to make you happy."

Veronica paused, and although Livvie wanted to run away from hearing all this, she forced herself to stay. Finally, she was getting some answers on what was going on between Drake and her. And she did see the caring and protective side of Drake that Veronica was talking about.

"That's what my son does, Livvie. It makes him feel good to help others. And if he sees he's making a beautiful woman happy, he's elated. That's my fault. I'm well aware that I'm the cause of Drake's relationship issues."

"You are?" Livvie blurted out. She knew Drake had told her the truth last night, but it was good to get confirmation.

"Yes. While he was growing up, he watched me become more and more miserable. There were days I was extremely depressed. He'd do anything to change that. I remember one day he wrote me a song. And then he started cancelling plans with his friends to be with me." Veronica sighed. "He always thought of different ways to make me happy, but nothing worked. And as his mother, I knew how I was harming him, how I was failing him, but I missed my family so much that there was nothing he could do. I loved my husband, too. Even though I had to leave him, my heart was still broken." Veronica seemed as if she was back in those days in

London until she shifted her focus to Livvie. "Most importantly, though, is how the two of you look at each other. I've never seen my son look at anyone the way he looks at you."

"Really?" Livvie asked.

"Yes, really," Veronica said.

"But I've only been here for a few days, and I'm leaving soon."

Veronica kissed Livvie on the cheek. "We'll see about that, darling."

And then Veronica walked away without saying another word, and that was okay as there was nothing left to say. She had helped Livvie understand Drake and why they were drawn to each other. She respected his mother for that.

Drake felt good being a knight in shining armor because of what happened with his mom, and even though Livvie was independent, she needed and craved a knight in shining armor. She only hoped her knight in shining armor wasn't a stubborn alpha-male.

She stood in the middle of the entrance hall by herself, processing everything his mom had said. Then she sat down on the stairs. It reminded her of when she was a little girl and she'd sit on her parents' stairs. It felt comforting. Kind of like mashed potatoes comforting. And she needed to feel that more than anything right now, because Drake made her feel the opposite, except when she was in his arms.

Feeling a sudden craving to write, Livvie opened her journal and took out her pen. Where had she left off…?

Haley noticed a movement inside the cabin. Who dared to be hiding in there, she wondered. Haley crept toward the cabin, rehearsing in her mind what she would say to this person, whoever or whatever it was. Her only fear was if it was an animal. She grabbed a stick along the way in case she needed to clobber him or her on the head with it. Not that the stick would do anything, but it made her feel safer. Although in her heart, she knew she was safe from whomever she was about to lay her eyes on. Haley took a deep breath and then pushed open the door, hoping to scare whomever it was. But when she locked gazes with the person, her heart felt as if it stopped for a moment. She dropped the stick, unsure what else she should do. The man was gorgeous. He must have been way over six feet tall and had the most beautiful green eyes she'd ever seen.

"You better breathe, beautiful. I don't want to be picking you up off the floor."

And when he spoke, chills ran up and down her body. His voice was deep but soothing at the same time, and he had a slight Southern accent. She could listen to him talk forever.

"So I've heard at length about how you've charmed my mother."

That wasn't something her character would say, so that meant another man with a deep, soothing voice must be standing right in front of her. Livvie looked up into his eyes and had to strain her neck.

"I really like your mom."

"And my mom really likes you."

"I'm glad that's settled then." Livvie pretended to return to her writing.

"I'm warning you, Olivia. Don't try to get information about me out of my mother. If there's something you'd like to know about me, ask me."

"Or what?" First of all, she hadn't asked Drake's mom anything. Veronica had volunteered everything she had told her. Second, why was he acting like such an asshole? She should be the asshole. He'd kissed her and then walked away.

"Or there will be consequences." Drake raised one eyebrow, infuriating her even more.

She wished she wasn't sitting. The way he was standing, right up against the stairs, made her feel as if she were trapped. And he knew it. Instead, she slammed her journal on the step, making a loud noise.

"If you want me to leave, then tell me, and I'll leave," Livvie said in a loud voice, making sure he knew how serious she was. She really missed the Drake she'd been with on the rooftop.

"Never raise your voice. Ever. And that wasn't the consequence I was thinking of."

Without another glance, Drake walked away, leaving her alone once again.

12

NEEDING TIME TO think without being interrupted again, Livvie ran to her room. Why was she so infatuated with a man she had only known for four days? Never in her entire twenty-nine years had she behaved like this. She had liked Zach from the start, but that had been different because she had met him through a friend. They had been friends for a few weeks before he asked her out on a date. His problem was staying monogamous. He was one of those guys who believed that men weren't supposed to be monogamous. When he casually told her that he had been with another woman, he couldn't understand why she was so angry with him. But she was. Obviously, they weren't right for each other. She believed in being monogamous, but he had looked her straight in the eye on their third date and told her he had never been a one-woman man and had no intention of changing. For some reason, she'd thought they had such a strong connection that he wouldn't want to be with anyone else. She completely lost herself in that relationship.

After Liam broke her heart, she'd gone to a therapist who'd told her she had a habit of falling for a man's potential. Not who he truly was in the present. And the therapist was one hundred percent correct. She fell in love with the idea of Liam's potential. And then there was Zach. But was she doing the same with Drake?

Livvie's eyes grew heavy. She was exhausted. Not only from waking up at the crack of dawn these last few days, but exhausted with the state of her life. She sat down in an overstuffed chair by the window. She would miss this chair when she left. It was white, so if she bought the same one for her house, she would worry about it getting dirty. It wasn't the comfort of the chair that she loved as much as the view the chair faced. She would miss looking at the beautiful vineyard. In Los Angeles, she loved her ocean view, but Drake's vineyard was beautiful in a different way. This was his vision. His baby. Livvie inhaled deeply and closed her eyes. She hoped that maybe he'd take her for another walk in his vineyard if he ever stopped being mad at her. Or maybe he'd take her to the rooftop, and they could look at the stars again.

The last thought Livvie had before she dozed off was how Drake's lips had felt on hers as he'd brutally kissed her earlier. As she slept, she dreamed of them kissing again. The kiss started out with Drake pressing his lips against hers. He grabbed her bottom lip and gently bit it, causing her a little pain until his tongue brushed over the exact spot and moved back and forth, bringing such pleasure that chills erupted in her body. She ran her hands through his hair, loving the feel and texture. His hair was thick and smooth and smelled amazing, which drove her crazy. He grabbed her even tighter, so there was no room between them. As his tongue slipped into her mouth, she raised to her toes, wishing she were taller. She craved getting closer to him, and the more his tongue played with hers, the more she burned for him. Inside and out, she felt as if flames were eating her alive. He had created the fire, and he was the only one who could extinguish it. He gracefully picked her up, and she instinctively placed her legs around his waist. Finally, she was his height, and she pushed her pelvis into him. She pushed into him again, desperately wanting him to be inside her, but he kept on kissing her. He moved, pressing her up against the wall. She knew he could no longer wait. Drake balanced her against the wall and then unzipped his pants. He took out his rock-hard penis, lifted up her sundress, and moved her panties aside. He pressed his cock against her entrance, but he didn't thrust inside. He was teasing her badly and driving her crazy. She groaned out of pure frustration. She had never wanted anything as badly as she wanted him.

"Please."

She begged him, yet still he remained motionless.

"Please," she begged again.

If he didn't fuck her soon, she thought she would die, but instead of heeding her, he continued the torment. And in her dream, someone was rudely knocking.

"Please, Drake, I need you."

She continued to beg, and the knocking continued, as well. Why wasn't Drake telling whomever it was to go away? But the knocking went on and became louder. Loud enough that Livvie opened her eyes, realizing the noise was real and not a part of her dream. Disappointed beyond belief, she ran her hands through her hair. She wasn't ready to face the outside world, but she couldn't afford the luxury of not answering.

"Coming!" Unfortunately, Livvie wasn't, but if the dream had been allowed to continue, maybe she would have. That dream had messed with her mind. Livvie opened her door but couldn't even get herself to smile.

"Ah, there you are," Mr. Birkshire said, stone-faced as ever.

"Is there something I can help you with?"

"Yes, I'm sorry to disturb you, but the guests have arrived, and lunch will be served shortly."

"Lunch?" Livvie stood up straighter and glanced back at the clock on the night table. Wow. She had been sleeping for over an hour.

"Mr. Birkshire?" Livvie sighed. "Does Mr. Morganthal want me to be at the lunch with his guests, or would he prefer I ate up here in my room?"

The look he gave her was unlike any look she had seen from him before. It was filled with compassion, which made her feel off balance. There was no way she would cry in front of anyone else today and humiliate herself again.

"As a guest yourself, I assume he'd like you to be there."

"I don't think we should *assume* anything, especially when it comes to Mr. Morganthal." Livvie looked down at her hands.

"Please, Ms. Collins, I'd like you to be there. And knowing Drake as well as I do, I know he'd want you there as well."

Livvie sighed. "Thank you, Mr. Birkshire, but it seems I'm always making him angry."

Mr. Birkshire paused before he spoke. "And that's why I know he wants you there. You make him feel *something*, Ms. Collins. And most women, his mother excluded, make him feel *nothing*."

"But he fights with me," Livvie whispered.

Mr. Birkshire nodded. "Yes, he does. And what's that saying, Ms. Collins? 'Only the good things in life are worth fighting for?'"

Livvie smiled. "Something like that." Livvie felt eternally grateful to Mr. Birkshire. He had given her hope, which, on one hand, was a good thing, but on the other hand could be dangerous. Hope led to fantasies, and fantasies led to heartbreak.

"Will you come to lunch, Ms. Collins?"

"Okay," she said.

"Excellent, I'll see you down there then."

Mr. Birkshire turned and left. Livvie closed her eyes and took a deep breath. If she was going to meet everyone downstairs, she needed to look presentable. She looked down at her sundress, and luckily, it hadn't wrinkled.

A few minutes later, Livvie walked into the dining room and all heads turned toward her. Should she have changed after all? Six unfamiliar faces and one face she was very familiar with were looking her up and down. There were a total of eight people in the room standing around the table, which left Drake's mom, who was staring directly at him. Livvie felt so self-conscious, she didn't know what do. To cover up how uncomfortable she felt, she smiled as warmly as she could.

"Darling, there you are. I'm so happy you joined us."

Livvie had never been so grateful for another human being in her entire life. Thank goodness for Veronica. Having an excuse to move, Livvie walked up to her and gave her a big hug, not caring that the remaining seven people were still staring. Didn't they have anything better to do?

Veronica hugged her back hard and whispered in her ear. "Don't worry, darling, just continue to smile. They're all wondering who you are. My son, on the other hand, would stare at you whether they were here or not."

Livvie laughed. Between what Mr. Birkshire had said and what Veronica had said maybe everything would be okay between her and Drake, and he would want to continue seeing her after her week was up.

"What's so funny?" Drake commanded.

"Nothing. Now are you going to introduce this beautiful woman, or would you like me to do the honors?" Veronica said.

"Of course not. I seem to have lost my manners."

Veronica rolled her eyes, causing Livvie to smile. She adored Veronica. Whatever happened between her and Drake, she would like to keep in touch with the older woman.

"Excuse me, everyone, I'd like to introduce you to Miss Olivia Collins. She has been a guest in my home as a result of winning a raffle held by a charity that's dear to my heart."

"A raffle?" An absolutely gorgeous, tall, longhaired blonde woman asked while giving Livvie the evil eye.

"Yes. The charity raffled off a one-week stay here at my vineyard, where the winner gets an extensive tour and learns what it's like to own a winery."

Livvie felt even more embarrassed. He didn't make her sound special at all. Last night, she had felt special. Maybe Mr. Birkshire was wrong, and Drake only considered her a random raffle winner. At least that's how his words made her feel.

She walked up to him and placed her arm around his waist. Her pride was at risk, and she couldn't afford for her self-worth to take another dive, especially over another man.

"And I've enjoyed every second of it. Right, Drake?" She looked up at him innocently.

He responded by placing his hand on her ass and pinching it. She jumped slightly from the surprise but covered it up by placing her other arm around the front of his waist, making it appear that she was giving him a big hug. This time she didn't look at Drake but instead looked around the room. Everyone appeared shocked and uncomfortable by this public display of affection, especially coming from a random raffle winner. But she couldn't blame them. She was shocked, too. She never behaved this way, and she hated being affectionate in front of others. And to make matters worse, Drake had no choice but to place his arm around her.

She noticed that the hot blonde was looking at Drake's arm and then back at Livvie with even more hatred. Obviously, the woman was attracted to him. And in that moment, a very depressing thought occurred to Livvie. Had they slept together? Was she an ex of his?

"Everyone, please have a seat, and we will begin the lunch and taste some of my delicious wines," Drake announced. He must have had enough of Livvie's immature behavior.

"It really is delicious. All of it," the hot blonde said.

What the hell does that mean? Livvie wondered.

As everyone sat at the table, Drake gracefully moved her arms away, no doubt not wanting to not cause another scene, and then he went and sat at the head of the table. His mom sat on his left, and the hot blonde sat down next to him on his right, which technically had been Livvie's seat. Livvie was left with no choice but to sit at the end. She wished she had stayed in her room and not allowed Mr. Birkshire to give her hope things might work out. Hope was a dangerous thing, and Drake had just squashed it—and her heart—into a million pieces.

Veronica looked at her across the table with compassion in her eyes. It felt as if she was telling her she was sorry, but there wasn't anything to be sorry about. If Drake wanted her to sit next to him, he would have made sure it happened. Instead, he was talking and laughing with the hot blonde.

Livvie placed her napkin on her lap as the salads were served. Mr. Birkshire gently touched her shoulder, causing Livvie to jump.

"Wine, Ms. Collins?"

"Yes, please."

She smiled at Mr. Birkshire, and he winked at her. Once he had poured her wine, he did the same for everyone else at the table. She watched the others swirling the wine around their glasses and then sniffing it. Livvie always thought the wine-tasting process was absurd, but she didn't want to look as if she didn't know what she was doing, so she swirled her wine, sniffed it, and then closed her eyes and took a sip.

Mmmmmmmm. She loved Drake's wines. It was red, so she assumed it was a merlot, but she wasn't sure. She also had no idea of the year, but she didn't care. It was delicious. Her eyes remained closed as she took another sip and swallowed, savoring every moment, until the man next to her laughed.

"Enjoying the wine, are you?"

"Yes, it's lovely." Livvie smiled at him. If Drake could flirt with the hot blonde, then she could flirt, too.

"I'm sorry, Drake gave everyone your name, but he never introduced us to you."

Livvie smiled wider and placed her hand on his arm. "I guess Drake doesn't want me to know who you all are. After all, I'm only the raffle winner," Livvie said with a twinkle in her eye.

The man laughed. Not only did he have a nice laugh, he was also handsome. He wore his brown hair a little long, and she loved that look. His big brown eyes twinkled back at her, causing a warm feeling to erupt in her belly. She liked him. And she didn't even know his name.

"Well let me introduce all of us to you."

"Please don't make a big deal about this." She wasn't ready for everyone's eyes to be on her again.

She simply wanted to have a conversation with this very nice man next to her.

She glanced briefly at Drake, who was fully engaged in a conversation with the blonde. The woman had her hand in his hair, playing with it as if she had the right to touch him.

The man next to Livvie gently touched her chin. "Hey, don't worry; I'll whisper who everyone is."

Livvie giggled softly, but Drake must have heard. He was glaring at her.

Before the nice man could tell her who everyone was, Drake chimed in.

"I'd like to make a toast."

Everyone raised his or her glasses, and Livvie followed suit. Drake then continued in that deep, strong voice of his that she adored.

"To lifelong friends, and, of course, to my mother."

Everyone at the table laughed.

"May we all drink my wine together for many years to come."

The man next to Livvie said, "Salute", someone else said, "Cheers", another person said, "Thank you." Drake's mom said nothing, and Livvie smiled softly. What else could she do when the blonde grabbed Drake's face and kissed him on the lips? It wasn't a long kiss but long enough for Livvie to feel sick. Those lips were hers to kiss. The blonde ran her hands up and down Drake's arm and then looked directly at Livvie and raised her glass.

"And we can't forget the raffle winner."

Ouch. The bitch should have just punched her in the stomach. The pain would have gone away quicker. Everyone raised his or her glass toward

Livvie except for Drake, who leaned back in his chair and looked at her with a blank expression. She wished she could read his mind.

Then everyone returned to eating their salads and drinking Drake's wine. Livvie, on the other hand, couldn't eat a thing. She wanted to leave the table and run upstairs to her room to pack her bags. Seeing him with another woman brought up terrible feelings.

"Don't worry, Olivia, she means nothing to him."

Livvie swallowed back the tears and looked up at her guardian angel next to her. "How do you know?"

The angel placed his hand on her knee and gently squeezed.

"She's my sister. I know everything about her."

"Your sister?" What a shame the nice man had to be related to the woman sitting next to Drake.

"Yes, my name is Stephan Brenson, and that's Kayla Brenson, and we're co-CEOs of Kayla Brenson Cosmetics."

Livvie put her wineglass down and stared at him. Kayla Brenson Cosmetics was the trendiest makeup line out there. She had been using them for years, but they became so popular that they'd raised their prices, and even when she was making great money on the television show, fifty dollars for a tube of lipstick was way too much.

"That's impressive." Livvie had no idea what else to say, but apparently, that was okay, because he squeezed her knee again and kept his hand there.

"Thank you. Kayla has always loved makeup, and I've always been great at business, so we found investors, and our parents gave us a chunk of cash, so we started the cosmetics business. My sister is great once you get to know her. She just has a habit of wanting what she wants when she wants it."

"That doesn't make me feel any better."

Stephan laughed and began rubbing her knee. It started to feel awkward, so she shifted her legs, forcing him to remove his hand.

"So I gather you're a fan of Drake's wine?" Livvie smiled up at him and took another sip. She hoped she hadn't offended him, but she was tired of men thinking they could touch her whenever they wanted. She wasn't a doll. She was a living, breathing, woman, with a brain in her head.

"A huge fan. I have a wine cellar in my house in New Jersey, which is mainly filled with his wines. My sister has one, too. We buy it by the case, as does everyone else at the table. So that leaves four other people who you don't know."

As the salad plates were cleared and prime rib with a side of mashed potatoes and asparagus were served, Livvie looked up at Stephan and smiled, encouraging him to continue with the other names at the table.

"Eat, and I'll tell you. So far, I've watched you drink a glass of wine and take only one bite of the salad."

He was right. There was no way she would humiliate herself at the table by getting drunk, and she was already buzzing. Not a good sign. But right now, as she watched Kayla continue to run her hands through Drake's hair, she really needed the wine. But there was no way she could get sick, so she listened to Stephan and started eating her prime rib slowly. The very first bite seemed to melt in her mouth. She closed her eyes and savored every moment. *Only the best for Drake.*

Stephan looked down at her and laughed.

"I thought I was blessed watching you drink your wine, but watching you eat the steak is just as sexy. In fact, I've never seen anything sexier."

"Is that so?"

"I never lie, Olivia."

Livvie looked into his eyes, and they were serious. Maybe he was telling her the truth. "Please, call me Livvie."

Stephan responded by placing his hand on her knee again. But now she was feeling the effects of the alcohol, so she pushed his hand away. She hoped he got the point.

Stephan chuckled under his breath. "As I was saying, the man across from us is Jeff Laden, and sitting next to him on his left is his wife, Melanie. He created some hedge fund and made billions. Now he enjoys his life and drinks Drake's wines. And the man next to me is Aidan Kreslin, who's a huge real estate tycoon, but he's very secretive with his identity. And next to him is his wife, Leslie. And you know Drake's mom already. So now you know who everyone is."

"Are you friends with everyone here?"

"We all attend the same wine dinners, so we've known each other for years. It was my idea to come here. I have some business I need to deal with in San Francisco and other parts of California. I randomly mentioned that at a previous wine dinner, and they all decided to join me on my plane."

"You came here on your private plane?"

Livvie tried to make it sound as if it wasn't a big deal, but it was. She was used to people having money since she worked on the television show, and she had money herself, even though her savings account was quickly diminishing. But she'd never met anyone who was as wealthy as these people were.

"So what do you do, besides being a lucky raffle winner?"

Livvie knew he was just making conversation, but how was she supposed to answer him?

"I'm a writer." Livvie swallowed hard.

"A writer? That's great. I always wanted to write, but I'm no good at it. What do you write?"

Livvie hated being asked that question. When she wrote for *Raven's Edge*, she'd felt proud. And now, even though she was finally following her dream and writing a novel, most people would judge her because she wasn't making money from it yet. But Stephan had asked the question, so she had no choice but to answer.

"I'm writing a novel, but I usually don't like to talk about what I'm writing until I'm finished, if you don't mind."

"No, not at all. In fact, I completely understand."

Livvie smiled up at him, unsure what else to say, so she delved back into her decadent meal. She had never tasted anything so good. Well, those scones Drake had fed her yesterday were equally delicious. Or maybe it was his fingers that had tasted so yummy. Feeling a sudden urge to look at Drake, Livvie glanced out of the corner of her eye at him and Kayla. His head was thrown back, and he was laughing. It made her feel bad. She wanted to be the one who made him laugh. With her appetite completely gone, Livvie put down her fork. What a shame.

Veronica cleared her throat loud enough that everyone around the table went silent.

"Livvie, dear, why don't we change seats for a bit? I'm dying to pick Stephan's brain about the latest lipsticks."

Livvie hated the idea. She'd feel uncomfortable sitting next to Drake right now, and she felt sure Veronica had no urge to talk about lipsticks. Stephan had been like her lifeline at this horrific meal. How could she leave him and make it through dessert? But she had no choice, as Veronica was already standing, and Livvie didn't want to make an unnecessary scene. Instead, she glanced at Stephan and gave him an apologetic look. He looked upset too. Then she grabbed her wineglass and stood. All eyes at the table were fixed on her once again. She couldn't understand why. Drake and Kayla had been flirting like crazy. Shouldn't everyone be staring at them?

Veronica passed her and winked at her. Livvie smiled. What else was she supposed to do? She didn't want to move. The idea of sitting next to Drake and watching him with Kayla made Livvie sick. And she didn't know if she could behave herself since she was on her third glass of wine.

Slowly, she sat down and avoided eye contact with Drake, who seemed to be glaring at her again. Was he mad at her? Why? She wasn't the one flirting shamelessly. She and Stephan had been having a normal conversation. And it wasn't her fault he had touched her knee. Besides, Drake wouldn't have seen what Stephan was doing anyway. And that brought up another thought. What were Kayla and Drake doing under the table?

Unfortunately, it didn't take long for her to find out. Mr. Birkshire placed a napkin on her lap. By mistake, Livvie dropped it. When she picked it up, she looked under the table and saw Kayla massaging his upper thigh. Another half an inch higher, and she'd be massaging his penis. Drake might as well have punched her in the stomach right there and then. If he intended to remind her that she was nothing more than a raffle winner, then his plan had worked. But on the rooftop he'd told her if he were going to try to commit to a woman, he would try with her. Was he purposely trying to push her away?

Livvie placed the napkin back on her lap and stared at her hands, feeling defeated. In the big picture of her life she knew she would get through this, but in the immediate future—and in the present moment—she didn't know how.

"Congratulations on winning the raffle."

Livvie looked up and realized Melanie was trying to make conversation with her. She wasn't in the mood for small talk, but what choice did she have?

"Thank you. I was excited to win, and it came as a complete surprise."

Melanie smiled. "I love that feeling. Everything in life that is unexpected is usually life changing. In a good way. I met Jeff on a miserable rainy day in a long line at a bagel store."

"Really?" Livvie loved hearing stories like these.

"Yes, I'll never forget how we met. I was in a bad mood because the night before I got into a meaningless argument with my roommate at the time, and the rain was falling hard. My umbrella had turned inside out, and my hair was drenched. I was also running late to work, but I needed my morning bagel and coffee. I walked into the café and groaned.

"The man in front of me, Jeff, turned around, took one look at me, and said, 'Some days it's better to just stay in bed'. We started talking, and since the line was so long, we spoke for a while. He gave me his phone number, and six months later we were engaged."

"Thank you, but I'm not sure how this week will change my life."

Melanie grabbed Livvie's hand and squeezed.

"I think it already has. It may look dismal, as my day had looked when I walked into the café, but it changed into something beautiful. I believe yours will, too."

Livvie was speechless, but luckily, Melanie's husband was trying to get his wife's attention.

Having no one else to talk to, Livvie glanced at Drake again. And in that moment, he crushed what little hope she had left. She forced herself to watch him gently caressing Kayla's hair. When we kissed, hadn't he caressed her hair like that?

She watched Kayla touch his thigh under the table again, but this time she moved her hand even higher. When she caught Livvie watching, Kayla winked. Livvie forced herself to listen to Drake inhale and hold his breath, as he obviously enjoyed the feeling of having his dick rubbed. Livvie glanced around the table to see if anyone else could see, but they were all engaged in conversation. Only Veronica caught Livvie's attention, looking at her with deep compassion. One thing Livvie hated more than anything was when other people felt sorry for her.

When she had been let go from the television show, the writers who stayed on gave her the "compassion" look. Yes, she had been upset when she was let go, but at the same time she felt relieved. In truth, she hated that show, and it felt good to remember that. Even though the pay had been amazing, and she could afford a small but beautiful house by the Pacific Ocean, the actors were high maintenance. She would write a scene for them, and they would do nothing but complain. All they cared about was winning an Emmy. But all Livvie cared about was writing from the heart, which she had not done again until Drake had given her the journal.

When Mr. Birkshire started serving dessert, Livvie had never been so relieved in her entire life. In just a few more minutes, she could excuse herself, go upstairs, climb into her big, fluffy bed, and put an end to this day. Day number four had been the worst day yet, and she only had three more days to go.

Mr. Birkshire placed a slice of cake in front of her then bent down and whispered, "Your favorite cake, Ms. Collins."

Livvie smiled at him. She would miss Mr. Birkshire. She would miss this castle. The idea that she would be leaving soon really upset her. Not even a scrumptious piece of cake would make her feel any better.

"Aren't you going to eat your cake? Yesterday, you seemed to really enjoy it."

Livvie looked up from her cake and realized Drake was talking to her. When she looked into his eyes, she saw a twinkle in them, but his tone sounded cocky. He was behaving like a jerk. She guessed that was to be expected. They had been arguing a lot, and he had already moved on to the next woman. Livvie wasn't surprised. She had only hoped she wouldn't have to know who the woman was. And she wished the woman wasn't as beautiful as Kayla.

"Livvie, isn't the cake as good as yesterday?"

Trapped in her thoughts, she had forgotten to answer Drake. She took a quick bite of the cake, and the sugar exploded in her mouth. It tasted decadent, but instead of making her happy as it had yesterday, today it made her feel sad. In fact, everything at this lunch made her sad.

"It's delicious. Thank you." Livvie smiled. Not the type of smile where her teeth were showing; she didn't have energy for that.

"If it wasn't for you, I'm not sure I would have hired the baker."

"Why?"

They stared at each other for a moment, but Drake wasn't the same warm man she had seen yesterday. Now his eyes were cold and distant, as if they were strangers.

"You seemed to have enjoyed the cake yesterday, so I hired him."

"If I wasn't here, you wouldn't have hired him?"

"Probably not. He didn't have the strongest of resumes."

When it came to Drake, Livvie felt conflicted. His actions confused the hell out of her. One minute he was flirting with Kayla, and the next he was telling her he had hired the baker because of her opinion.

"I've been dying for him to hire the baker at my country club. He makes the most phenomenal desserts. And he has recently moved out west," Kayla chimed in, much to Livvie's infuriation.

"And I was scheduled to meet him next week," Drake added.

"But unfortunately he was too late."

So they were finishing each other's sentences? This felt wrong.

"You could still hire him," Livvie suggested.

Drake looked at her, and for a split second she saw warmth return to his eyes. And then, just like that, it disappeared.

"From the way you were devouring the cake and scones yesterday, I thought I had found *the one*."

Drake lifted one eyebrow, as if he were daring her to issue a comeback. But what could she say? Besides, she didn't think the baker was *the one*. Deep down, she had thought maybe Drake was.

When she failed to respond, Drake turned his head away from her and continued speaking with Kayla. After a few more dreadful minutes, he spoke to Stephan. Then Mr. Birkshire came back in and poured more wine in everyone's glasses. Everyone had a comment.

"This one tastes like vanilla."

"This wine tastes like licorice."

"This one is divine and would give Bordeaux a run for their money."

And then everyone was comparing Burgundy wines to Bordeaux wines, and so on and so forth. Livvie simply sat there and smiled when appropriate, but other than that, she remained silent. She only cared about Drake's wines because he had created them. From now on, no matter how painful it would be, she would only drink Morganthal wines. Luckily for her, not all of his wines were expensive.

She noticed Stephan glancing at her every so often, and mostly, those were the moments when she smiled. Other than that, Drake ignored her. Kayla only had eyes for Drake, and Melanie was drunk and flirting shamelessly with her husband. Livvie thought it must be nice to A) have a husband, and B) flirt shamelessly at a lunch because you were drunk.

When there were no more bottles of wine left, and everyone was sipping what remained in their glasses, Livvie rose, ready to exit. She was nervous to be the first, but she didn't fit in at this table. Everyone was nice, and she had enjoyed their company, but she couldn't stand watching Drake and Kayla flirt and touch each other.

So she made an excuse about wanting to take a walk after the meal. She smiled as warmly as she could.

"It's been a pleasure meeting you all," she said.

There were a few murmured responses, and everyone returned her smile. A moment later, she left the room, managing to avoid Drake's gaze altogether, but she felt his eyes on her as she walked out the door. What did he expect? That she would stay until the end and continue to be tormented, watching him and Kayla? No way would she subject herself to that willingly. She came to eat lunch. Not to be humiliated or shamed.

The second Livvie left the dining room and stepped into the entrance hall, she sighed with relief. She had gotten through the horrid lunch and without visibly falling apart. No tears. Nobody had made a scene. She'd suffered in silence. Livvie reached the stairs, dying to go to her room, when a hand touched her arm. She jumped, not because she was scared but because she didn't want anyone to physically touch her.

"I'm sorry, Livvie. I didn't mean to startle you."

Livvie turned, relieved to see Stephan and not Drake. She honestly didn't know what she would have done if it had been Drake, especially if he touched her.

"Oh, that's totally fine. I was just in my head." Livvie smiled at him.

"I'm sorry about how badly my sister behaved."

Livvie could see the compassion in his eyes, and she hated that.

"Please don't. Drake and I aren't together. And I think they make a beautiful couple."

"They're not together, either."

"But I'm sure after this afternoon they will be." Livvie turned around, no longer wanting to talk about Drake's love life. She also had no intention of breaking down in front of a man she had only just met.

"Wait. Please."

Already on the middle of the stairs, she stopped climbing and turned back toward Stephan. He hadn't done anything wrong, and she shouldn't be taking her frustration out on him. He had only been nice to her.

"I'm sorry. I guess I'm just a little tired from all the wine."

"That's a lie. I think you're tired of watching Drake and my sister flirting."

"And there's that," Livvie said as she looked down at her hand gripping the banister.

"They've been friends for years. I don't know what got into my sister today."

Livvie walked back down the stairs and rubbed her hand on his arm.

"Hey, it's okay if they want to be together. They're adults."

"But she's usually distant when it comes to men. She likes them worshipping and pursuing her. Today, she was pursuing Drake."

"And you're surprised?" Livvie laughed. Well, she tried to laugh, anyway. It came out as more of a humph.

"I guess women find him good looking," Stephan said quietly.

"Yes, women find him very good looking."

"I don't know why."

"What do you mean?" Livvie's hand rested on his arm.

"I think it's odd that women would be attracted to a man who has a track record of breaking women's hearts."

Livvie dropped her hand. He was right. But she had fallen for him anyway, as many women, including Kayla, had done.

"You're right," Livvie whispered.

"Well then maybe I can give you my phone number, so you know what it's like to be with a different type of man."

Livvie swallowed. "And what kind of man is that?"

"A man who isn't afraid of a commitment. I've had long-term relationships before, Livvie. I just haven't met the right woman to marry, but I'm open to the idea."

Livvie smiled. "And you're good looking, too."

They both laughed, easing the tension until Stephan became serious again.

"Will you take my phone number? I live in New Jersey. And you?"

"Los Angeles."

"I think you're beautiful and warm. I enjoyed the short time Veronica let us sit next to each other. I'd like to get to know you better."

Livvie inhaled deeply, as she tried to figure out the right thing to do. Although he was a really nice, successful, and handsome man, he wasn't Drake. She'd only known Drake a few days, so her feelings didn't make sense, but it didn't make them any less real. And even though she knew the chances of Drake being her future husband were slim, she wasn't healthy enough within herself to date another man. She wasn't talking about forever, only for now.

"I'm sorry, Stephan," she said. "I don't think I'm the woman you deserve."

"Right now," he responded.

She nodded. "Right now, I have a few things I need to figure out, and it's not only about a man."

Stephan gently touched her hair. "I think you're wrong. You are the woman I deserve, but for now, I will give you what you need."

Livvie didn't know what to say to that, so she smiled softly. She felt relieved that she didn't take his phone number, even as he walked out of the entrance hall and didn't look back. Stephan was a great guy, but it would have been wrong to take his phone number when her mind and heart were all jumbled.

It felt good to do the right thing. It felt better that she took care of her own needs. Maybe she was getting back to her old self. Just that alone made coming here worth it.

13

WHEN STEPHAN LEFT, Livvie ran up to her room, stopping momentarily when she saw Drake's bedroom door. She placed her hand on the doorknob as if she was touching Drake. Her heart felt like it was aching, as sadness consumed her. Drake touched this doorknob every day and slept behind this very door. Then she touched his wooden door and closed her eyes. When the week had started, she didn't think she'd be this torn about leaving and never seeing him again. But with only three days left she was a complete emotional mess. Maybe she should have chosen Plan A. Maybe then he wouldn't have felt the need to be with Kayla. Maybe if Livvie slept with him, she'd get him out of her system. She wished she were one of those women who could sleep with a man and stay detached.

Livvie pressed her head against the door and took a deep breath. She was dying to go inside. So fucking badly. She wanted to touch the bed he slept in and run her hands through his clothes. She knew that was inappropriate. But then suddenly, she thought, what the hell? Who cared what Drake thought of her? Who cared if she was invading his private space? He'd done far worse to her when he'd kissed her.

With surprisingly steady hands, she turned the knob, but the door was locked. Livvie groaned, but deep down she knew she would be better off not going in there. He probably had cameras all over the place. Instead, she opened her own bedroom door. She closed the door, leaned against it, and closed her eyes. She was finally safe. Safe from having to watch Drake with Kayla, and safe from having to pretend she was happy in front of a group of strangers.

Livvie walked to her bed and grabbed her purse. She rummaged through it until she found her cellphone. She needed to hear Carly's voice. But then Livvie stopped herself again. What would she say? That she had fallen for the most beautiful man who ever lived, a man who had been pursuing her until Kayla Brenson, of Kayla Brenson Cosmetics, came to lunch? And how did Livvie expect Carly to respond? No, this was something Livvie would have to handle herself. Maybe Livvie would fess up once she was back in Los Angeles.

Livvie placed the cellphone back in her purse, peeled off her clothes, and climbed into bed naked. She loved sleeping naked, but she rarely did. Living in Los Angles, she went to bed each night, knowing there was always the chance of being awakened by an earthquake. Running out of her house naked while debris fell down all around her didn't sound like a great idea. But she didn't care if there was an earthquake tonight. She felt buzzed from the wine, depressed, and exhausted. She glanced at the clock on her night table. 4:00 p.m. She would probably wake up in an hour, shower, and then write. She definitely wouldn't leave the sanctuary of her room and chance running into Drake. Or worse yet, Drake and Kayla. If he brought that woman to his bedroom, and Livvie heard them having sex, she would be devastated. So she did the only thing she knew to do. She pulled the blankets around her and went to sleep.

When Livvie next opened her eyes, it was dark. She must have slept for a long time. She felt warm, so she pushed her blanket off and stretched. Much better.

"Mmmmmmm, so beautiful."

Livvie screamed, sat up, grabbed the blanket around her, and turned on the lamp on her night table. Her heart was beating out of control, but she knew that voice. And then she remembered him and Kayla.

"What are you doing in here?" she whispered.

Drake was sitting on the couch opposite the bed, leaning back with a glass of wine in his hand. He looked relaxed…and drunk.

"I was wondering if Stephan was here."

"Really?" Livvie said. Of all things for him to say, especially after what he had put her through—the man had nerve. Where was Kayla? And why did Livvie feel as if he had cheated on her? She recognized this feeling all too well.

"Yes, really. You two seemed to have gotten along great at my lunch, and from the way he was looking at you, I thought you'd both be up here fucking."

Livvie's eyes widened. "You thought because of the way he was looking at me we would be up here *fucking*?" she said through clenched teeth.

"Why are you repeating my words?" Drake took another sip of his wine.

Livvie sighed. Even drunk he was sexy.

"Where's Kayla?"

"Where Kayla should be."

Livvie swallowed. "And where's that?"

Drake sipped more wine. "Jealous, my little raffle winner?"

Livvie wasn't sure how to answer. She ran her hands through her hair in frustration then nodded. "Yes. Were you jealous of Stephan?"

Drake took another sip of his wine and then another and another. The silence was killing her. She had been honest, which was hard to do. Why couldn't he be honest, too? Livvie pulled the blanket tighter around her. She hated that she was naked underneath. She hated feeling this vulnerable. And she hated that he was sitting there all cocky and fully clothed.

"No."

"No?"

"That's what I said." Drake took another sip of wine.

If Livvie had clothes on, she would take the glass and pour it over his head.

"Okay. Then why are you here? And why would you care if Stephan was in here, and we were fucking?" If he didn't care that a man could be in her bed, then he didn't care about her. At all.

"Kayla wanted to go home, and he drove her here in his rental car."

Livvie placed her head in her hands and took a deep breath.

"Stephan isn't here, Drake, so you can leave now." Livvie's voice sounded strong and steady.

Drake remained sitting and sipping his wine, as if he had all the time in the world. But he didn't. If he didn't admit he was jealous, his time was running out.

"I don't want to leave. I'm enjoying the view."

Livvie felt the tension rise in the room. Her mind was trying to downplay what he had just said, but her body burned for him. She still wanted him even though he could have just been with Kayla.

"Kayla has the same thing," she said.

"You're wrong."

They were both silent, and Livvie didn't know what to do.

"Take the blanket off all the way," Drake said in a quiet but stern voice.

"Were you with Kayla?" If he had been, his seductive talk and behavior was going to stop right now. And if he hadn't? Livvie couldn't answer that.

Drake continued to sip his wine.

"Were you?" Livvie demanded.

They stared at each other as if fire was coming out of their eyes. But Livvie refused to budge. This topic was too important to her. Drake having been with another woman was definitely a deal breaker. She swallowed and pulled the blanket farther up her body, clinging to it as if it could add another layer of protection around her heart. Then she looked down at her lap. He wasn't going to tell her, and she wasn't going to give in. It wasn't his fault, really. He had no idea that two of her ex-lovers had cheated on her.

"No," he responded in a strong tone.

"No?" she whispered again.

"I wasn't with Kayla." He took another sip of his wine, not once breaking her stare.

"But I saw her," Livvie said louder, finding her voice once again.

"You saw her touch my cock over my pants."

"And you seemed more than happy with her attention."

"And what about you and Stephan?"

Livvie's heart sank. "What about us?"

Drake raised an eyebrow. "So there is an *us*?"

"What? No," Livvie responded.

"Yet you seemed more than happy with him touching your knee."

How does he know? "I hated every moment of it, and if you hadn't noticed I pushed his hand away," Livvie responded honestly.

"But you still allowed him to touch you?"

"Maybe for one second, because he was the only one at the table at the time who was being nice to me."

"My mother was being nice to you."

Livvie groaned. "But she was sitting on the other side of the table, next to you. Why do I have to explain myself? Stephan may have been touching my knee, but Kayla was touching your cock. Big difference, Drake."

The room was once again silent. But there was something Livvie had to know. It would make the difference between her staying for the remainder of the week or leaving shortly.

"Drake?" Livvie paused.

He took another sip of wine. "Yes?"

She inhaled deeply. "Did you fuck Kayla?"

"You asked me that already."

Livvie sighed. "Yes, but after she touched your cock, what happened?"

Drake didn't say anything right away, and the sick feeling inside her intensified.

"I subtly removed her hand, and then the moment you left, I took everyone outside to my vineyard, except for Stephan. Because at that point, he conveniently disappeared."

"I wasn't with him, Drake, I swear. He came to talk with me, and that's it." Livvie sensed that Drake was telling the truth, so she needed him to understand that Stephan wasn't with her either.

Drake resumed drinking. Without any further response from him she felt uncomfortable. But feeling as if she was no longer being attacked, she loosened her grip on the blanket.

Mid sip, Drake paused, and the intensity in his eyes grew.

"I lied." Drake paused.

Livvie waited with baited breath for him to proceed.

"I hated watching Stephan touch you and flirt with you."

Livvie swallowed, feeling relieved. "And I hated watching Kayla doing the same thing with you."

"She means nothing to me, except she's a good customer."

Livvie smiled softly. "Ditto, except for the customer part."

Drake chuckled. After another few seconds of silence, he said, "Drop the blanket, Olivia."

Livvie swallowed and shifted slightly. Should she succumb to Drake's charms? Her heart thudded like crazy. Either way, she would leave here devastated. Livvie looked around the room, avoiding his gaze, trying to find her answer.

"Look at me," Drake ordered.

Livvie did as Drake instructed. The moment their eyes met, she dropped the blanket she had been holding on to for dear life. She reminded herself it was only sex, and she needed it badly.

The blanket fell into her lap, keeping her most intimate spot hidden. But her breasts with hardened nipples were revealed to Drake's intense green eyes. And then they became even more intense, darker, and dangerous.

His reaction should have calmed her and made her feel powerful. Instead, it made her crazy. She couldn't think straight, she couldn't breathe, and her entire body was experiencing an unending yearning.

"Shh, it's okay, Olivia."

"No, it isn't."

"Yes, it is."

"No. I chose Plan B."

Drake raised an eyebrow. "And you chose wrong. Now slide the blanket all the way off."

Livvie didn't move. She couldn't.

"Olivia, if you don't want to do this, you can tell me to leave. But your entire body is on edge with unfulfilled desires. And I'm the only one who can fulfill it."

"But you've been drinking," Livvie stated.

Drake sighed loudly and put down his drink.

"That's it, I'm leaving." He stood.

Feeling panicked, Livvie jumped off the bed and ran toward him, not caring that she was completely naked. She was tired of craving him. If he was drunk, the sex could be bad and not how she envisioned. But right now, bad sex was better than no sex. She needed to get laid. Period. Once she left here, she had no idea when she'd have another opportunity. There had been so much sexual tension between them this week; her vibrator at home wouldn't cut it.

"Please don't leave," she said.

Drake looked at her, but he wasn't touching her. "Only if you give up control, Olivia. You want this. You want me to tell you what to do. You don't want to think. Whatever assholes you chose to be with in your past caused you to second guess everything. I'm taking that away from you. Let me. At least for tonight."

She did what she'd been longing to do with all her heart since she'd first laid eyes on him… She agreed to sleep with him.

"Lie back down on the bed." Drake walked over to the bed and swiftly removed all the blankets.

Livvie did as he instructed. She passed Drake on her way, but they didn't touch. It was killing her, but she knew that if she listened to him, eventually, they would. She was grateful she didn't have to think about the why, the how, and the "what if…?" All she had to do was lie down naked on the bed. So that's exactly what she did.

"On your back."

As the mattress hit her back, she felt incredibly sensitive. Part of it was cold, but the part where she had recently sat was warm.

Drake sat back down on the couch and picked up his wineglass.

"Open your legs," he said in that deep, dominant voice she loved. "Wide. I want to see all of you. I want to see your entire pussy and your hole, where my cock will be soon."

As if in a trance, Livvie spread her legs open wide. She felt herself becoming wet, and she didn't care. There was no going back now.

"Wider."

She spread them even wider.

"Now tell me why you didn't fuck Stephan."

She hadn't expected that question, so she closed her legs.

"Don't. You. Dare."

Livvie immediately reopened her legs. Drake had revealed that he was jealous and a little bit possessive. So she answered honestly.

"I didn't want him."

"Why?"

Livvie inhaled deeply.

"Because I wanted you."

She couldn't see Drake from her current position, but she was dying to know his expression.

"Wanted?"

It took a second for Livvie to understand what he was asking her.

"Want," she whispered.

"I see." Drake paused. "Even though I go from woman to woman, never making a commitment?"

Livvie's body trembled. "Yes."

She could hear Drake taking another sip of wine.

"Please," Livvie begged.

Drake took another sip. How much is left in that fucking wineglass, thought Livvie.

"Spread your pussy lips. Let me see how wet you are."

Without hesitating, Livvie spread the lips of her pussy wide. She felt her clitoris swell and then pulse. If he didn't hurry up and touch her, she would truly die.

Drake put his glass on the coffee table and stood. He slowly walked toward her. When he was standing right next to the bed his finger delved inside her pussy and then he glided it up to her clitoris.

"You're dripping wet, my little raffle winner." He lifted his finger to his mouth and sucked it dry. "Delicious."

He then stuck a second finger inside her, thrusting it so hard it felt as if he was touching every sensitive area down there at the same time.

"Drake?" Livvie had never experienced a feeling like that.

He then stuck a third finger inside, and then a fourth.

She moaned and raised her pelvis off the bed.

Seconds later, Drake kneeled down and replaced her fingers that were keeping her vagina lips wide with his, spreading her pussy even wider. Without warning, he leaned over and placed his mouth directly on her clit. He sucked her clit and licked downward to the place where Livvie craved his cock. He licked his way back to her clit and then circled gently at first and then hard.

"Have you touched yourself while thinking about me in this bed?"

"Yes," she answered breathlessly.

"And have you come in this bed, in my guestroom, in my house?"

"Yes," she said, catching her breath.

"You will come for me now, Olivia," he demanded.

But Livvie shook her head back and forth. She couldn't come with Drake watching her; she'd feel too self-conscious.

"You will if I demand it. But don't worry; I'll make you come. Get out of your head, Olivia."

Drake resumed licking her clit with an intensity he didn't have earlier. He used one hand to grab her nipple and gently pull and massage. Livvie moaned louder as he continued. And then he found the sensitive place by her clit that always drove her crazy when she touched herself. How did he know? While he was licking, he pinched her nipple hard. She felt the orgasmic wave start, but she wasn't sure if it would continue. It never had in front of a man. But then with his other hand he thrust three fingers inside her and rubbed about an inch upward. The orgasm hit her so hard; she lifted her pelvis high in the air and screamed. She had never felt the wave this intense, and her vagina muscles clenched his fingers tightly, causing another mini orgasm. When her orgasm finally died down, and Drake stopped licking and touching her, she sat up slightly. He was gazing at her, and his eyes had grown even darker.

She looked at him then stared at his cock, hoping he'd get the hint.

Finally, he started taking off his clothes. *God, he has a beautiful body.* But before she had a chance to stare at each part, he pulled her down farther on the bed. Drake held her legs by his sides and moved his penis so it was right against her vagina but not yet inside. She leaned over to look. His cock was a work of art. Maybe one day she'd write about it.

"Olivia, I've seen your medical records, but if you'd like, I can show you mine."

Livvie understood what he was saying. She was grateful that he was clean, and she was not surprised he had seen her medical records. Apparently, he was asking her if she wanted to have sex without a condom. Was she ready to feel him without any barrier? Was she ready for the feelings that would invoke? So after a much-needed deep breath, she looked at him straight in the eye and nodded.

She heard Drake's exhale, and then he thrust powerfully inside her. It felt so fucking good that she moaned loudly. Slowly, he pulled out and then thrust back in. Out and then back in.

"You're so fucking wet, Olivia," Drake said through clenched teeth.

"You make me that way," she responded softly.

"Let's see how wet you are when I fuck you harder."

Without warning Drake pulled back and then thrust so hard that Livvie's entire body moved slightly up on the bed. He thrust again and again in the same rough way. And with each hard thrust Livvie's mind stopped analyzing and obsessing.

"You feel so fucking good."

Livvie's response was a moan. He was being all dominant, all alpha male—all Drake. And she thrived on his essence. When Drake's cock hit that particularly sensitive spot that no man had ever touched, she came hard. And it felt so good to ride the orgasmic wave in the same way that a surfer rides the ocean.

Not even a second later, Drake made a groaning sound, and she felt the wetness from his cum overtake her womb.

"Olivia, your pussy felt so tight around me," he said while catching his breath.

Her vagina clenched in response to his words. *Will I ever not want this man?* Stupid question. She knew the answer.

Drake groaned, and then he pulled out of her. The second he was no longer inside, Livvie's brain once again took over. The sex was the best she had ever experienced, but she hadn't even touched him or kissed him. Why? And would they do this again? Looking at the clock on the night table, she saw that it was past midnight. With only two more days remaining what would happen?

Drake collapsed next to her. "Get out of your head, Olivia." Then he did something she didn't expect from someone who had a phobia when it came to commitment. He pulled her into his arms and held her tightly, with her head against his chest. How could she analyze when he did something like that? Instead, she closed her eyes and drifted to sleep.

Sometime later, she opened her eyes and found the blanket wrapped around her and Drake still holding her. She wished there was a class she could take on *How to Figure Out Drake Morganthal.*

The next morning, Livvie woke up with a pounding headache. Partly from all the wine she had consumed at lunch yesterday. And partly from waking up alone. She'd been so spent after they'd had sex that she'd only awakened once throughout the night. And he had been there.

She glanced at the clock on the nightstand. *9:00 a.m.*

"Fuck."

She had overslept, and Drake was probably already working in the vineyard. She wished he had woken her up. Now she was stressing that he'd be all *after sex weird* on her. And she hated that. Seeing his wineglass still sitting on her coffee table brought back memories from last night.

She sat up a little too quickly and closed her eyes, trying to steady herself. God, she was a mess. Livvie stared at the wineglass for a little longer. Drake had placed his lips on the glass over and over again. What she would do to have his lips on hers one more time. And when he'd ordered her to spread her legs and had stared at her vagina, it was one of the hottest things she had ever experienced. Thinking about it made her pussy wet.

She hoped to be with him at least once more before she left. There was no need to deny herself any longer. She had done the deed, so why stop now? She thought she'd wake up feeling bad about herself, but she didn't. All she had to do was change her mindset. This was only sex. Obviously, she had feelings for him, but if she kept that separate, she could have sex with him and then leave. Without regretting a thing. Then when she returned to Los Angeles, she'd find a man who was the opposite of an alpha-male and date him. Her only concern was if he'd be as good in bed as Drake was.

While she sat there obsessing over Drake, someone slid a note under her door. *Good morning, reality*, thought Livvie. Then her heart stopped, and panic set in. Was it from Drake? Was he giving her walking papers? Did he not have the courage to tell her goodbye to her face?

Livvie forced herself to walk over and pick up the note. With trembling hands, she turned it over and saw it was from Veronica.

Livvie,

I'm sorry we didn't get a chance to say goodbye. I had to leave to meet up with an architect. I've been debating about whether to redo my house. Maybe the hot architect will convince me? I also wanted to tell you I'm really sorry for how my son behaved at lunch. I know he hurt you, and I hated to watch it, especially as his mother. I want you to know I've never seen my son so enamored with another woman as he is with you. I know you've only known each other for a few days, but falling in love is instant. I know you feel it, too. My son doesn't flirt. He doesn't need to. Women fall at his feet, but when I saw him flirting with Kayla, I understood. He was trying to make you jealous. I have never seen him so troubled, as he was when he was watching you and Stephan talk. It drove him crazy, so if that was your intention, it worked! Brilliant, my dear.

Please don't give up on my son. You make him different — a better man. Please, Livvie, I know I'm asking a lot, but please fight for him. Fight for the both of you. Here is my phone number. I expect you to use it whether you need my help or to talk. I live in Marin County, so I also expect you to visit.

Until we meet again…and we will.

XO,

Veronica

And then she had written her phone number at the bottom, beneath her signature. Livvie inhaled and stared at the note. How was she supposed to fight for a man who didn't want to commit to a woman? How was she supposed to protect herself? Livvie didn't have the answers, but she had her journal. So after a quick shower, she began to write. She may not be able to figure out her life, but at least when she wrote, she didn't have to stress over falling in love with a man who had given her an expiration date, from the very first day they met.

14

BEING ALONE IN a cabin in the middle of the woods can be daunting. Being alone in the cabin in the middle of the woods with a drop-dead gorgeous man can be just as terrifying. Or at least Haley thought so at first, but the situation turned out quite the opposite. Blake made her feel rejuvenated, free in her own skin, euphorically happy, and most of all, alive. Just a fraction of those feelings was what she'd hoped she would feel by staying at this cabin alone for the week. She had never been so grateful in her entire life that her travel agent had double booked the week. Blake was tanning himself by the lake. Would tonight be the night? The sexual tension in the cabin was building. She wanted him badly. More than she had ever wanted anything in her life, including this one sought-after, peaceful week.

Haley watched as Blake rubbed lotion on his magnificent body. She could smell the lotion from here…or maybe it was Blake's intoxicating smell. She would miss this smell. Strong and masculine, just like the man himself. What would she do once the week was over? How would she rebuild her life? Could she rebuild her life? She knew it seemed strange. Mourning over a man she had met only a few short days ago. And yet she knew she would grieve. Big time. But she didn't know how. How should she grieve over a beautiful man? A man who seemed to get everything he wanted out of life, and for these few days, she'd believed she could, too. His ambition, determination, and fearlessness had rubbed off on her. Spending time alone in the cabin with him, especially at night, when the only light came from the moon's reflection, had created memories she would treasure for the rest of her life.

Livvie put down her pen and stretched her arms above her head. After reading Veronica's note, she had spent the rest of the day writing in her room. Actually, she was hiding in her room. At first, she had intended to find Drake, but she felt weird about it. She was a big believer that if a man wanted a woman, he would do everything in his power to get her. But from what he'd done yesterday—or, rather, hadn't done—he must not have wanted her that badly or even at all. She could understand why he had left in the early morning without waking her up, because if it were the other way around, she probably wouldn't have woken him, either.

At around seven o'clock, she heard a knock on her door. She hoped Mr. Birkshire was bringing her dinner. She was starved. Writing always made her hungry.

She was grateful she wouldn't have to go down to the dining room to eat. She was still wearing her blue tank top and comfy jeans, which she had thrown on that morning before settling in to write. But when she opened the door, Mr. Birkshire wasn't there with food.

"It's about time you showed your beautiful face." Drake was standing there in a white polo shirt and green shorts, looking sexy as hell.

Livvie opened the door wider. "Sorry, I was writing all day."

"That's only part of the truth. You were avoiding me, afraid the commitment phobic man wouldn't want to see the woman he slept with last night."

"And there's that." Livvie smiled softly, unsure of why he was here but relieved at the same time.

Drake put his hands in his pockets, looking almost uncomfortable. "Normally, you'd be right, but I had to see you. I've been dying to kiss you all day."

Drake stepped forward, grabbed the back of Livvie's head, and gave her such a warm kiss. He moved his lips gently over hers. Livvie stood on her tippy-toes and threw her arms around his neck, needing to feel him closer.

With obvious reluctance, Drake stepped back but held her around her waist. "Now I feel much better."

Livvie laughed. "So do I."

"Good. Are you hungry? I know you haven't eaten dinner."

Livvie's stomach growled. "As you can hear, I'm starved."

"Excellent. Come with me."

Drake grabbed her hand, and they walked out of the room. Livvie's heartbeat picked up with the anticipation of spending time with him.

She followed him through the same door as the other evening.

"We're going to your rooftop?" she asked as they climbed the steps.

When they reached the top, he turned and looked at her before opening the door, which led to the roof. "I hope that's okay."

Livvie couldn't respond. When she stepped out onto the roof, she was speechless. Drake had set up a small table with plates, wineglasses, and two chairs next to each other. A heating lamp was placed by the table to keep them warm. Not that they needed it. It was a warm night.

A tall white candle sat in the middle of the table with red rose petals surrounding it. Rose petals also covered the ground. Red candles sitting in glass jars were scattered around this part of the roof. The view in the background made everything even more beautiful. More perfect.

"Drake, it's beautiful," Livvie said, her tone breathless.

"As you can see, this is the only part of the roof that's flat. Once in a while, I like to eat up here. Since you enjoyed the rooftop the other night, I thought you'd like this, too. So I moved the couch and set this up instead."

Livvie tore herself away from the view and looked at him. "Thank you." And she meant it with all of her heart. She stood on her tippy-toes and pecked him on the lips. Not being able to help herself, she threw her arms around him and hugged him tightly.

He refused to offer her tomorrow, but at least he was being romantic. He made her feel special.

"I'm glad you like it." Drake was holding her just as tightly.

"I love it. I never knew you had a romantic side to you."

Drake broke the hug and led her to the table. Like a gentleman, he held the chair out for her. "I don't. This is the first time I've ever brought a woman up here. For some reason, you bring out a side of me I didn't know I had. You have from the moment we met."

Livvie sat down as she soaked in what he was saying. Drake was almost acting like her dream man. Almost. Even though his actions reflected his pretty words, he was still afraid of a commitment. But tonight, she didn't want to think about that. Tonight, she wanted to enjoy him.

Mr. Birkshire came out on the roof with a bottle of wine.

Livvie laughed. "You made Mr. Birkshire come all the way up here?"

Drake smiled. "He went to get the bottle of wine I requested. I installed a kitchen behind the door on the left. He won't have to keep going up and down the stairs."

"I don't mind," Mr. Birkshire chimed in as he poured wine into Drake's glass.

Drake sipped it and then nodded. Mr. Birkshire resumed pouring the wine in Drake's glass and then filled Livvie's.

Once he was done, he winked at Livvie and then exited through the door Drake had mentioned. Then another man, who she didn't recognize, placed halibut and a delicious, roasted corn dish on their plates. Once they left, Livvie felt free to talk.

"I see Andrew isn't serving us."

Drake gave her a deadly look. "He no longer serves meals while you're here."

Livvie couldn't help herself and laughed. "He's harmless, Drake."

"In my eyes, any man who goes near you isn't harmless," he said as he dug into his halibut.

She laughed even harder. "You're sexy when you're jealous."

"I'm sexy to you even when I'm not jealous. Now eat."

He took another forkful of food and Livvie followed.

"True," she said. "But your chef must be sexy, too. Any man who can cook this good is a god, at least in my eyes."

Drake stopped eating and picked up his glass of wine instead. "I'll make sure you never meet him." He took a large sip of wine.

"We forgot to toast." She picked up her glass.

"What would you like to toast to?"

Livvie inhaled. "To nights on your rooftop." Her heart felt heavy. Soon, she would be leaving, and there would be no more nights up here.

Drake's eyes looked intense. "To nights on my rooftop." He clicked his glass with hers and then resumed eating.

The rest of the meal went by quickly. He pointed out the different vineyards in the distance. He explained to Livvie about their different wines and who the owners were. Livvie asked him questions about the wines in France and what it was like when he'd worked in the vineyard in Burgundy. Drake told her story after story.

When they finished off the wine bottle, Livvie leaned back in her chair, feeling more relaxed than she'd ever been.

"Thank you, Drake," she said softly. "I'll remember this evening forever." She wasn't mentioning their expiration date, but they both knew it was coming.

"The evening isn't over," he said as his eyes darkened. He stood and held out his hand.

Livvie instantly took it, and he led her farther down the roof until they reached a section that was slanted.

"Careful," he told her.

Drake held her waist and helped her step over the slanted portion. On the other side, the roof flattened out again, and someone had laid out a thick blanket. Nearby stood another heating lamp.

"Drake," Livvie said. "Did you have Mr. Birkshire place this here?"

Drake chuckled. "No. I did this earlier this afternoon. I wanted to see you earlier, but I was swamped with work. I found a minute to place this here and set up dinner."

Livvie sat on the blanket, craving what was coming next. "Thank you." She couldn't find the words to express how touched she felt. She wanted to show him instead.

Drake sat next to her, and they immediately kissed. With the stars above, this was the perfect setting to show him how much she appreciated tonight.

The kissing didn't last long.

"I want you naked, and I want you naked now," Drake demanded.

Livvie obeyed. She took off her tank top and put it behind the heat lamp that was keeping her nice and toasty. As she unbuttoned her jeans, Drake was taking off his shirt and shorts. She loved him naked. And the more she got to know him, the more she loved him clothed, too. She'd have to analyze her feelings tomorrow, though…not tonight.

They both sighed with relief as Drake lay on top of her, his naked body pressed against hers. Always needing control, he placed her hands above her head. With his free hand, he reached to touch her between her legs.

He inhaled deeply. "God, I love how wet you are for me."

Livvie pushed her pelvis up into his hand, as Drake circled her clit, just the way she liked. At the same time, he thrust his fingers inside her.

"Drake," Livvie begged.

"I love how you beg when you want more. I love how badly you want my cock."

Livvie couldn't argue because he spoke the truth. After a few more minutes of this wonderful torture, Drake replaced his fingers with his cock.

Livvie moaned and raised her pelvis to meet him. "This feels so fucking good."

She couldn't say anything more because Drake kissed her. And for the rest of the time he was inside her, his lips never left hers.

Livvie woke up feeling better than ever, although she should feel exhausted. Last night, after they had sex on the roof, Drake pointed out all the different stars.

She'd had no idea he was so knowledgeable about astronomy. She didn't know a lot about astronomy, but she knew a lot about astrology. In Los Angeles, everyone did. It was almost like a prerequisite course you needed to take to move there. She learned that Drake's birthday was January 8th, which made him a Capricorn. The Capricorn men who she knew were hard working, successful, and struggled when it came to relationships, which pretty much described Drake to perfection. She was a Gemini. Gemini and Capricorn were compatible signs. When she'd told him that, he'd just laughed.

They stayed on the roof until three o'clock in the morning and then came back to her bedroom and had sex again. She'd wanted to go to his, but he had a conference call with some business associates who lived in France this morning and had to wake up super early. It meant he wouldn't be in the vineyard, so she was able to sleep until seven and then write for a few hours.

The only thing that depressed her was the fact she was leaving Morganthal Winery tomorrow, never to return. If she thought about it for too long, she would stay in bed all day, completely immobilized, so she decided to put her feelings to the side and deal with them when she was alone and back in Los Angeles. Besides, it was already past ten o'clock in the morning.

She looked at her last remaining sundress, relieved to see it wasn't wrinkled. It was black and white and sleeveless. Putting on her black sandals, Livvie left her room and closed the door.

As she walked down the grand staircase, Mr. Birkshire called out her name.

"There you are. We're so happy you've come down."

He still wasn't smiling, but he did seem abnormally relieved to see she had left her room.

"Sorry, I really needed to write."

"Did you accomplish a lot?"

Livvie smiled warmly at him. "Yes, I did. Thank you."

"We're happy to hear that."

"Who is '*we*', Mr. Birkshire?" Livvie hoped it was Drake, but she wasn't sure how long the conference call had lasted.

"I am."

Livvie froze as Drake appeared out of nowhere. She was so happy to see him, even though he had only left her bed a few hours ago. Had she based her character Blake on him? Probably. He was all she had thought about. He had consumed her every thought for six straight days. And it was exhausting.

"You're glad to see me?" she asked, her tone flirtatious.

Drake nodded. "Are you hungry?" He looked as if he wanted to eat her.

Livvie was starved but she didn't want to go into the dining room after what had happened the other day at lunch. She loved the rooftop, but the dining room brought back bad memories.

"I'm okay, but thank you." She smiled.

Drake smiled back with a twinkle in his eye. "Really? Because the baker made some fresh chocolate chip scones this morning."

"He did?" Livvie's mouth watered. There was no way she could turn down one of his decadent scones, and Drake was well aware of that.

"He did." Drake smirked. "If you'd like one…or two, you can join me in the *kitchen*."

Drake emphasized the word kitchen. How had he known? Livvie sighed. Of course he knew.

"I'd like that very much."

Drake placed his hand gently behind Livvie's arm. His easy touch made her heart do a little dance.

They walked in silence until they reached the kitchen. Livvie had never been in here before. It was beautiful, with dark wooden floors, white cabinets with glass, white granite counter tops, and a huge island in the center with bar stools. This kitchen was a dream. Her mom used to cook a lot, and she had taught Livvie. Livvie rarely cooked for herself, but this kitchen would definitely inspire her.

"Do you like it?"

Livvie beamed from ear to ear. "I more than like it." She laughed.

"Do you cook?' Drake asked, grabbing a large plate of scones from the counter.

He held out the plate, and she grabbed one.

"I cook, but I'd much rather eat."

Livvie bit into the scone and closed her eyes, savoring every crumb that hit her taste buds. Drake laughed. Her senses were out of control between her satisfied taste buds, smelling the delicious scones, looking at the man in front of her, and listening to the beautiful sound of his laughter. She was definitely experiencing sensory overload. As she took another bite of the scone she felt chocolate drip onto her chin, so she licked it off. Then she took another bite, and felt Drake's eyes on hers again. Gone was the laughter she had seen a few seconds ago. Instead, she saw such intense lust she had no choice but to stop eating and put down her scone.

"You're not eating?" Livvie whispered.

Drake's Adam's apple bobbed as he swallowed. Watching his throat move turned her on.

"I'd prefer to watch."

Livvie's heart was going crazy, and her entire body felt as if it was pulsing. She needed to do something, anything, so she jumped up on the island and sat there, swinging her legs as if he wasn't affecting her at all. She grabbed her half-eaten scone and placed it right under Drake's nose.

"Are you sure?"

Drake inhaled, staring at her the entire time. Livvie pulled the scone away from his nose and took another bite.

"Mmm, you don't know what you're missing."

"Oh, I know what I'm missing."

Livvie could no longer pretend. "But do you miss *me*?" she said softly as she put down the scone.

Drake exhaled. "You're here."

Livvie couldn't stop herself from pressing further. "But I won't be tomorrow."

Drake spread her legs slightly and then moved forward so he was standing between her thighs. He then grabbed her legs, which stopped her from swinging them.

"And I will miss you terribly."

Livvie's heart beat faster. "We could change that," she whispered. She wanted Drake to get over his fear of commitment and give them a real chance. He admitted he'd miss her. That had to mean something.

Drake was staring at her with such intensity. "Let's not think about tomorrow. Instead, let's make love as much as possible with the time we have remaining."

Make love? Where did that come from? It wasn't the answer she wanted, but did he make love to all the women whose hearts he'd broken? "I didn't realize we were making love. Making love is when two people come together, hoping they have a tomorrow. Even if they're scared. I assumed we were fucking." She had no right to say that. He had told her there would be no tomorrow. And she hurt him. She could tell from the look in his eyes.

But a second later, the hurt in his eyes had gone, replaced with danger.

Drake clenched his teeth and pulled her closer to the edge of the counter. He grabbed her hair in one hand and then pulled her head all the way back.

"So you think I'm a coward?" he said between clenched teeth.

He was hurting her, but she wasn't in pain. In fact, she was turned on beyond belief, and her nipples hardened against the soft cotton of her dress.

"No. I didn't say you were a coward," she said, her head completely bent back.

"You didn't have to. But you're wrong. I'm not a coward."

He pulled her head up slightly and kissed her hard. He held his lips in place, forcing Livvie to breathe through her nose, and then his actions grew gentle. He moved his lips slowly against hers, making sure he touched every part of her waiting mouth. His tongue slipped in gracefully and met hers. He licked her tongue as thoroughly as his lips kissed her mouth. Livvie moaned. He was the best kisser she had ever been with. He was the best at everything.

He touched her knee and then sensually caressed all the way up her to her inner thigh, to the piece of cotton that was protecting her most intimate spot. He placed his hand flat against her crotch over her panties. Holding his hand there, he spoke in a seductive voice against her ear.

"I wanted to continue making love to you, but clearly you'd rather fuck. So you win. We're going to fuck."

Without warning, Drake removed his hand from her crotch, and then, using both hands, he ripped her panties. Roughly, he touched her clit until it swelled under his finger. In that moment, he owned her body, and he could do with it as he pleased.

Once her arousal was evident, he unzipped his pants enough to take out his beautiful, thick cock. He pulled her hair again, this time causing slightly more pain, and thrust into her hard until she felt it all the way to her stomach.

Livvie moaned out of a mixture of pain and pleasure. And then he started to fuck her—over and over again, as if he didn't care if she came or not. This was just fucking. But it drove Livvie crazy. She moaned even louder, and in the back of her mind, she hoped Drake had locked the door to the kitchen. But even if he hadn't and someone barged in, there was no way she could stop this now. She wanted him with an intensity that scared her. So she grabbed onto his shirt, slipped her hands under it, and touched his chest all over.

"You slut," Drake said while continuing the beautiful torture. "All you want is to fuck, don't you?"

Livvie nodded.

"Say it," Drake demanded.

Livvie was so turned on she could barely speak, but she knew she had no option.

"I want to fuck."

He groaned and then, keeping one hand in her hair, he reached the other hand to touch her clit softly, his gentle strokes in exact opposition to the way he was fucking her. The two extremes combined set her on edge. She felt her orgasm build, but she wanted his permission before she came.

"Drake?"

"Yes, slut?"

She loved him calling her that and it made her even wetter. She couldn't hold back from coming, but she knew she had to.

"Drake, I need to come."

He pressed hard against her clit while continuing to thrust. "Come for me, Olivia."

Less than a second later, Livvie screamed as her orgasm took over her body. She desperately grabbed onto him, needing to hold on to something. And as she wrapped her arms around his neck, she heard him groan and felt his cum shoot into her body.

When they had finished, Livvie's arms remained around his neck, and Drake released her hair and hugged her tightly. It felt right. Magical. And she was leaving tomorrow.

He kissed the side of her hair. "Why don't we wrap these scones and take them to my bedroom? I don't know about you, but I think this will be the perfect day to stay in bed."

Livvie smiled. "What would Mr. Birkshire say?"

He pulled out of her and pulled up his pants. Livvie pushed down her dress and tried to fix the wrinkles that had formed.

"Mr. Birkshire will be relieved that he won't have to prepare the dining room for us and can instead leave a tray of food by my door."

Livvie didn't care anyway. She was sure that by now everyone in the castle knew they were fucking. Or making love. Or whatever. She was leaving tomorrow, so it didn't matter.

She jumped off the island. "Okay, let's go."

Drake smiled and grabbed her hand.

They may not have tomorrow, but at least they had today.

15

ON LIVVIE'S LAST and final day at Morganthal Winery, she woke up in Drake's bed, but this time, when she opened her eyes, she wasn't alone. Drake was still there, lying beside her, fast asleep. She let out a sigh of relief. If she had woken up alone, she would have been devastated. She was grateful he was still sleeping as it gave her a chance to take in her surroundings.

After they had shared amazing sex in the kitchen, Drake had taken her up to his room for more sex. He kept on referring to it as making love, yet Livvie refused to call it that as she was leaving today. He had previously made it very clear that after the week was over, so were they. And since they had spent the entire day and evening fucking, all she saw was Drake's gorgeous body. It wasn't even until the evening that Drake picked up the tray of food Mr. Birkshire had left outside his door. After looking around, she realized this was definitely a bedroom for a man. If he ever decided to get married or live with a woman, he would have to add a feminine touch to it. But that thought depressed her, so she focused on the dark wood dresser, the largest flat screen television hanging on the wall, and the black leather couch on the side of the room. His hardwood floors were covered with a beige rug, and his enormous bed had a wood and leather headboard. The furniture was obviously expensive and obnoxiously masculine. She thought Drake would have better taste. Livvie smiled to herself. She'd finally found his first flaw.

"I swear I didn't decorate my room myself," Drake said, half asleep.

Livvie laughed. "No?"

"No. I decorated the rest of the house, but when it came to my bedroom, I was closing a big business deal, and the interior decorator I hired to help me was getting on my nerves. So my assistant at the time on Wall Street picked all this out."

"And do you like it?" Livvie had to bite down on her bottom lip to keep from laughing.

"I hate it."

"Then why not change it?"

"When it was finished and I received the bill, I discovered it had cost me a fortune. I honestly didn't want to spend any more money on this house. And clearly, you can see how well my assistant knew me. And hated me, I might add. She put me in the category of an egotistical, wealthy man with bland taste."

Livvie laughed again but then stopped herself as Drake rolled onto his back and grabbed her hand. Then reality crept in.

"I'm leaving soon." Livvie swallowed tears that formed.

"What time?"

"What time is it now?"

Drake turned toward his night table and glanced at his clock. "It's eight o'clock in the morning."

Livvie paused before she spoke. "My flight leaves at noon."

Drake squeezed her hand. "And it takes about two hours to get to the airport."

Livvie inhaled. "I know. I should go," she whispered.

Drake climbed on top of her and pressed his lips against hers. A goodbye kiss. She could feel it in the intensity of his lips against hers. She broke the kiss by moving her head to the side. She didn't want to cry in front of him.

"I have to go," she said.

Drake nodded and moved off her but not before he gazed down at her naked body. And the look in his eyes spoke volumes. He wanted to remember her as she was now. Yesterday, he told her he'd miss her terribly. She had to cling to that.

Filled with pain, Livvie stood and gathered one of the blankets that had fallen. She didn't care that she was naked in front of him, but she had to pack, and she had no idea who would be in the hallway.

"Thank you," she said once the blanket was firmly in place.

Drake lay back down and clasped his hands behind his head. "For what?"

"For showing a random raffle winner a great time." She laughed, trying to keep the moment light, but she knew she had failed. The tension in the room only grew thicker.

"Thank you for being the one who won the raffle."

Drake smiled, but Livvie didn't think the expression was genuine. She could feel him detaching. Drake did not want a commitment. Period. She needed to leave before it started to feel weirder.

"Okay, well I'm going to quickly pack my things and then go."

"Take care of yourself, Olivia. And make sure you continue to write."

Livvie smiled and then turned and left his room, closing the door behind her. He hadn't even gotten up and walked her to the door. How awkward, how…*final*. The man she'd seen these last few days, was gone.

In the hallway, she stood there a moment and held the doorknob. She closed her eyes as a tear slid down her cheek. *Only a few more hours.* And then she'd be back at her house, and she could break down and cry. So she inhaled, let go of his doorknob, and opened her door for the last time. But before she walked in, she kissed her hand and placed it back on his door.

"Goodbye, Drake," she whispered. Then without a second glance she went inside her own room to pack and get out of there as quickly as possible.

Standing in the entrance hall for the last time, Livvie felt numb. This was the best and the most torturous week she'd had in her life, and she was afraid she would wake up tomorrow in her own bed in Los Angles and discover it'd been a dream.

She lifted the handle of her suitcase, mentally preparing herself for the reality that awaited her once she was on the other side of this door. She inhaled deeply, wanting to remember what the castle smelled like. She looked around for the last time and took little mental pictures. She knew she needed to leave. The longer she delayed her departure the harder this would be.

"Ms. Collins, I didn't realize you were leaving so early. Please don't leave without these scones. The baker made them specifically for you."

Livvie released the handle and graciously took the paper bag out of Mr. Birkshire's hand.

"Thank you, Mr. Birkshire. I'll miss seeing you every day." Livvie tried to smile. "But if we meet again, please call me Livvie." Without thinking about it, Livvie put down the scones and wrapped her arms around Mr. Birkshire, giving him a warm hug. She swallowed back the tears. Even leaving Mr. Birkshire was hard. He very carefully placed his arms around her, but she could tell he felt uncomfortable. Not wanting to make it worse for him, Livvie ended the hug, and Mr. Birkshire instantly stepped back.

"Livvie, you *will* come back."

Looking into his eyes, for one solid second she believed him. Then again, hope could be rearing its ugly head again. And hope was an illusion.

Knowing she was about to break down, she smiled at Mr. Birkshire and then quickly picked up her scones.

"Thank you," she said softly.

Swallowing back more tears, Livvie rolled her luggage to the door. She glanced back at Mr. Birkshire, who had that compassionate look in his eyes that she hated, and she smiled. He didn't smile back but the look in his eye said it all. Then she glanced up at the grand staircase, secretly hoping she would see Drake once more. But she didn't.

Mr. Birkshire stepped in front of Livvie and opened the door. "Please let me."

But as he held the door open for her, she couldn't even look at him. The minute the Napa air hit her skin, she ran to her rental car that was awaiting her. She didn't care what Mr. Birkshire thought of her or even if Drake was staring at her through the window. She simply needed to get out of there as fast as she could. She threw her luggage and the scones into the back seat, and then opened the front door and sat down. Once she closed the door and turned on the car, she was tempted to look back at the house. But she couldn't. She was barely holding it together as it was, and if there was even a small chance that Drake was looking, she didn't want him to know how much leaving him was affecting her. Instead, she gripped the steering wheel hard because if she didn't, she would run out of the car and back into Drake's arms. However, he was clearly already done with her. He hadn't even offered for them to stay in touch. So Livvie drove down the long road back to Main Street. Once there, she stopped and pulled over to the side of the road. Without realizing it, she had stopped at the exact point where she first saw his castle. And then the tears began to pour down her face. She had just left a man who had broken down all her walls in one week and who she had fallen deeply in love with. And the reality of her life, which she had managed to keep at bay, was creeping back in.

Livvie cleared her throat and wiped away the tears with the back of her hand. It was time she drove to the airport and dealt with whatever reality awaited her. Her dream was clearly over.

16

DAY ONE, DAY one, day one, day one, Livvie repeated to herself over and over again. She sighed loudly and dropped her suitcase onto the floor. As she looked around her living room, she gripped the bag with the scones. She wished she had remembered to take a bottle of wine before she left Morganthal Winery. The scones were the only thing—besides her new journal—that she had from there. She would need to rebuild her life, and today was the first day of that journey.

Strange, thought Livvie. Everything in her house looked the same. Nothing was disturbed. No one had broken in. But it felt different. She had moved into this house three years ago, a year after she was hired to write for the television show. She remembered the first time she walked into the house after she'd signed her lease. It was similar to this moment, yet it felt so different. The place had come furnished. She remembered Carly saying that Livvie should buy a house. And Carly had been right.

Financially speaking, Livvie would have been smarter to buy, but deep down, she hadn't been sure she'd want to put down roots in Los Angeles. She'd never really felt at home there. So she'd insisted on leasing and finding a place that was fully furnished. She had always envisioned herself buying furniture and a house with her husband. But when everything with Liam blew up in her face, her life track had changed.

Livvie plopped down in her big, fluffy chair and placed the bag of scones on the coffee table. Then she slumped back on the chair with her hands hanging over the arms and closed her eyes. Already, she missed Morganthal Winery like crazy. Or maybe she just missed Drake.

She must have dozed off because when her text message went off, she literally jumped in her chair. When she opened her eyes, she thought she was still at Morganthal Winery, but then reality hit her. And an intense feeling of despair consumed her. Yet she knew how the mourning process worked. On day one it was hard to breathe because the sadness was so overwhelming, but each day would become better. She would get through this. She had survived through all of her other disappointments.

She found her purse, which was by her suitcase, and grabbed her cellphone. She remembered turning on her cell when her plane landed, but she had been too tired and depressed to check her messages. Sitting back down in her chair, Livvie took a deep breath, ready to face her life again.

Glancing down at her screen, she sucked in a breath, and her heart flipped. The text was from Drake. She wouldn't have known it was from him except in the scone bag Mr. Birkshire had left a note with both his cellphone number and Drake's. She'd thought it odd that there wasn't anything else on the note, but she had been touched by his gesture. She had no intention of calling either one of them, but now she felt thrown. She had assumed there would be no further contact. Or maybe he had sent a message out of nothing more than politeness. After all, he was a gentleman, and this text was definitely the gentlemanly thing to do.

Livvie read and reread the text about ten times.

Please let me know when you arrive home safely.

There was nothing emotional about his text. No, *I miss you*, or, *I miss you more than life itself* or *come back...I realize I can't live without you*, or, *you are my soul mate*. So Livvie exhaled and responded in the same tone.

I'm home safe. Thank you for asking.

She placed the phone against her heart and closed her eyes. There, that was it. Now he would go on with his day and never text her again. A tear slid down her cheek, but she didn't care. She had cried in her car, in the airport, and on the taxi ride to her house.

She gripped the phone a little tighter, and then she felt it vibrate. Her heart did a little leap. She immediately checked to see if it was Drake, and it was!

The week was beautiful and perfect. Just like you.

He went there, thought Livvie. *He actually went there.*

She quickly typed a reply.

Thank you. I thought the week was beautiful and perfect, just like you, too.

She hit "send" and then groaned. Had her response been lame? Maybe she should have come up with something more original. She sighed. Yeah, her response was stupid.

Once again, the phone vibrated.

That's good to know.

Livvie stared at her phone. Was she supposed to respond to that? What could she even say? So instead, she took a deep breath and didn't text back. She hated being the last person who texted, especially with a man. Now she had no idea if or when she would hear from him. Livvie sighed. It would be best if she never heard from him again. That way she would heal faster.

Needing to keep herself out of her head, she finally played her voicemail.

God, Livvie thought, *Carly is definitely going to kill me.*

There were six messages from her, all absolutely frantic. Then she received a message from her mom, checking in on her, and three messages from Zach. The last one was enough to make her want to stay in bed for rest of the week. And these latest messages didn't include the messages she'd played the first few days at Drake's. But Zach's last message was the worst.

"Hey, Livvie," he said, "Look, I know you're not returning my calls for whatever fucking reason, but I miss you. I miss us, baby. Where are you? Why are you not calling me back? I know I fucked up. I know it, baby, but don't ruin what we have. I love you. I love you, Liv. Please talk to me. Just talk to me. I can come over anytime, day or night. Please, Liv. I need you. I love you."

Livvie wished with her entire heart and soul that Drake had left her that message. But Drake wouldn't leave a message like that. But then again, his text messages were really nice, so maybe there was hope?

Livvie sighed. Drake wouldn't leave a voicemail like that. From the text he sent, it sounded as if he was done with her. They had a great week, and now it was time to move on. But she had no idea how to do that, especially being unemployed. At least if she had a job maybe it would help her get over him. Maybe it would give her something else to think about.

Why had Livvie slept with another unavailable alpha-male? Because there was a side to him that was humble, caring, and warm. But he still didn't want a commitment. Her next man needed to be humble, caring, warm, and ready to commit. She was getting closer, though, right?

Livvie quickly called her mom to let her know she was okay, which ended up being a lot more difficult than Livvie had thought. Her mom knew her well, and it was hard to cover up her emotions. And there was no way she wanted to start crying on the phone. Then she would have to explain everything. She ended the call with the excuse of having a headache due to the hot flight, and then she went into her kitchen to grab her emergency pint of Heath Bar Crunch ice cream. Unfortunately, someone was knocking on her door, and she wasn't ready to see anyone.

"Livvie, I know you're in there!"

Livvie sighed. She should have called back Carly the minute she got home. It was wrong of her to make her best friend worry. Carly had a way of knowing what was going on inside Livvie's mind, even if Livvie didn't. So she placed the ice cream on the kitchen counter, ran her hands through her hair, took a deep breath, and opened the door.

"Hi, Carly." Livvie put on the best smile she could.

"Oh, God, you look like shit. What the hell happened to you?" Carly walked right past Livvie and plopped down on the couch. "So are you just going to stand there, or are you going to grab the ice cream on the counter in the kitchen, sit your ass down, and tell me why you haven't called me all week?" Carly softened her words with a grin.

Livvie sighed. She could never escape the wrath of Carly even if she tried. And she didn't try. She loved Carly. They had been best friends since childhood. Then when Carly was fifteen, her dad had gotten a job in Los Angeles editing movies, and Carly had moved. Livvie had been devastated, but they'd remained closer than ever. Carly had been one of the main reasons Livvie had wanted to move to Los Angeles after the whole Liam incident. Knowing Carly was here made everything much easier. She was like a sister, and Livvie trusted Carly with everything. Livvie didn't have a lot of female friends. She found most women competitive and had no time for that, but Carly was always legitimately happy for Livvie when things went well for her and sad for her when things turned to shit. They had such a special friendship, and Livvie had no intention of ruining it by lying to her, so she walked back into the kitchen, grabbed two bowls, two spoons, and a bunch of napkins and placed them on the coffee table. She then went back for the ice cream and surprised Carly by taking out two chocolate chip scones—one for each of them.

"Scones! I love scones." Carly grabbed her plate and took a bite.

Considering the noises Carly made as she closed her eyes and chewed, Livvie would swear her friend was having an orgasm.

"Yeah, Drake's new baker made them." Livvie thought that was a perfect place to start. "And you won the bet."

Carly stopped eating and stared at Livvie, wide eyed and obviously shocked.

"You bitch. You saw Drake Morganthal, and you didn't immediately call and tell me?"

Livvie bit her bottom lip. Carly was right. Livvie should have called. "I'm sorry."

"And he was there for the entire week?" Carly's mouth was practically hanging open.

Livvie nodded. "Yes."

Carly sighed. "Please tell me you didn't fall in love with Drake Morganthal."

Livvie sat down, looked at her very best friend, and started to cry. In between sobs, she began to tell Carly how she fell for another unavailable man.

Hours later, Livvie awoke to someone pounding on her door.

"Who is it now?" she said, putting the pillow over her head. She was exhausted. After crying for hours on Carly's shoulder, Livvie had barely been able to keep her eyes open and had passed out shortly after her friend had left.

As the pounding on her door continued, Livvie groaned. She lay there for a few more minutes, contemplating what she should do, including calling the police. Where was Mr. Birkshire when she needed him?

Groaning even louder, she forced herself out of bed. She was afraid the pounding would wake up her neighbors. She'd felt so much safer at Morganthal Winery. If it were some random drunk guy, she'd totally freak. Looking at her clock on her night table, she saw it was two o'clock in the morning. She wasn't dressed appropriately for answering the door at this time of night...well, the morning. She could wrap a blanket around her shoulders, but there was a strong chance she'd call the police. If that were the case and they showed up, she'd feel a lot better if she was dressed. There was also a chance she wouldn't answer the door at all, but it could be Carly making sure she was okay. Carly had a huge problem sleeping. Livvie was used to her coming over at weird hours.

Her black tank top with matching silk pajama bottoms would have to do.

Her best bet was to grab her cellphone in case she had to call someone. She hated living alone at times like this.

Livvie picked up her cellphone from the coffee table and then tiptoed to the door. It was hot in her house, so she was sweating. Her heart was also beating like crazy. Livvie stood on her toes and looked out her peephole.

"Oh, fuck," Livvie said out loud. *Why is Zach here, and what the fuck am I supposed to say to him?* Should she leave him standing outside? No, she couldn't do that. He would just continue pounding on her door, and then she would get in trouble with her neighbors. They weren't the friendliest group of people. Not that it mattered. Without bringing in any money, she wasn't sure how much longer she could afford this place anyway.

Livvie sighed and then opened her front door. "What do you want, Zach?"

Catching Livvie off guard, Zach pushed her away and stormed into her house.

"Where is he?" Zach shouted.

"Who are you talking about?"

Zach ran his hands through his short blond hair and walked through her house as if he was looking for someone.

"Your new man," Zach said through a clenched jaw.

There was something different about Zach tonight. Livvie couldn't put her finger on it, but his behavior made her uneasy. Just in case, she left her front door open, so she could make a hasty exit if she needed to get out of there.

"I don't have a man, Zach."

"You're lying."

"I never lie. You know me." But her uneasy feeling intensified because she was kind of lying. No, she didn't have a new man, per se, but her heart was still very much connected to Drake.

Zach stopped walking and then stood in front of her, staring at her as if he was looking through her. This wasn't good and so not like him. Was she safe? Zach looked at her for a few more seconds, smirked, and then walked into her bedroom. Livvie stayed still while he opened her closet door and then slammed it shut. She then heard him going into her bathroom, opening the shower door, and then closing it again. What was she supposed to do?

Zach stormed back into her living room and grabbed her shoulders. Livvie gripped her cellphone harder.

"If you don't have a new man, then why have you been avoiding my calls for a whole week?"

Zach was grinding his teeth, but it was the look in his eyes that scared her the most. They were glazed over and haunting. Livvie swallowed hard and gripped her cellphone even harder. If she could get away from him long enough, she could call the police. Something definitely wasn't right.

"Zach, let me go," Livvie said quietly.

Luckily, Zach let her go and began pacing around her living room. She sighed with relief.

"I'm not going to hurt you, Livvie. I know that's what you're thinking." Zach appeared calmer, but she still didn't trust him. They were together for one year, and she had never felt like he would physically hurt her, but she had heard stories that he had a dark side. When they first started dating, he was five years sober from alcohol. She thought that was long enough for him to be in a relationship, but his addiction cropped up in different ways, such as cheating on her. He couldn't be with only one woman, and she should have known better. He refused to go to therapy, and he wasn't part of a recovery program. He had just decided one day that drinking made him sick, so he stopped. At the beginning of their relationship, he spent hours telling her stories of his past drinking habits. None of the stories were pretty, but she believed he was on a healthy path. He worked hard as a successful talent agent with many celebrity clients, and that's how she had met him. Zach represented one of the actors on her television show…a guy she'd become friends with and who had spoken very highly of Zach. Livvie met him one day on the set, and they had clicked. At first, she wanted to just be friends with him, but their attraction was too strong. They'd started dating, but he didn't believe in being monogamous. And foolishly, she'd thought she was different from all of his past women. That she was special. But she was wrong. Out of the blue, he'd told her that he had been with his assistant the night before…as if he had done nothing wrong. And in a way, he hadn't, as he had made himself very clear regarding how he felt about such things, right from the beginning of their relationship.

"That's what you're thinking, aren't you, Livvie? I know you pretty well."

Zach's question jarred her out of her thoughts. She had to figure out a way to get him out of her house. Her only sanctuary.

"Yes. You scared me for a sec." Livvie took a step back toward her front door.

"Liv, please close the door and sit down. We need to talk."

Livvie's heart began to thud. If she closed the door, how would she escape if she needed to?

"I promise I won't hurt you. I'd never hurt you." Zach ran his hands through his hair again.

Livvie looked up into his eyes to see if he was telling her the truth. She saw tears. He was crying over her? This was getting stranger by the second. But she did believe him, as he had never hurt her physically. Why would he? Livvie inhaled, closed the door, and sat down on her big chair.

She nodded toward the couch, indicating for him to sit down. Zach sat close enough that their knees were touching. Livvie hadn't planned for that. She also hadn't planned for Zach grabbing her free hand and holding it.

"Liv, I'm sorry. I'm sorry for being with other women when I was supposed to be with you."

Livvie looked at him but felt numb. Tears were pouring down his face.

"Women? I thought there was only one," she whispered.

"No, I'm sorry. There were a few."

Luckily, she always insisted he use a condom, and thank goodness she had been tested when they broke up.

"You fucked them all?"

"No, I mainly got them off with my fingers, and they would blow me, except for one. The one I told you about."

"Why are you telling me this?"

"Because you scared me this week, Liv. I thought I'd lost you."

"Zach, we broke up four months ago."

"That's not true. I mean, yes, technically, we broke up, but we continued talking. Our connection never died. And we have a rare and powerful connection, Livvie."

"Zach, you cheated on me over and over again, and I'm supposed to be okay with all of that?"

"I promise you, I'll never do that again. I can't lose you. I'll do whatever you want. Do you need money? I'll put money in your account first thing tomorrow. And besides, I didn't technically cheat. I told you right from the beginning that I'd be with other women. I thought I'd made myself clear. But if you want me to be monogamous, I will." Zach gripped her hand harder.

"No, I'm fine. Thank you," she said.

"Liv, let me explain. When I hadn't heard from you, I felt something different when I thought of you. I felt as if there was another man around you. Like you were fucking another man. I came here every night for the last three nights, but you never answered your fucking door." Zach's voice became louder.

"I wasn't here. And can you please lower your voice? I don't want my neighbors to hear you."

She shouldn't care what they thought of her, but she did. Maybe because when she was growing up, her family was friends with all the neighbors. Here, they all ignored her, and she tried so hard to be friendly. She even baked them all brownies when she moved in. Maybe that was why they didn't like her...she was a terrible baker. Speaking of baking, Livvie saw the bag of scones still sitting on her coffee table. She'd been too tired to clean up when Carly left earlier. Livvie needed to get Zach out of her house. It somehow felt wrong that he and the scones were in the same room.

"Sorry. So are you going to tell me where you were?" Zach smiled but it didn't reach his eyes.

"I went to some charity event with Carly, and I won a raffle ticket for a week in Napa. That's where I was," Livvie said as nonchalantly as she could.

"You went by yourself?"

Zach was smart, and after dating Livvie for a year, he also knew her well.

"Well, sort of. I mean, I stayed at a winery, and there were a lot of other people staying there, as well." Livvie wasn't exactly lying. Drake did have a lot of staff staying there.

"Really? Huh, and what were the other guests like at this winery?" he asked.

"I don't know. They were nice, I guess. I mainly wrote while I was there." Livvie looked down, which was a bad idea, as she had forgotten how revealing her pajama outfit was.

Zach followed her gaze and practically stared at her chest, which was fully on display. It made her feel too exposed. She still felt the need to grip her cellphone as if it was her lifeline, while her other hand was still in Zach's.

"You wrote?"

"Yes," Livvie said a little too cheerfully.

"And what was the name of the winery you stayed at?"

"Why the fucking twenty questions, Zach?" Livvie had to get him out of her house.

"I'm entitled to ask my girlfriend as many questions as I'd like. Who were you fucking at this winery?" Zach yelled.

"No one. I fucked no one," Livvie yelled back and yanked her hand from Zach's grasp. She stood and walked to her front door once again. Panic started rising, and she swallowed hard to try to calm herself down. What would Zach do if he found out she had sex with Drake? She hadn't cheated on Zach. They had already broken up, but she never thought Zach was the jealous type, until now.

"Don't. You. Lie. To. Me." Zach stood and crept toward Livvie like an animal hunting his prey.

"I talked to people, but I mainly wrote."

"Uh huh." Zach paused, standing only a few feet away. "And what was the name of the winery? I asked you, and you decided not to answer." Zach eyes became darker, more dangerous.

She could lie to him, but he would probably find out some other way. Morganthal Winery was listed on the school's website as one of the prizes. He knew where Carly worked, so it wouldn't be that hard for Zach to put two and two together... Livvie felt trapped, but what would Zach do? He would never suspect that someone like Drake would be interested in her. That was reassuring at least.

"Morganthal Winery," Livvie said, trying to keep her tone as normal as possible.

Zach smirked, a much different smirk than Drake's. Drake's smirk was seductive while Zach's looked as if he was mentally preparing to kill her.

"So you fucked Drake Morganthal," he stated.

"No," Livvie blurted out and then swallowed hard. *How does he know?*

Zach nodded slowly a few times and then pursed his lips before roughly pushing her aside and opening her door. "I never thought you were a liar, Livvie."

"Where are you going?"

Zach turned around and looked straight into her eyes. "To get rip-roaring drunk, which is what I've been doing since I suspected you'd been with another man." Zach stepped out of her house and then once again turned around. "I don't have to hurt you, Livvie. Drake Morganthal will never commit to you. And knowing you, I'm sure you're hoping he will. He'll break your heart far worse than I ever could. If it was any other man, I'd rip him to shreds, but this is way more perfect." Zach laughed in a creepy way and then stopped and looked at her as if she had grown horns. "What I don't understand is why you're attracted to men who have no interest in being in a committed relationship. You'll never get married this way, and forget about ever having kids. And since you can't find another writing gig, you'll probably move in with Carly and spend the rest of your life dating men who have no intention of being with you long term." Zach smiled wide. "Good luck, Liv." He winked and then turned around and walked down her walkway.

Livvie leaned against her front door, watching him, and began to cry. She was surprised she still had any tears left. He was right, and he knew it. He also knew how badly his words had hurt her.

Livvie had tears running down her face as Zach pulled away. She looked up at the stars in the sky. She couldn't see many with all the streetlights, but she could see a few. It wasn't Drake's rooftop, though.

It was a peaceful night outside, except she thought she heard a bird. She looked around but didn't see anything. Maybe it would be smart to close the door. But she heard the noise again, this time even louder.

"Hello? Olivia?"

Livvie jumped and almost dropped her cellphone. She held it up. The name on the screen was Drake's. *Oh, no!* She'd been clutching the phone so hard—had she called Drake, of all people, accidentally? What should she do?

"Olivia, is everything okay?"

Livvie quickly pressed end. Maybe he would think she'd drunk dialed him or something. God, this was so humiliating. She'd promised herself she would never call him, no matter what. And now she had gone and called him by mistake. Had he heard Zach? Had he heard anything? How long ago had she called him? She walked back into her bedroom, pressed his name on her recent call list, and saw that the call had lasted eleven minutes. Livvie threw herself down on her bed. This was one of the worst days and nights she had ever had.

Again the phone rang. It was Drake.

Fuck. What should she do? She let the call go to voicemail. Seconds ticked by as Livvie stared at her phone, waiting to see if he had left a message. She waited. And waited. And waited. Then her phone buzzed, indicating she had a voicemail. With trembling hands, Livvie pressed the button to listen.

"Livvie, I'm calling back in two minutes. If you don't answer your fucking phone, I'm going to call the police, my lawyers, and anyone else I need to fucking call to make sure Zach stays away from you."

And then he'd hung up. Livvie's heart was beating like crazy. What would she say to him? Something like, "Don't worry, Zach is on his way to a bar, and there's no way he'll show up again?" That was a lie, as she had no idea if Zach would show up again. And that terrified her. She didn't think he would harm her, physically, but she had also never seen him this mad or this evil.

Livvie jumped when the phone rang again, and this time she knew what she had to do.

"Hey, Drake."

She heard Drake breathing loudly on the other end.

"Hey, Drake? You called me by mistake at two o'clock in the morning because some asshole was in your house, and then I call back, and you ignore my call, and all you can say is, 'Hey, Drake'?"

Livvie sighed. "I'm okay. Everything's okay. I'm sorry to have woken you."

Silence filled the line for a few moments, and she wasn't sure if that was good or bad, but she was ready to hang up the phone.

"Do you have any idea how much you scared me? Do you have any idea how worried I was when I saw your name on my phone at two o'clock in the fucking morning?"

Livvie swallowed. She was missing him like crazy. He had no idea how much she was missing him. "No."

"And do you have any idea how it felt when I answered your call, and there was a fucking man at your house screaming at you? I thought he would hit you at any minute. And do you know how it felt for me to realize I could do nothing to help you?"

Livvie's heart felt as if there were a ton of bricks on it. She didn't want Drake involved in her drama. In the big picture, he had no intention of being part of her life. He had made that clear. She didn't want to make the same mistake with Drake as she had with Zach. Both men had spoken their truth. It was up to her to listen.

"I'm sorry," Livvie whispered. "He wasn't going to harm me. Please, don't worry. I can take care of myself."

She heard a bang on the other end of the line. It sounded as if Drake had punched the wall.

"And how do you know he won't harm you? You're five foot nothing, Olivia. If he tries to hurt you, how are you going to take care of yourself?"

Livvie sighed. "He has never hurt anyone, and I know a lot of people in his circle. If he physically harmed me, I'd make sure they found out. And he knows this."

"But I didn't know that, Olivia. All I heard was your ex screaming at you. If he really is your ex, that is. He doesn't seem to think so. And worse than that, I heard the fear in your voice. Do you know what I wanted to do to him? Do you?"

"No," Livvie whispered.

"I wanted to break every bone in his body."

Livvie swallowed. "Why, Drake?"

Livvie heard Drake inhale loudly.

"Because we're friends."

Livvie's heart sank. "And yet yesterday morning, we were more than friends." She had no interest in having more male friends. She wondered if Drake had heard Zach's rant about never wanting to commit.

"You're wrong. We were friends then, too," Drake replied.

So was that all he thought they were? Friends with benefits? She had absolutely no interest in that. She didn't need that bullshit in her life.

"We're not friends, Drake," Livvie said a little too loudly.

"I disagree. And that's why I came up with a brilliant idea."

"And what's your *brilliant* idea?" she asked, her tone sarcastic.

"Stay here with me until Zach calms down or is in jail."

"He's not going to jail." Livvie rolled her eyes.

"I disagree."

Livvie laughed. "You've been doing a lot of that in this conversation."

"Olivia, I can't stand the thought of you living alone with this stalker pounding on your door at all hours of the night." Drake raised his voice.

Livvie was surprised he was so angry, especially since he only considered her a friend.

"Thank you for the kind offer, Drake, but I'm okay here."

Drake was breathing so loudly; it almost felt as if he was in her bedroom.

"Fine, you win. But if Zach bothers you once more, I want you on the first flight to Napa. Do you understand, Olivia?"

"I think the flights only go to San Francisco," Livvie said, biting her bottom lip.

"Fine, then I'll send my private plane. No arguments, Olivia. You may have won this time, but when it comes to your safety, I win."

Drake hung up without saying goodbye. She knew he was frustrated over not getting his way. And he did sort of ask her to come back to Napa. But he was wrong about one thing. She hadn't won. She collapsed onto her bed and prayed Zach would stay away.

17

LIVVIE SAT AT her kitchen table, feeling awful and exhausted, which wasn't a good combination. The only thing she felt relieved about was that Zach hadn't shown up again. She doubted he would, but she was a little frightened that he might come there again after he got drunk at the bar. Drake was right; she wouldn't be able to defend herself if Zach tried to hurt her. When she had first moved to Los Angeles, Carly had begged Livvie to learn self-defense, but she hadn't felt like it. She had just left Liam, and she needed to find peace.

But it was time she started to take better care of herself. And if that meant a self-defense class, then she was game.

Today was day two of being away from Drake, but it was day one all over again because she'd spoken to him early in the morning, which had halted her healing process. So she would make today her fresh start. That meant doing something she loved, something that made her feel whole again.

Livvie reached for the journal Drake had bought her but then stopped. If she was trying to get over Drake and start fresh, she should continue writing her novel, but she should use a different journal. The idea devastated her, and for ten solid minutes she was completely immobilized, but she'd made the right decision. So she opened her kitchen cabinet where she kept her office supplies and found an old journal she had bought when she had first moved to Los Angeles. She had gone to a therapist, who had told her she needed to journal every day about what was happening in her life in order to release emotions. But every time she'd sat down to write she hadn't been able to do it. Some days, it was easier to not feel and to pretend she was okay. Now she was ready to write in this journal. Instead of writing about her life, she would write about Haley's and Blake's.

Livvie sighed. She also had another epiphany. If her agent called, she would tell her she no longer wanted to write for a television show. It was gutsy, considering how her savings account was dwindling, but also necessary. Finally, she had control over her life again. And nothing or no one, including Drake Morganthal, would take that away from her.

Remembering where the story left off, Livvie took a sip of her iced coffee and opened her new journal. Already, she felt calmer. She picked up the Tiffany pen Drake had bought her. It dawned on her that maybe it would be a good idea if she also used another pen, but she loved this pen. And she didn't have the heart to part with it. So she began to write…

Blake picked up Haley and threw her onto the bed. She had anticipated this moment from the second she'd laid eyes on him. He was so beautiful. With his rugged looks he fit into her log cabin fantasy perfectly. When his lips locked with hers and he roughly ripped her shirt, Haley groaned. His calloused hands immediately found her hard nipples, and he rubbed them between his fingers. Wetness slid down her thigh. Haley pushed her pelvis into him, hoping he'd get the hint and rip off her jeans the same way as he had her shirt. Instead, he stopped what he was doing and laughed.

"Patience, beautiful."

And then he smiled, and Haley forgot how much her clit was pulsing. She could only pay attention to his perfect white teeth that she had to lick at this very moment. So that's what she did. He responded by biting her lip, causing pain to shoot through her mouth, and then he passionately kissed her. His lips were intoxicating, just like the man himself.

Livvie put down her pen and stared out her kitchen window. Maybe it wasn't such a smart idea, starting with a sex scene. Running her hands through her un-brushed hair, she was admiring the prettiness of her neighbors' front yard flowers when something strange caught her eye. She went to get up to take a closer look, and in doing so, she moved too quickly. Her chair slid back across the hardwood floor, and fell with a thump, loud enough to make her jump. There was a man pacing in front of her house, but when he saw her looking at him, he ran behind the nearest tree. Who the hell was he? Completely freaked out, Livvie ran into her bedroom and threw on a pair of jeans, a sports bra, and her pink tank top. When she ran back to the window, the man was no longer there, but her intuition told her something was wrong. And with her new fresh start in life, she was going to start listening to her intuition more. Livvie opened the door and stepped outside.

"Livvie Collins?"

The man stepped out from the side of her house, and Livvie screamed.

"Who are you?" she asked.

"Hey, hey, hey, calm down. It's okay."

The man looked to be well over six feet tall. He was wearing jeans and a white t-shirt, and to say he had big arm muscles was an understatement. Livvie thought he was a nice-looking man, more the rugged type. Not rugged like her novel character, Blake. Blake oozed confidence and sexuality. This man wasn't oozing anything.

"I'll ask you once more before I call the police. Who are you, and why are you stalking my house?" If men were going to make a habit of stalking her, she would need to take that self-defense class, after all. Walking around clutching her cellphone all the time would not solve her problems.

The stranger with extremely dark eyes walked toward her.

"If you come any closer, I'm calling the police; I mean it." Livvie's heart was thudding.

Luckily, the man stopped walking and ran his hands through his dark-brown hair.

"I'm supposed to watch you," the stranger said while looking at her house and then her neighbor's house…anywhere but straight in her eyes.

One thing she had learned as a child was that anyone who can't look you in the eye, should either not be trusted or they were hiding something. Livvie thought that in his case it was both.

"Says who?" Livvie said with more confidence than she was feeling.

"Says your guardian angel," the man said, a little too smugly.

Okay, Livvie didn't like this. If he didn't start talking in one more minute, she would call the police, and that would only make it more awkward between her and the neighbors.

Livvie placed her hands on her hips. "Start talking, mister."

"I wasn't paid to talk to you." He mimicked her by placing his hands on his hips.

"So this is how you're going to play it." She lifted her cellphone and started dialing Carly's number but pretended she was calling the police. If she called the cops, she would add even more drama to her life, and right now, that's not what she wanted.

"Okay, stop," the man shouted.

"There's no need to yell at me." Livvie stopped dialing. Thank goodness she had only pressed two numbers. The last thing she wanted was to get her best friend involved in whatever this was.

"Look, I'm supposed to watch you to make sure you're safe."

"Okay, but who's paying you?" Livvie had a feeling she knew, but she needed to hear it directly from this stranger.

"The man who's paying me wanted to remain anonymous." This time, the man did look her straight in the eyes, and his gaze was filled with what looked like panic.

"And is the man who's paying you a nice man?"

"Put it this way, I've worked for him on and off for years. He's an honest guy who always seems to get what he wants."

"And how do you know he always gets what he wants?" she asked.

"Because he said that if you found out he hired me, you'd get all mad. He then said that no matter how mad you got, there was no way you'd win this one."

"Win what?"

"I'm your new bodyguard. My name is Mitch. Nice to meet you." Mitch held out his hand, as if she would actually take it.

"And why do I need a bodyguard?"

Looking offended, Mitch rubbed his hand down his jeans. "Because some guy named Zachary Kagin tried to assault you at two o'clock in the morning."

"And so Drake decided he needed to be my knight in shining armor?"

"Hey, lady, you said his name, not me."

"Look, Mitch, one way or the other, you're not watching me, so either Drake is going to fire you, or I am." Livvie ran her hands through her hair.

"You can't fire me because you didn't hire me," Mitch said, sounding a little too cocky.

"Listen, mister cocky asshole…"

"Hey, you don't even know me. Don't take out your hatred for Mr. Morganthal on me."

Livvie looked up at the sky and groaned. Did all of his employees call him *Mr. Morganthal*? "Look, I don't want you watching me. I also don't want to call Drake, but apparently, I have no choice." Livvie didn't want to call Drake after what happened at two o'clock in the morning, so she decided to send him a text instead.

Fire Mitch. Now! She typed.

No. His response came quickly.

Livvie groaned again and stomped her foot. *YES! I DON'T NEED OR WANT A BODYGUARD!* She shouted at him in all caps.

TOO BAD. WHEN YOU BEHAVE LIKE AN ADULT, I WILL TREAT YOU LIKE ONE. SINCE YOU REFUSE TO COME TO ME, I'VE SENT SOMEONE TO YOU.

Livvie sighed. She knew she wouldn't win this battle, so she would have to figure out a way to make Mitch quit. And she hated that Drake kept offering her to return to Napa. It's not like he was offering her a commitment. What Drake didn't realize was that she was done listening to men. She was taking charge of her life. In all areas.

She unlocked the caps button and typed: *Fine. Thank you for the bodyguard and for your concern.*

You're very welcome, he responded.

Perfect, thought Livvie. What could she say to that? He was probably sitting in his big leather chair in his office, feeling all smug and thinking he had won. Livvie glanced at Mitch, who was shifting on his feet, definitely more arrogant than confident. Besides, how good of a bodyguard was he? She needed to figure out a way to deal with him, but now was not the time. She had a novel to write.

"Okay, suit yourself. But I'm not inviting you into my house for coffee or even water, for that matter." Livvie turned around and stormed into her house. "Oh, and Mitch?" she said before she slammed her door shut. "Please call me Olivia. You haven't earned the right to call me Livvie."

Mitch raised his eyebrow. "Oh, and Drake Morganthal has?"

"No. He calls me Olivia, too." She slammed the door before he made another snide comment.

At least she'd had the last word. That was a start. And as far as she was concerned, the game was on. Apparently, Drake didn't think she could take care of herself. She was sick and tired of men thinking they could control her. When they wanted to spend time with her, they did, and when they didn't, they ignored her. And they would go on to the next woman, as if she hadn't given them her heart and soul.

Livvie grabbed her cell and called Carly, who answered on the first ring.

"Hey, Carly, meet me at Le Club at nine. We have some work to do."

"I can't wait!" Carly squealed with excitement before hanging up.

Livvie ran to her closet to look for something sexy to wear for the night. After all, this was the first night of her fresh, new life.

18

LIVVIE ARRIVED AT Le Club, relieved when she saw Carly waiting.

"What's going on, Liv?"

"Drake hired a fucking bodyguard to watch me after what Zach did. He gave me two choices; either I agreed to the bodyguard or I returned to his winery." Livvie had called Carly first thing in the morning to tell her what happened with Zach.

"Drake wanted you to go back to his house?" Carly asked.

"Yes, until Zach left me alone. But then Drake would want me to leave again. No, thank you. I'm through with men who refuse to commit," Livvie said. "We need to lose the bodyguard."

"Where is he?"

Livvie half nodded toward the left, and Carly smiled. Livvie had pulled out of her garage and had driven fast down the street before Mitch even knew what she was doing. After their little talk, he had spent the rest of the day in his car. He was super good at following her. She would give him that.

Livvie and Carly nodded at the bouncer. Livvie knew she looked good in her skintight, off-the-shoulder black mini-dress and high heels. Carly looked beautiful as usual in a white miniskirt and matching white silk shirt. They both wore their hair straight and down. The bouncer instantly let them in, but Mitch had to wait in the long line.

"He's hot," Carly yelled over the music as they were walking to the bar.

"You think so?"

Carly winked and then resumed walking. "I know so," she yelled back.

When they reached the bar, Carly took out her credit card and handed it to the bartender.

"Drinks are on me, Livvie. Should I ask to see if they have any Morganthal wines?"

Livvie's heart felt as if it stopped beating. Just hearing *Morganthal* made her edgy. "I'll have a Stoli Vanil and ginger ale," she shouted to the bartender.

"You've had the same drink since college. Aren't you in the mood for something new?"

Livvie was in the mood for a lot of new things, but drinking one of Drake's wines was not on that list. At least, not tonight. As she grabbed her glass, she looked around the club. It was crazy tonight. Music pounding, lights flashing on the dance floor, and tons of people dressed to kill. Livvie loved it here. There was something about this place that ignited her soul. She loved the black walls and the white marble floor. The glass chandelier circled above the dance floor, shining lights down on it. And she was dying to dance. It made her feel free, wild, fearless.

Once Carly had her vodka tonic, Livvie grabbed her friend's hand and pulled her onto the dance floor. And that's when she noticed a very pissed off Mitch walking toward them.

Carly saw him, too. "Hey, Mitchy, drinks are on me." She nodded toward the bar, winked at him, and resumed walking toward the dance floor.

She and Livvie both laughed.

The music sounded amazing. Livvie raised her arms in the air with her drink and her purse in her hands and moved to the music. Carly grabbed Livvie by the waist and swayed with her. But she felt a pair of very pissed-off brown eyes staring at her. He was also looking Carly up and down, and suddenly, he didn't seem nearly as angry. Livvie wasn't surprised, as Carly was beautiful.

Livvie bent down and whispered in Carly's ear, "I think Mitchy wants you."

Carly smiled. "Of course, he wants me. Don't worry, Liv, I'll use it to our advantage."

Livvie had no doubt. Feeling much better, she closed her eyes and danced to the music. It felt so good to dance and be free. When was the last time she had felt free? Probably at Drake's house when she'd finally given in to her attraction to him. And she still craved him like crazy.

As Livvie was dancing, a random man placed his hands around her waist. Normally, she would hate that, but as she was starting her life over, she let him. He grinded his hips into her behind, and Livvie pushed back. With her eyes still closed, she heard Carly laugh. When Livvie opened them, she saw

Carly had some guy doing the same thing to her. It felt good to dance like this…at least until Livvie felt the guy's dick become hard against her ass. She stopped dancing and then realized how silly she was being. It wasn't as if anything could happen in the middle of the dance floor. She closed her eyes again and began dancing, but at some point, she realized the man behind her had disappeared. She frowned, wondering why he'd left, and turned around to see a very angry Mitch standing next to her.

"Ladies, we're leaving now," Mitch demanded.

Carly went up to him and began caressing his arm. "Come on, handsome, let's dance."

She smiled up at him so sweetly; Livvie had to hold back her laughter. Mitch stood completely still in the middle of the dance floor while Carly danced around him and caressed a part of his body every so often. Livvie thought Carly even touched his penis. A waitress approached them and handed her and Carly two more drinks.

"They're from the men up there," the waitress shouted.

Livvie looked up to see two very good-looking guys smiling at them, and she smiled back.

"We could get any guy we want tonight," Carly said in Livvie's ear.

She thought about that for a second. She could choose a guy, fuck him, and then never have to talk to him again. All on *her* terms. But the idea of a man inside her freaked her out. Because he wouldn't be Drake. She was here on a mission. That mission didn't include fucking. When Livvie felt another man behind her, Mitch snapped his fingers, and the man left. Mitch was a complete buzz kill. She hated him, and she had a feeling she'd have to do something drastic if she wanted to get rid of him.

Livvie eyed Carly and nodded. A few years ago, Carly had taught Livvie little ways to silently communicate when they went out to bars and parties. Carly nodded back and laughed. Apparently, she remembered.

"When?" Carly shouted over the music.

"Thirty minutes. Let's make him wait."

They both laughed and continued to dance wildly with Mitch staring at them from the side of the dance floor. Livvie turned around and found the guy who Mitch had intimidated moments earlier. She could tell he was debating approaching her again. And that's when she formed her plan. She slowly and seductively danced up to him and grabbed his shirt.

"Do you want to dance again?"

Livvie had to admit, out of all the guys in the club, he wasn't the best looking, but she had to make her point to both Drake and Mitch.

The man could barely look her in the eyes. He had probably just turned twenty-one. Funny how he hadn't seemed this shy when he had grabbed her waist and pushed his pelvis against her.

"Hey, I don't wanna make trouble, ya know? I don't want your boyfriend to slit my throat or nothing."

Livvie turned around and saw Carly trying to stop Mitch from coming over, but it didn't work. Mitch was walking fast and literally pushing aside anyone in his way.

Well, it's now or never, thought Livvie. She took her cellphone out of her clutch purse and turned it so she could take a selfie. Then she grabbed the boy from behind his neck and smacked her lips into his while simultaneously taking their picture. She pretended she was really into it when she felt Mitch coming closer. The boy seemed surprised and a little too eager to kiss her back. He tried to stick his tongue in her mouth, but that grossed her out. She finally allowed it only because she knew it would piss off Mitch.

Then all of a sudden, the music stopped, and the crowd fell silent. She heard Carly say, "Fuck." And then she heard footsteps. Loud footsteps. She stopped kissing the poor boy, and chills ran up and down her spine. Her heartbeat picked up, and her body went into fight or flight mode. If she turned around, she would know exactly what was causing this, or rather who, so she chose not to look.

But then everyone cleared the dance floor, including the boy.

"Don't let him leave."

She recognized that voice well, and she knew she had to turn around. She had no other option. What was she thinking, pissing off a man who had enough power and money to control anyone and everyone?

"Turn around, Olivia. Playtime is over."

Livvie swallowed and then slowly turned. The sight that awaited her almost made her turn around again. But she knew that would be a bad move. Instead, she tried to look Drake in the eye. But that was another bad move. To say he appeared angry would have been putting it mildly. Irate was more like it, but he looked even angrier than that. He was standing with his feet hip-width apart, and his arms were crossed over his chest. He wore black slacks that he looked incredibly hot in and an olive-green, button-down shirt. But it was the look in his eyes that made her want to run. She chose not to, because at the same time, she felt euphoric to see him standing in front of her. And if she hadn't been drinking, she would be obsessing over why, especially since she hadn't thought she would ever see him again. She had been devastated about that prospect for the last two days, and that awful feeling alone made her want to rip those angry eyes out.

"Did you come here to dance?" Livvie asked.

Drake stared at her, breathing loudly. Livvie could have sworn she saw fumes coming out of his ears. "You're drunk, Olivia. That's not an attractive sight."

"That's ironic, coming from a man who owns a vineyard. And since our expiration date is up, it shouldn't matter how attractive I am."

Livvie paused, trying to get a hold of herself. She looked around the club and noticed that everyone was off the dance floor and watching the two of them. She looked at Carly for help, but she was just standing there, mouth wide open as if she were in shock.

"Olivia, come here," Drake said through clenched teeth, emphasizing each word.

"And what are you going to do if I don't want to?" she asked.

He nodded at Mitch, and then Drake strode toward Livvie. Without any warning, Drake picked her up and threw her over his shoulder. She noticed that Mitch did the same to Carly.

Livvie and Carly both hit the backs of the man carrying them, all the while screaming to be put down. Livvie also pinched Drake on his backside. He walked up to the poor boy Livvie had been making out with.

"Would you like me to beat the hell out of him, Mr. Morganthal?" Mitch asked.

Livvie panicked. She was the one who had put the kid in the middle of this.

"No," Livvie yelled from her upside down position.

Drake slid one of his hands over her ass and moved it in circles. She felt her cheeks flush beet red.

"Do you want to fuck him?" he asked, turning his head to look at her.

She wished he would put her down.

"No," she responded.

God, she had never been so mortified in her entire life. And what made matters worse was that she saw people taking pictures and videos of them. They probably loved seeing the famous Drake Morganthal carrying some random woman upside down.

"Are you sure, Olivia? I have no problem watching."

Livvie looked at the boy, who was probably redder than she was.

"No. I'm good." She really wanted to get out of here.

Drake stepped closer to the kid—God, she didn't even know his name… She couldn't really see his expression from her position, but she noticed his knees trembling.

"How old are you?" Drake asked in a stern voice.

The boy cleared his throat. "Twenty-three. I look underage, but I'm not. I swear."

Drake nodded. "Then heed my warning. If I ever see you near Olivia again, I'll do more than watch the two of you fuck." Drake immediately turned and walked toward the front of the club.

She mouthed the word "sorry" at the boy, but he wasn't looking her way.

Although she was tempted to hit Drake in the behind again, it was no use. Instead, she looked at Carly, who seemed to be massaging in between Mitch's legs. Only she would think to touch a guy's penis at a time like this. Livvie laughed and rolled her eyes.

When they finally reached the front door, Livvie saw the bouncer who'd let her in. Drake handed him a wad of cash and his business card.

"Thanks, man. And next time you see Olivia at this club, please notify me immediately."

"Asshole," she said under her breath.

"I heard that," Drake said back.

A limo seemed to be waiting for them. Drake opened the back door and literally threw her into the back seat. Then he got inside, closed the door, and slammed the partition shut between them and the driver. Livvie moved to the far end of the seat, away from him.

"Where's Carly?"

"Mitch is taking her home."

"Why?" They both had their own cars. Drake had no right to do what he was doing.

"Because I said so."

Livvie groaned. "We both came in our own cars."

"And I took care of that."

She knew it wasn't smart to keep pestering him. He had looked angry in the club, but now his anger seemed to be radiating off of him.

"What the fuck, Drake? Why are you even here?"

Drake's gaze remained forward facing, and he was clenching his jaw.

"Why aren't you looking at me?"

"I'm not looking at you when you reek of other men touching you, and your lips are full and red from kissing that boy. And I won't be looking at you when you've had more to drink than you had during an entire week at my winery." Drake paused. "You misbehaved, Olivia."

"Misbehaved?" She looked at him in shock.

Finally, he looked back.

"Yes."

He grabbed her arm and pulled her over, so she lay facedown over his lap. He pulled up her short black dress and pulled down her black silk thong. He rubbed her ass in circles, making her horny and wet.

"Did you like all those men touching you and pushing their hard cocks into you on the dance floor?"

"Yes," she whispered.

"Louder," he demanded.

"Yes," she said louder.

"Really?" Drake stopped caressing her backside and moved his hands in between her legs. His fingers touched her clit and then moved back up her vagina toward her hole.

Livvie instinctively pushed her pelvis against his lap and moaned.

"Are you horny already, Olivia? Is that why?"

Drake thrust two fingers inside her, causing her to moan again.

"You're sopping wet, Olivia. Were those men making you wet? Did the twenty-three-year-old boy turn you on?" He kept thrusting his fingers. "You haven't fucked in two days, Olivia. Did you come here to find a man to fuck? Do you need it that badly?"

Livvie hoped he wasn't waiting for her to answer. He was making her so crazy that she couldn't speak. Instead, she spread her legs a little wider, desperately needing to come.

"No, Olivia. Only good girls get to come. This is what bad girls get."

Drake took his fingers out of her and spanked her right cheek hard.

"Ouch," Livvie shouted.

Drake didn't seem to care. He spanked her left cheek and then her right, alternating back and forth. She was really grateful for the partition between them and the driver. If he saw, she'd be mortified. Drake continued spanking her but not as hard. If anything, it turned her on even more.

"I can smell your arousal, Olivia. Maybe my belt would take care of that."

Livvie panicked, thinking he was really going to hit her with his belt, when he stopped spanking her and thrust his fingers back inside her. She moaned even louder, so close to coming.

Drake removed his fingers, pulled up her thong, and pushed down her dress.

"We're here."

Livvie groaned and slowly got up. If he touched her for one more second, she would have come. But they were at her house. "Are you coming in?"

Drake grabbed the handle and then looked at her. "Of course. Zach is stalking you, and you refused a bodyguard. Do you just expect me to go to a hotel?"

She did, but by the time she opened her mouth to say anything, Drake was already out of the car and walking toward the door. The limo driver gave her purse to Drake. That was weird. Where had she put her purse, and how had the limo driver gotten it? She must have had way too much to drink.

Drake paused and turned toward Livvie, obviously exasperated.

"Come on, Olivia."

She got out of the car and slammed the door. Then she remembered her neighbors and cringed before she addressed Drake. "Someone woke up on the wrong side of the bed."

"You're wrong. I woke up at my vineyard in my comfortable bed, thinking about how much I was going to accomplish today. And then I got a call from the bodyguard, who I hired specifically for you, who said you refused to allow him into your house. Mitch had to remain in his car all day and had to order food."

"I didn't realize I needed to feed him. Besides, when I first saw him, he was hiding. What kind of bodyguard hides from the person they're supposed to protect?"

He sighed loudly. "He wasn't hiding, Olivia. I told him not to get in your way. And I expected you to be courteous and helpful, considering he was protecting you," he said in a raised voice.

"Shhhhhhhh, you'll wake my neighbors," she whispered loudly.

Drake rolled his eyes, opened her purse, and rummaged through it until he found her key.

"Hey." Livvie grabbed her purse out of his hand.

Drake opened her door as if he owned the place. Livvie slid around him, wanting to make a point.

"Ladies, first," she said.

"I don't see any ladies."

Livvie turned around and slapped him with her purse. "Drake."

He followed her inside. "When you start behaving like a lady, I'll treat you like a lady."

She would have had another snide remark, but she found Mr. Birkshire sleeping on her couch with a huge black suitcase next to him. "Mr. Birkshire?"

He literally jumped up off the couch. "Yes, yes, I'm sorry."

Drake shut the door behind him and locked it.

"Are you okay?" she asked Mr. Birkshire. This night was getting weirder and weirder.

"Yes, Ms. Collins. Mr. Morganthal, where would you like your luggage?"

"In the master bedroom, please."

Mr. Birkshire nodded and rolled the suitcase into her bedroom.

Livvie stood in place, absolutely stunned. "How does he know where my bedroom is?"

Drake walked into her kitchen and grabbed two bottles of water from her fridge. He then walked back to Livvie, unscrewed the cap, and handed her the bottle.

"Drink, and I'll answer."

Livvie obeyed, but only because she was extremely parched.

"Good girl. By the time I was able to fly down here, you'd just left for the club with Mitch chasing you. So Mr. Birkshire and I opened your door and started to make ourselves at home until Mitch called me and said that every guy at the club was practically waiting in line to touch you."

"That's so not true," Livvie yelled.

"Be careful, Olivia, or you'll wake up your neighbors." Drake took a large sip of water.

Livvie rolled her eyes. "So how did you get a key to my house?"

"Tsk tsk tsk. So many questions." Drake took another sip of water. "You doubt my abilities. Just because I have no interest in being in a committed relationship doesn't mean I don't always get what I want."

Livvie's heart sank. "Then what is it that you want?" she whispered.

"I want you in the shower. Now."

She badly wished he had said something else. Anything to give her hope. But all he'd done was reiterate that he didn't want a relationship.

"I can't. Mr. Birkshire is in my bedroom."

"Right. Mr. Birkshire?" Drake shouted.

Mr. Birkshire immediately came out into the living room. "Yes, sir?"

"Have you finished unpacking?"

Livvie looked right at Drake. *Unpacking?*

"Yes, sir. I placed all your clothes in the walk-in closet and everything else in the bathroom vanity."

Livvie's mouth hung wide open.

"Thank you, as usual. Please check yourself in to any hotel you'd like."

"Thank you. I appreciate that. Will you need me tomorrow?"

Drake shrugged. "I'm not sure yet. I'll keep you posted."

Livvie was having a hard time speaking, as she couldn't believe what was happening. But she was glad to see Mr. Birkshire. She truly hadn't thought she'd see him again after she left the vineyard. In a way, this felt like a dream come true, and in a way, it was her worst nightmare. She needed to work on healing from her encounter with Drake. And she had no idea what he intended, but she knew it wouldn't help her in the long run. But she couldn't deal with how she felt about him leaving right now, especially because her buzz from drinking was starting to fade.

Mr. Birkshire left her house and closed the door behind him. Livvie wanted to sob, but she didn't, especially because Drake was standing a few feet away from her. Right now, she didn't feel safe with him. Just the other day, she'd been thinking that the only other place in the entire world where she felt safe was at Drake's. She felt safe with him physically, but emotionally, she didn't.

"Are you planning on standing there looking all pitiful, or do you plan to get in the shower?"

Livvie swallowed and turned toward Drake. "Actually, I don't need a shower. Thank you very much. I'm going to change, get into bed, and you can sleep in the guest bedroom."

Livvie started to turn around, but Drake grabbed her and threw her over his shoulder again. Livvie wished she had longer legs.

"Drake. Put. Me. Down. Now."

Drake spanked her on the ass as he walked her to the bathroom.

"No. No. No."

She remained over his shoulder as he opened her glass shower door, turned on the water, and waited until it was hot enough. "I won't be sharing a bed with a woman who has the smell of every man in the club on her."

"That isn't true."

Once the water was warm enough, Drake placed her in the shower fully clothed.

"Drake, you asshole. My clothes are soaking wet."

He stood outside the shower with his sleeves rolled up. "Put your hands over your head."

Livvie did not want Drake to see her naked. He hadn't earned it. "I'm more than capable of undressing myself, thank you. You can leave now."

Drake grabbed her foot, removed her sandal, and threw it onto the bathroom floor. He did the same with her other sandal. Then he grabbed the bottom of her dress, forcing her to lift her arms above her head.

"I've seen you naked before. There's no need to be shy."

Standing in nothing but her strapless, black silk bra and black silk thong panties, she felt completely exposed. She moved her hair away from her eyes and allowed the water cascading down her body to soothe her.

"I'm not being shy. It's just that you saw me naked before our expiration date. And now it feels...wrong."

"Olivia, I'm only helping you shower." He unclasped her bra, exposing her C-cup breasts. Her nipples hardened from the water and from Drake's lustful gaze. He grabbed the sides of her panties and slowly pulled them down.

She stepped out of them, leaving herself completely naked and trembling.

"Is the water cold?" he asked.

"No."

Drake threw her panties on the bathroom floor and looked her up and down. "You're trembling."

"Yes." She wanted him badly, but not like this.

"I can help you with that."

He could help her if he agreed to compromise. She wasn't asking for marriage, only to date and to see where that led. Instead, he grabbed her vanilla and cinnamon body wash and squirted a substantial amount in the palm of his hand.

"Turn around."

"Drake, you don't have to do this."

"I know."

Livvie turned. She heard him rub the palms of his hands briskly together, and then he gently touched her shoulders. Fearing she would fall over from the sensations that seemed to ignite her body, she braced herself on the tiled wall.

"You don't need to lean against the wall. I've got you," he whispered in her ear while continuing to massage her shoulders.

Livvie removed her hands from the wall and tried to relax. She closed her eyes and allowed his hands to work their magic on her body.

Once she calmed, Drake massaged the middle of her back and then her lower spine. He moved his hands in circles, kneading and pressing. He then moved his hands lower to her backside, and she felt her body tighten.

"Relax."

She took a deep breath and focused on his hands instead of the negative thoughts in her mind. He massaged her backside. It didn't feel erotic, but when he brushed his fingers down her crack, it did. He grabbed more body wash, rubbed the palms of his hands together, and moved to her upper thigh. As turned-on as she was, when he neared her vagina, she thought of anything but his hands. She wanted this man, but she wanted all of him. He slid his hands farther down her legs and then massaged the outside of her feet.

"Hold on to the wall."

She did as she was told, and then he lifted her foot and massaged underneath in all the places she needed. He did the same to her other foot.

"Let go of the wall now, and turn around."

Livvie's heartbeat sped up, and her clit was pulsing like crazy, even though she was fighting it. When she turned, Drake inhaled. He poured more body wash in his hands and washed her right arm and then her left. She was dying for him to touch her nipples. But the rules had changed.

Drake grabbed her left breast and washed her gently. He was so close to her hard nipple.

"Do you know what it was like, watching you kiss that boy?"

Livvie opened her eyes but didn't say anything. She wanted to tell him she watched Kayla Brenson touch his cock under the table, but now wasn't the time to bring that up.

He went to work, cleaning her other breast.

"It was torture," he said through clenched teeth. "And do you know how I felt when Mitch called and told me how random men were dancing behind you and grinding their hard dicks into your ass? My ass?"

"You were the one who gave us an expiration date."

He got more body wash and then washed her stomach. "It had only been two days, Olivia. Two days."

It was nice to know he probably hadn't been with another woman yet. That was something.

"Were you doing it to punish me?" he asked.

Drake moved his hand above her pubic bone, and Livvie's vagina muscles clenched.

"Were you?" he demanded.

Livvie had an answer; she just didn't know if he'd like it or not. "Yes and no."

"So let me get this straight. You liked the men paying attention to you, and you liked that you knew I'd find out."

"Yes," she whispered.

"Louder."

"Yes," she screamed.

Drake brushed her clit and then stopped and moved down to wash her knees.

"Are you a slut, Olivia?"

He was washing her calf, so she couldn't see the expression in his eyes, but she did notice his clenched jaw.

"No, Drake, I'm not."

"You acted like one."

"You called me a slut when we were in your kitchen."

Drake put down the body wash and grabbed her favorite shampoo.

"You were *my* slut, Olivia."

Livvie didn't respond to that. But she definitely needed to stop him from washing her hair.

"Drake, you don't need to wash my hair."

He resumed pouring the shampoo into his hands, and then he grabbed all of her hair and placed it on top of her head before massaging her scalp, doing a better job than the people at her hair salon.

"Did a man touch your hair tonight?"

She had to think about it for a second. "Yes."

"Then it needs to be washed."

Drake rinsed her hair and then applied conditioner. She was almost surprised he didn't shave her legs with her razor. She waxed her pussy bare, so there was no need to shave there at least, although she found the thought pretty erotic.

By the time he rinsed out the conditioner, she wanted to scream. Her entire body felt on high alert. She looked at Drake to see if he was also affected, but he didn't seem to be, and that upset her. But his shirt was sopping wet, which made her feel a little better. She tried to look down at his pants to see if he was at least hard, but he wasn't. If she was suffering, he should be, too. He stopped her staring by grabbing her arm.

Then he turned off the water. "Get out."

Livvie stepped out of the shower. He grabbed a fluffy white towel from the vanity. Wait, that wasn't her towel.

"Drake, did you take towels from your house?"

"Yes, I had no idea what kind of towels you had."

Livvie rolled her eyes as he placed the towel around her and rubbed to get rid of the water clinging to her body. He then secured it in place and grabbed a smaller white towel to wring out her hair.

"Were you worried my towels would be too rough for your body?"

Drake chuckled. "Yes." He finished getting the water out of her hair. "Do you need to blow dry it?"

"No, I'll let it dry naturally."

"Then get into bed."

"I'm not tired."

"Olivia you've been drinking all night, and you look like you're about to fall asleep on your feet."

He was right. She just didn't want to admit it.

"Okay, well let me throw on my pajamas." She turned to leave.

"Naked, Olivia." Drake's tone was totally dominant.

She loved that tone, but not right now.

"No, Drake, this is my house. I don't want to go to bed naked, and I don't want you in my bed."

Drake grinded his teeth. "I won't be sleeping in another bed while Zach is stalking you. I also don't want you wearing anything that you may have had on with another man."

"Like, any man, ever?"

"Yes, ever."

Where was all his jealousy coming from? She was about to ask him, but when she looked in his eyes she no longer saw anger. She saw hurt. And she had caused it, even though she technically hadn't done anything wrong. They were no longer together. Still, if she saw him with another woman two days after she had left, she would be devastated, so she took a deep breath and walked into her bedroom. Mr. Birkshire must have pulled down her blanket. She dropped the towels from around her, leaving them in a pile on the floor. The moment she lay down, she sighed. The silk sheets felt delicious against her naked body.

Drake closed the door and took care of his business in the bathroom. When he came back out, his chest was bare but he was still wearing his boxer shorts. Too bad she wouldn't be running her hands down his chest.

He went into the living room and returned with their bottles of water.

"Take these."

He gave her the water bottle and two ibuprofens, and she gratefully took them. A headache was already starting.

"Move over," he demanded.

"Why?"

"I want to be closest to the window."

Livvie scooted over. "Drake, what do you think is going to happen?" He was making Zach out to be some kind of psycho ax murderer.

Drake pulled off his boxers and left them on the floor. Livvie stared at his dick that had started to get hard.

Drake noticed her staring and raised his eyebrow. "I wasn't hard when you were in the shower because other men had been touching you. But now since I personally know how clean you are, I want you again."

Livvie glanced at his beautiful body once more before he got into her bed and put the blanket around him. He lay on his back with his hands behind his head, so Livvie turned on her side.

"It's nice to know you're suffering as much as I am," she said.

Drake ignored her. He seemed to be deep in thought. "Zach isn't giving up on you without a fight," he said, almost to himself.

"Oh, no. Zach doesn't fight."

"I disagree. Think like a man. He may not be physically fighting for you, but when he suspected you were with someone else, he called you incessantly, and he stopped by your house late at night, drunk."

"Is that how men fight for a woman?"

Drake turned his head toward her. "When he's emotionally unstable, it is."

Livvie paused. "But I'm not with another man. I was, but we had our expiration date."

"And yet we're both lying here, due to unforeseen circumstances, wanting to fuck."

"I'm glad to see you, Drake, but it's not happening," she said, even though she wanted him with every fiber of her being. "I think I'm going to bed. If you see Zach, send him my love." She rolled onto her side, away from Drake, and closed her eyes.

The energy in the room seemed to shift. She felt Drake stiffen, and the tension between them thickened.

"Do you still want him, Olivia?" he asked softly.

"No. He's my ex for a reason."

"Are you sure? Because he may be able to give you exactly what you need."

"I'm sure," she whispered as a tear slid down her cheek. She wanted Drake so badly. But he was offering her nothing, which was pretty much the same story with Zach.

19

LIVVIE MUST HAVE dozed off because she awoke to pounding on her door. She felt Drake immediately get out of bed.

Then she heard Zach screaming at the top of his lungs. "Livvie! Livvie! I know you're in there."

Drake ran to the door naked.

"Drake, put on some clothes."

He ignored her and opened the door. This was Livvie's biggest nightmare come true, and to make matters worse, she saw her neighbor's light come on. How embarrassing.

"Get in here, Zach," Drake said sternly.

She cringed, as she threw her blanket around her and ran into the living room to join them.

"What the fuck, Liv?" Zach could barely stand.

Drake grabbed Zach by his collar. Zach wouldn't fight Drake, but Drake would definitely fight him.

"Drake, stop. We're adults."

Drake turned toward Livvie with a look that could kill. "Leave us alone. This is between me and your ex."

"No. You're wrong. It's between me and Zach."

"Dude, you're naked. Can you stop touching me, please?" Zach asked.

If Livvie hadn't been so worried, she would have laughed. This was getting worse by the second.

"And by the way, Mr. Naked, she's not my ex. She's just fucking you to get back at me for fucking around on her," Zach said, sounding all cocky.

Livvie's eyes widened. "Zach, stop. Both of you."

Drake released Zach. "Is that true, Olivia?"

She swallowed and looked Drake in the eye.

"No, I swear it isn't," she said softly.

"Is that what you were thinking when we were together at my vineyard?"

"No."

"And what about the boy you were making out with tonight?"

"Liv, you get around," Zach chimed in.

"I did that to make you mad."

"Hello? Did everyone forget about me?" Zach said, visibly swaying.

Livvie turned to Zach. "Zach, we're through. You were right, and I was wrong."

Out of the corner of her eye, she saw Drake grab her throw blanket that was over the arm of her couch, and he placed it around him. Inside, she sighed with relief.

"What the fuck are you talking about?" Zach asked.

"Can we refrain from cursing? You were right. At the beginning of our relationship, you told me you had no intention of having a monogamous relationship."

"Were they the exact words I used?"

Livvie rolled her eyes. "I'm being serious. Even though you may be too drunk tomorrow to remember this."

"I may have been drinking, but I'm not drunk." Zach swayed on his feet again.

Feeling uneasy, she turned toward Drake, who was leaning against her living room wall with his arms crossed. This was getting awkward. But she had no choice. She needed to handle this like an adult.

She took a deep breath. "You told me you didn't want a monogamous relationship and that you didn't even believe in them, and I want those things. I thought maybe I was special. That maybe you'd want to be that way with me."

Zach leaned against the arm of the couch to steady himself. "There was a moment, Liv, when I thought I did, too. I thought that with you I could be in a normal relationship. I was even hopeful. I love you. But I'm not in love with you in the way you want me to be."

Tears welled up in her eyes. Zach telling her he wasn't in love with her was one thing, but it was another having Drake witness her humiliation.

"Then why have you called me over and over again? Why did you come here last night, wanting to be with me?"

"Stop the questions," Zach said sternly.

Dick, she thought.

"You fucked another man, and I wasn't done with you." Zach paused. "So then I wanted you because you became a challenge. And you hadn't been a challenge the entire year we dated. If I told you I was working late, you were cool with it, even though I always lied. If I had to cut a dinner short, you were cool with it. If I cancelled a date, you were cool with it."

"I get the idea," Livvie said. She had come to those same conclusions herself. She'd lost herself.

"And then when you moved on from me and didn't tell me where you were, you became exciting." Zach cleared his throat. "But then when I figured out that you'd fucked Drake Morganthal, the challenge was gone. Because of all men to fuck, he was the one man who would hurt you worse than I ever could, so then you became pitiful to me."

Livvie was trying desperately not to cry, but his words were slicing through her. She wasn't pitiful. She'd resisted Drake until she'd gotten to know him better. Drake had issues, but he wasn't an asshole. *Zach* was an asshole.

"Enough, Zach." Drake was going to punch Zach.

She knew it in her gut. She had to put an end to this.

"Then why are you here?" she asked.

"Because you and Drakey boy are all over the Internet. Look." Zach swayed up to her and showed her his phone.

"Oh, no." She had thought things couldn't get any worse, but seeing herself thrown over Drake's shoulders was much worse.

"And there's a video of you guys." He grabbed the phone out of Livvie's trembling hands and scrolled to find it.

Drake walked over and gently placed his hands on her shoulders. She was still hurt and angry with him. But right now, feeling comforted was more important than hanging on to her anger.

"We're all over the Internet." When she turned toward Drake, she couldn't help the tear that ran down her cheek.

"Fuck," Drake said when Zach showed him the picture.

"He cursed, too, Liv," Zach said.

"Shut up, Zach."

"Yeah, you're right. If I had a video and pictures like that all over the Internet, I'd curse, too."

Livvie ignored him and watched Drake run into her bedroom.

"What are you doing?" she asked.

He returned with his cellphone and started dialing. "I'm taking care of this." Then he stopped dialing. "Olivia, everything will be okay. I want you to know this."

Livvie nodded while swallowing back the tears. Everything wouldn't be okay...not between them, anyway. But she knew he would take care of the current situation. He was a powerful man, after all.

"Mr. Birkshire, there has been trouble. I want you to call Seth at the PR firm, and tell him we need to do damage control. I don't care about me, but I don't want this to harm Olivia. She has been harmed enough."

Livvie stood there, too stunned to speak. Drake spoke for another few minutes, and then he hung up. He looked briefly at Livvie and then at Zach.

"Why did you feel the need to show her these?"

"Because no matter what, we're friends."

"I think you wanted to show her these yourself, so you could see her reaction. Because that's what sociopaths do."

"Drake, it's okay. I would have seen them sooner or later."

"But that's not the point." Drake grabbed Zach by the collar again and threw him against the wall.

Livvie was too tired to stop him.

"You never fell in love with her because you're not enough of a man. And you could never remain monogamous for the same reason. She's extraordinary, asshole. You can only handle weak women."

Zach laughed right in Drake's face. "And you're any different?"

Drake paused, and Livvie felt as if her heart was beating out of her chest.

"I am different. Because I'd make sure that the look in her eyes right now would never happen because of me. I'd make sure that no matter how weak I am, I'd tell her how brave and strong she is. And every moment I'm with her, I would celebrate her, not show her pictures to add to the scars around her heart."

Drake tightened his grip around Zach, but Livvie couldn't speak. Drake wouldn't hurt Zack because her ex wasn't worth it.

But he pushed him against the wall once and then twice.

"If I ever find out you were anywhere near Olivia, I'll personally come after you. If I ever find out you did anything malicious with those pictures and videos, I'll come after you. If I ever find out you did anything at all to hurt her, I'll come after you. I have enough money and power to crush you, and let me tell you, I'll definitely use it."

"Okay, man, chill."

Drake let go, and Zach practically fell to the floor. He swayed a little and then tried to focus on Livvie, but he was looking everywhere but at her.

"Have a nice life, Liv."

She nodded, only because she felt the need to acknowledge him, and also because this would be the last time she saw him. Drake would make sure of that, but so would she.

Drake opened the front door, and Zach left.

Livvie didn't know what to do or say, but she was feeling dizzy. She leaned against the wall for support and then slid down and placed her face in her hands. This had to be one of her worst nights, ever. She sighed with relief when she heard Drake close the front door.

"What time is it?" she whispered.

"A little after two in the morning."

"He came here at the same time last night." Her face remained in her hands. "Did you sleep a little at least?" She wasn't ready to look at Drake.

"Olivia, it's okay." Drake kneeled on the floor beside her.

He grabbed her and held her in his arms and started rocking her back and forth. She moved closer into his arms and said nothing, as there was nothing left to say. She needed this. He wasn't better than Zach because he wouldn't commit to her, but as a man, there was no comparison. Drake was the most honorable and loving man she knew. And she loved him. So much, it hurt. He was wrong about what he had said earlier to Zach. But she clung to him anyway, because he was a good man. And because she had fallen in love with him in less than seven days.

Her hands dropped from her face, and she was only inches away from his mouth, so she gently kissed him, and he gently kissed her back. Once. Twice. And then he leaned his forehead against hers.

"Olivia, are you sure you want this?"

She nodded against his forehead, not wanting to speak. She needed him. He was warm, comforting, and he was here. He wasn't offering her a tomorrow, but she needed him now. When their lips met again, it wasn't gentle. Passion stored deep inside her that she never felt free enough to let out was pouring out in waves. And Drake met her passion with his. They kissed as if they couldn't get enough of each other. Their lips connected over and over again, their tongues becoming one. Livvie inhaled through her nose, barely able to breathe, but when she did, she was breathing Drake's air.

He released her lips and kissed her forehead, her nose, and her cheeks. He licked inside her ears, and then he grabbed the blanket around his waist and placed it on her living room floor.

"Lie down." He doubled the blanket over so it became a pillow for her head, and she lay down. In one quick motion, he removed the blanket she'd wrapped around her. And then he looked at her. Really looked at her. She licked her lips as he leaned by her side and touched her face as if she was the most beautiful woman in the world, as if he was in love with her. And then he glided his hand around her neck and in between her breasts, over her heart. He laid his full hand there and kept it there. A sensation unlike any she had ever experienced consumed her. Her heart had calmed and was infused with love. Her breath caught in her throat. Drake smiled down at her and then moved his hand down her stomach, over her pubic bone, and swept it down to her vagina, causing her to moan.

Then exactly what he did to her heart, he did to her pussy. He placed his whole hand there and stilled. Her vagina muscles clenched under him, but a feeling of warmth consumed her. And then he moved his hand by rubbing his fingers up and down her pussy, grazing her clit and then thrusting inside her and grazing her clit once again.

Livvie looked into his brilliant eyes and grabbed his face as his fingers danced inside her. She touched his face in a way that echoed how she felt toward him. She ran her hands through his hair and scraped his scalp. Then he leaned down and kissed her, as a prince would kiss a princess in a fairy tale. His fingers were doing their magic, and she was close to coming, but she needed for him to come with her, inside her. So she stopped the fairy tale kiss, and he nodded. Without words, he stopped touching her and leaned over her instead. They locked eyes, and then in one swift motion he thrust inside her. She could have bent her knees. She could have thrust her pelvis up, but she didn't. Instead, she pushed her legs closer together, as if her legs and vagina were hugging his penis exactly where she wanted it to be. Where she needed it to be.

Drake groaned, thrusting deeper. Pulled all the way out and then went all the way back in. He did that over and over until Livvie could barely think, which was fine by her. Then he pushed up slightly and hit the spot that pushed her over the edge. Her vagina pulsed, and her muscles clenched hard, and then unclenched and clenched again. Orgasmic chills graced her entire body, and she was lifted into another realm. A higher realm. A more peaceful realm, where only love existed and where there was no pain. And then she felt Drake come. His wet sperm was taking over her womb and she loved that feeling.

Drake fell on top of her. He moved her hair away from her eyes and kissed her on her nose.

"There are no words," he whispered.

"I know," she whispered back.

Drake pulled out of her, and the loss was overwhelming. But then he scooped her up in his arms and carried her to her bedroom. Carefully, he laid her down on the bed and then ran into her bathroom and wet some washcloths. He cleaned himself and then gently washed her vagina.

"Thank you," she whispered.

He threw the washcloths on the bathroom floor, grabbed her blanket, and then climbed into bed. After putting the blanket around them, he wrapped her in his arms and pulled her close, forcing her to lie on her side. He threw his leg over hers and spooned her, his arms tight around her.

She couldn't believe how affectionate he was being. And how much love she was feeling. She desperately wanted to tell him, but she couldn't. As minutes turned to hours and she heard his breathing become even, she still wanted to tell him, but she didn't have the courage. Or maybe she was afraid he wouldn't say it back? Even though they had incredible sex, it hadn't changed the fact that Drake didn't want a committed relationship. It hurt like hell, but it was the truth. She would get over Zach not being in love with her, but she wished Drake were different. And then after another hour or so, she joined Drake in sleep.

WHEN LIVVIE WOKE up, she was alone. At first, a rush of panic came over her, but then she felt relieved. She needed time to think and process everything that was going on in her life. She stretched and yawned loudly for no other reason than she could. The feeling of exhaustion consumed her, but it felt more emotional than physical. Through barely open eyes she glanced at her clock. And then she glanced again. It was eleven o'clock! The last time she had slept that late was when she was a kid at her parents' house.

She also saw a glass of water on the night table, along with two more ibuprofens. Livvie laughed. Drake had thought she would wake up with a huge hangover, but she hadn't been that drunk last night. And what she was feeling was more of an emotional hangover. They were similar and yet so different.

Drake had also left her a note against the glass. Why hadn't she heard him leaving? The feeling of panic set in again. But her bathroom door was open, and she could see his stuff on her vanity. She exhaled with relief. He hadn't left her yet. So she sat up in bed, grabbed the note, and kissed it. And then she began reading.

Olivia,

I have to meet Mr. Birkshire early, and then we are going to Seth's. Need to do a lot more damage control than I thought. I don't want you to worry about it though. I want you to write. All day, Olivia. Stay out of your head, and stop thinking so much.

Love,

Drake

P.S. I would have much rather woken up to you and your gorgeous, naked body.

Her heart practically melted. Livvie sighed. She missed him terribly. And she had no idea when he would be leaving for good. They had to be missing him at his winery, as well.

But there was no point in feeling sorry for herself. Drake was right; she would feel much better if she wrote. He knew her so well and yet refused to give her what she ultimately wanted. Him.

Hours later, she sat at her kitchen table, writing ferociously. At first, she had struggled to write. Zach's words had really hurt her. He *loved* her, but he was never *in love* with her. A part of her understood that how he felt had nothing to do with her. He was a man who was never faithful to one woman, and when he lost interest in one, he would go to the next. But a part of her wanted to know what she had done wrong. Maybe that was just her ego talking. Besides, she loved Zach, but she wasn't in love with him, either. The only reason she had dated him to begin with was because she was attracted to him, and he had a good sense of humor. He made her laugh. And after what happened with Liam, she had really needed to laugh. And he was right that she'd been okay with him walking all over her.

Livvie heard her door opening, and she jumped up.

"Who is it?" she yelled, gripping the edge of her kitchen table. No one had a key to her house except her, unless…

Drake walked into the kitchen, holding a large bag of food.

"Hey, beautiful. You okay? You look as white as a ghost." He placed the bag on her counter and started to unload the food.

"How did you get a key?" She hated that he had one. Playing house with a man who didn't want to commit felt as if she was she was living in an illusion. She wasn't living in an illusion. She understood the situation very well.

"Ah, that's why you're so uptight."

"I'm not uptight." Although she was still gripping the kitchen table.

"In my experience, most people keep spare keys in a kitchen drawer, so this morning before I left, I found one." Drake smiled in that charming way.

How could she be mad at him when he smiled at her like that?

"You never told me how you got in last night when I was at the club. Or for that matter, how did you even know where I lived?"

"When I heard Zach at your house the first night, I made it my business to know where you live. As far as how I got in? I picked your lock. A trick I learned from my roommate in college. It's an excellent skill to have. If you behave yourself, maybe I'll teach you." He winked and then turned back to the food.

Livvie inhaled. "No, thanks, I'm good." She sat down and opened her journal again. She read and reread the last paragraph she had written. Haley and Blake were arguing.

Drake opened her kitchen drawers and took out forks, knives, and plates. He seemed to know her kitchen very well.

"What are you doing?" She put down her journal and gave him her full attention.

"I figured you had barely eaten today, except maybe a scone. And whenever I'm forced to come down to LA, I always get Thai food from my favorite restaurant."

Drake was right; all she had eaten all day was one scone, and a glance at her watch told her it was already five o'clock. The day had flown by. "Thank you. Do you need any help?"

"Nope. I hope you like Thai food."

Livvie smiled. "I love Thai food." She got up and started clearing her kitchen table. Then she grabbed the plates out of Drake's hand. "I'll take them."

He turned, and when she looked back at him, his expression had changed.

"What it is? What's wrong?"

"Where's the journal I bought you?"

Livvie's heart sank.

"When I got home from your vineyard and started to write, it made me sad, knowing you'd given me the journal, and I'd never see you again. And I needed to get over you. I needed to heal."

Drake stared at her. "What made you think we'd never see each other again?"

Unable to look him in the eye, Livvie put the plates on the table and grabbed some napkins. "Because you made it clear that we were through once the week was over."

"But I didn't say we couldn't remain friends."

"Right. Friends." Livvie looked at the table. She couldn't talk about this now. "So what happened with Seth today? Was his PR firm able to help?"

Drake placed two wineglasses on the table and uncorked a bottle of his red wine. Livvie laughed.

"What?" Drake asked.

"You brought your own wine?"

Drake winked at her. "I never leave home without it."

She continued to laugh as he poured them both wine. She picked up her glass. Should she pretend she was a wine connoisseur and swirl the wine in her glass and then sniff? She decided not to put on any airs, and instead, she took a sip. It was delicious.

"Good?"

Livvie nodded, smiling. Drake, on the other hand, did the whole swirling, sniffing, and tasting thing. And he looked ever so hot doing it. No one had ever looked as sexy tasting wine, but then again, Drake looked sexy doing everything. When he sat down, he smirked at her, and she blushed.

"I gave you a little bit of everything. Eat while it's hot."

Livvie was famished, so she dived right in, and Drake joined her.

"Back to your question. The meeting with Seth went great, but you and I were all over the Internet."

Livvie paused, fork raised to her mouth. "What about your reputation?" Drake was a successful businessman. This could ruin him and all because of her temper.

"What about it?" Drake asked, mid-chew.

"I don't want you to have a bad reputation over me kissing that guy."

The fun look in Drake's eyes vanished instantly, and the cold, distant look replaced it. Fuck, she never should have mentioned what had happened at the club last night, but she'd had no choice.

"Olivia, if you hadn't noticed, I already have a bad reputation. The media has convinced the entire world that I'm some billionaire playboy who dates famous women and breaks their hearts."

"And that's not true?" She was pushing his buttons, but she didn't care.

Drake dropped his fork loudly onto his plate and clenched his jaw. "It's not true at all. Most of the women I've dated are through with me around the same time I'm through with them, usually when they realize I have no interest in taking them to expensive restaurants and going to the latest party. I like to stay home, in my castle, have my chef make me dinner, and afterward, fuck hard. But the actresses and models want to be seen, and I want the opposite. So, no, I don't care about my reputation."

"But I thought you leave them before it turns into more."

"I do. You know that. But these women are also extremely high maintenance. We have fun, and then when they expect more, I give them less. At that point, a few of them throw temper tantrums, and that's what you read about. What you don't read about is that those same women are no longer interested in me, either. They would rather be the one to blow me off first. Do you understand?"

"I do." She understood she would be the next to be blown off.

"Good." Drake picked up his fork and resumed eating. And then he paused. "But I'm very touched that you're more concerned about my reputation than your own."

Livvie thought about that for a second, but she didn't care about her reputation. She was a writer. The only way this could be bad is if her family found out. Her sister wouldn't care. She'd just want to know in detail how she knew Drake. Her mom would be devastated, though. And if Liam found out…would she even care?

"Why are you so deep in thought?"

Livvie was always amazed by how well Drake seemed to know her.

"I was just worried that my mom will find out."

"She won't, unless she was online last night a little before midnight until three in the morning."

"No. They're in New York, which is three hours ahead. I'm sure my parents were fast asleep at six in the morning their time."

Drake nodded. "Good, then you have nothing to worry about. And luckily, no one knew your name. Drink."

Livvie had another sip of Drake's fabulous wine, and he followed suit.

"Seth was able to remove the videos and pictures from the Internet."

"How?" she asked, mid-sip.

"He has his ways."

The odds that Liam had seen the video and pictures were slim. A part of her would have liked him to see them. To see she had not only moved on but that a man such as Drake Morganthal was interested in her. Did that make her a bad person? She considered the question briefly but decided she was only human.

Throughout the rest of dinner, they made small talk. Drake talked about his concern over his vineyard and that he had a few customers stalking him, hoping to be the first to own one of his rare bottles. His stories made her laugh a few times. Drake kept pouring her wine. She wasn't sure if that was a good thing, but it helped her to relax. And she needed to do just that.

When the bottle of red wine was empty and the meal over, they both cleared the dishes and placed them in her dishwasher. Then they sat down on the sofa in the living room, and Drake opened up one of his bottles of dessert wines. Livvie had never tasted anything so delicious.

"I have this theory," Livvie said, sipping the dessert wine.

"Yes?" Drake took a sip, too.

"I think Carly and Mitch fucked last night."

Drake choked on his wine. "Why do you think that?"

"Well, Carly told me she thought he was hot, and I saw Mitch checking her out. And then under your orders, he threw her over his shoulder. And unlike me, she wasn't all that upset about him acting like a caveman. I even saw her grabbing his cock. I tried calling her earlier to make sure she was okay, and her phone went right to voicemail." Livvie had a feeling the wine might be getting to her head, but she felt so good.

"When Carly calls you back, let me know. If you're right, which I have no doubt you are, then I'll never use Mitch again," Drake said as he picked up his wineglass and took another sip.

"Why?" Even though she was annoyed at Mitch for watching over her, she felt guilty for the way she had treated him.

"Because I hired him to watch over you, not to fuck your best friend."

"But he was off duty."

"That doesn't matter to me. If he did fuck Carly, I'll never hire him again. End of discussion."

"But you don't know Carly. If she wants to fuck someone, she will. No matter who they are. End of discussion." Livvie smiled to herself.

"I don't hire weak men, Olivia. And no matter how seductive your friend can be, if one of my employees succumbs to that, then they're weak."

Livvie rolled her eyes and took another sip of the wine. It felt so strange and yet so natural to be sitting here with him like this. And yet she'd left his vineyard days ago and never thought she would lay eyes on him again. Life was strange.

"So if Zach doesn't come to my house again for a few days, are you going to leave?"

Drake finished his wine in one gulp and poured more into his glass. Livvie held out her glass for him to pour more into hers, also. Last night, she had drunk Stoli Vanil and ginger ale, and tonight she was drinking Drake's wine. She'd drunk more in the last ten days than she had in her entire life—not a good habit to get into.

"What kind of men did you date before Zach?" Drake asked out of nowhere, ignoring her last question.

She wished he had answered. If he was going to leave soon, she needed to prepare herself again.

"I don't know; all types of men, I guess. Why?" Livvie hadn't decided if she wanted to tell him about Liam. She felt humiliated enough, knowing Drake had heard Zach's harsh words.

"Because you wouldn't have dated a loser like Zach if a man hadn't hurt you before him," he said. "Please, Olivia."

Livvie sighed. How could she refuse him when he asked so nicely? She took one more sip of wine before she delved into the tale about her love life or lack of it.

"I dated Jared briefly when I first moved to Los Angeles, before Zach. I liked him. He wanted to be an actor, but he was struggling—financially as well as emotionally. And I couldn't handle that, so I ended it."

"Before him," Drake demanded.

"Before him..." Livvie paused. *Here she goes*, she thought. "I dated Liam." She paused again and looked down at her wineglass instead of into Drake's eyes. "I met him in college during my freshman year. We dated for about four years. He asked me to marry him, and I said yes." Livvie exhaled and sipped more wine, still unable to look at Drake.

But Drake touched the bottom of her chin and slightly raised her face.

"I'm not Liam. I'm not Zach, and I'm not Jared. You can look me in the eyes," he said softly.

As Drake released her, she swallowed and nodded.

"I loved him," she continued.

Drake had a blank expression. He wasn't judging, so she felt safe to continue.

"I really did. When we got engaged, our families were so happy." Livvie smiled as she remembered her mom jumping up and down when she heard the news. "His parents were both successful lawyers, and they liked my family. We shared the same friends, and they all bought us gifts." Livvie took another sip of wine. This was harder than she thought, but it felt important that Drake knew her history, even if they didn't have a future. "Going to an Ivy League school, I felt very hopeful about everything. Liam majored in prelaw for undergrad, and then he went to law school at the university. After law school, he planned to work at his dad's firm, which was one of the top in New York City."

"What was he like?" Drake asked.

When Livvie looked into his eyes, she felt as if she was back in college with Liam, reliving all of it, and in a way, she was.

"He was brilliant. I could ask him any question, and he'd have the answer. He was also a talented athlete. He played lacrosse, and I'd go to his games and cheer him on." Livvie had loved going to those games. She'd been so proud to be his girlfriend.

"How did you two meet?"

"When I was a freshman, my roommate sucked me into joining a sorority. I didn't want to, but she was scared to do it by herself, so I joined with her. I met Liam at a fraternity party. He was an attractive junior. And he wanted me. As a freshman, I thought that was a pretty big deal. He said that the moment he saw me, he knew I would be his wife one day."

She looked down. Drake's hands were clenched into fists.

"Go on," he said.

"He was the only man I dated in college. And I lost my virginity to him."

"You did? You didn't have sex in high school?"

"No, I was pretty sheltered until I left for college. My parents sent me to a strict private school. No one would have dared had sex...or even drank, for that matter. I dated someone, but we were more like friends. That's how it was in my high school. We all pretty much stayed innocent."

"You had a lucky upbringing." Drake unclasped his hands and continued drinking his wine.

"I did." Livvie smiled, but then her smile disappeared. "Liam proposed to me right before my graduation. He was in law school, so he told me to plan the wedding over the summer and we'd be married on Christmas break when he had a few weeks off. I had time to plan everything because Liam wanted me to postpone getting my Masters of Fine Arts in creative writing until he was working for his dad, and then I could go to a school in New York City. And then we'd get pregnant." Livvie took a much-needed breath. "It all made sense to me. So I moved in with him after graduation, which wasn't a big deal since I stayed over almost every night anyway. And I planned our wedding. Invitations were made, and I was ready to send them out." Livvie paused and put down her glass of wine, staring at her empty hands.

"It's okay, Olivia." Drake grabbed her hands and squeezed.

She inhaled and continued. "Then I came home from yoga one day, and I caught Liam in bed with my old roommate. The one who wanted me to join the sorority with her? Strangely, he knew the exact time I'd be home, so I think he wanted me to know."

Drake looked compassionate, so she continued. "When I saw them, they weren't fucking. I think I would have been able to get over it if they were doing that. You know?"

Drake nodded.

"They were sleeping, cuddling naked. I didn't even care that they were naked. It was the cuddling that devastated me. Liam wasn't the cuddling type. He told me how much he hated cuddling, yet he seemed more than fine cuddling her."

"Did you confront the bastard?" Drake's tone sounded harsh.

"I didn't have to. I was so shocked; I dropped my yoga mat. They both heard and woke up. My old roommate, my ex friend, panicked and said over and over again that she was sorry. That they had fallen asleep and she had never wanted me to know about them or see what I'd seen. I didn't say a word to her. I wasn't mad at her. She had betrayed our friendship, which hurt, but what he had done was worse. Then she got up, grabbed her clothes, and left. And then Liam apologized and said he still wanted to marry me.

"And in that horrific moment, where I saw my life destroyed, everything made sense. Liam grew up in a family where career and image was number one. I didn't know that men like Liam had a resume for the perfect woman — the perfect wife. I fit his resume. But *love* wasn't listed anywhere on his resume. I think he loved me, but as with Zach, Liam wasn't *in love* with me. I think he was actually in love with my roommate. But she didn't fit his resume at all, so there was no way he could take her as a wife. She was a middleclass girl from Texas, and he was looking for an East Coast girl from an affluent family."

"So what happened?" Drake asked.

"He wanted the wedding to go on, as planned, and I remained silent. I couldn't speak. So I left. There are some women who would have told him off or thrown things at him, but how could I have done that to a man who was in love with a woman his career and family wouldn't have allowed? That was punishment enough. And I thought my actions spoke volumes. I cancelled the invitations, the other wedding details, and mailed back every gift we had received from my registry. It was too late for me to apply to graduate school, so instead, I came here."

"And then you dated that actor?"

"I wasn't into him at all, but I was told that if you sleep with another man after a break up, it's easier to forget about your ex. So that's what I did, except Jared was struggling financially, so he was depressed and stressed all the time. I was trying to get over Liam, and I was also struggling in my own way. I didn't want any more drama in my life."

"And then you met Zach."

"Yes, and then I met Zach. I mustn't have learned my lesson from Liam because Zach cheated on me, too. But I guess you can't call it cheating if he tells you on the third date that he doesn't believe in monogamous relationships." Livvie sighed. "I liked Zach a lot. He made me feel good about myself, and after what had happened with Liam, I didn't."

Livvie leaned her head against the back of the couch and closed her eyes. The next thing she knew, Drake was scooping her up in his arms. She expected him to at least give her his opinion on her past, but she didn't expect this. And she was too tired to ask if he had any more questions.

He held her tightly in his arms as he carried her to her bedroom. Then he laid her on the bed and took off each shoe. He unzipped her jeans, and she instinctively clenched her vagina.

"I'm undressing you, so you can sleep."

Livvie blushed, and at the same time, she panicked. Had her story turned him off? He slid her jeans down her legs, and Livvie helped him to remove them. Then he grabbed her tank top and lifted it above her head as Livvie raised her arms. As he unclasped her bra, her breasts were on full display for him, and her nipples hardened. Did he notice?

He went into the bathroom and returned seconds later with liquid soap on a cotton ball.

"Close your eyes."

Livvie did as instructed and felt the cotton brush her eyelids, her cheeks, and her forehead. He was so gentle she even drifted to sleep for a quick second. Then she opened her eyes.

"Do you need to use the bathroom before I put you under the covers? I should have asked you before."

She nodded, ran into the bathroom, and came out a minute later. Drake had pulled down the blanket enough for her to crawl into bed.

She pulled off her panties, causing Drake's eyes to darken. And then she crawled into bed fully naked.

"Are you coming?" Livvie needed to feel his arms around her.

"Would you like me to come in?" he whispered in her ear.

Livvie nodded, feeling more vulnerable than ever.

Drake took off his shoes and then walked into the bathroom. She heard the sink water go on and then stop a minute later. When Drake came out, he wasn't wearing a shirt or pants, only his boxers. He looked hot, as usual. He placed his clothes in her closet and then walked to the other side of the bed. As his body hit the mattress, it sank down slightly. Not including last night, the last time she had experienced a man being in her bed had been over four months ago with Zach.

"Come here." Drake motioned for her to scoot over.

He grabbed her so she was lying on her side, and he pressed his body against hers so they were spooning. He held her tight around her waist. It was still early, around nine o'clock, but she felt exhausted. Drake would probably rather be working. But she was grateful he wasn't.

He kissed her hair gently. "Go to sleep, baby."

Livvie shook her head. "No."

As exhausted as she felt, not being intimate wasn't an option. Spilling her past wasn't supposed to turn Drake off. She would die if that were the case.

Livvie turned toward him and silently pleaded with her eyes, telling him what she needed from him.

She watched Drake swallow hard. From the look in his eyes, she could tell he was debating what to do, but if he weren't intimate, she would regret everything she'd said.

Drake leaned down and kissed her on the forehead. Then he gently caressed her hair. "I think both men were fools. Zach and Liam, I mean; you can't count Jared, since you never gave him your heart."

Livvie gasped, as the meaning behind his words seeped into her soul. She wasn't the type of woman who made the first move, but she couldn't help herself. She raised her head off the pillow and pressed her lips firmly against his. But Drake instantly pulled back.

"You need your sleep."

"No. I need *you*," she demanded. "I want you."

The look in his eyes was breaking her heart. He was indecisive.

Holding his face, she licked her tongue along his bottom lip.

Drake pulled back again. "Olivia," he pleaded.

He didn't want to be with her tonight. Livvie understood. That was how she'd felt the first night he was here, before Zach showed up. Drake had no intention of committing to her. Having sex was prolonging the inevitable, and he didn't want to hurt her like the others had. She respected him for that. At the same time, having confessed about Liam brought back feelings she had stuffed down. She wanted Drake to make her feel good again. For one more night, she wanted to feel him inside her. It wasn't the healthiest decision, but she'd deal with the ramifications later. So Livvie placed her hand on his cock, over his boxer shorts, and waited.

Finally, Drake groaned loudly and pulled her hair back. He brutally smashed his lips against her before releasing her.

"You sure you want to fuck?"

Livvie nodded.

Drake looked at her for a brief second before clenching his jaw. Then he released his cock from his boxers, but instead of thrusting inside her, he rubbed the head of his dick against the outside of her soaking wet vagina.

"Do you think you'll forget how those men treated you if I fuck you hard enough?" Drake said through clenched teeth.

He pulled her hair tighter as he continued torturing her with his dick. She needed him inside her now.

"Yes," she said softly.

Drake pulled her hair even tighter. It hurt, but at least she could feel something other than frustration.

"Please," she whispered.

Drake kept rubbing against the lips of her vagina, but every so often, he brushed his cock against her clit. It was so swollen that the lightest touch brought her closer and closer to climax. Then he pushed her on her back and resumed the torture.

"I want you," she practically cried. "Since the moment I stepped foot into your winery." She panted hard. If he didn't fuck her soon, she'd be forced to touch herself. She needed to come, and she needed to come now.

"Look at me, Olivia," Drake demanded.

Livvie swallowed and then obeyed. But she reined in her emotions. She had to. Drake looked serious, not the type of look that made a woman have an orgasm. But rather the type of look that made a woman want to run.

His cock glided against her clit and then down to her hole. Without warning, he thrust inside her, hard and deep, the way she wanted him to. The way she needed him to. Livvie moaned as he sped up the tempo. He bent her right knee, which made him go in so deep it felt as if his cock was touching her soul.

"Is this what you wanted?" Drake said through clenched teeth.

"Yes." In this position, she couldn't thrust with him. Instead, she rubbed the sweat pouring off his forehead with her fingers and then placed her fingertips into her mouth.

Drake's eyes became huge.

"Thank you," she whispered.

Drake grabbed her nipple and pinched hard. Livvie screamed. The pain made her feel wild, and she welcomed the feeling. She moved her head from side to side and gripped his hair. He pushed her other leg up and then spread her knees wide. Livvie felt open and exposed in this position. Raw even. She screamed again, and then pushed her pelvis up, even though she couldn't go that far. She kept doing it until Drake pinched her clit as hard as he had her nipple.

An orgasm, the likes of which she'd never felt in her entire life, ripped through her body. She moaned and shook as a wave of intense chills overtook her body. She couldn't breathe. She couldn't swallow.

Livvie hated to admit it, but she wanted to fuck him because she was terrified of losing him. Yet, she didn't have him. The irrational part of her was hoping he'd want to stay because of their incredible sex. But she was wrong. That wasn't how you kept a guy. And she should've known better by now. Apparently, it was a lesson she needed to relearn.

She didn't know how to apologize, so instead, as her orgasm was waning, she clenched her vagina as hard as she could. Drake groaned and then thrust hard a few more times, and then she felt his seed bathe her womb. She'd wanted to make him feel good because inside she felt awful.

As guilt consumed her, she kept her eyes closed. Drake pulled out of her. Then he kissed her on the forehead gently, surprising her.

"Thank *you*," he whispered in her ear.

She heard him put his boxers back on.

To her relief, Drake didn't leave her bed. He moved onto his side and then pulled her with him, causing her to also lie on her side. He kept his arm tight around her waist. Once again, he was spooning her.

"Goodnight, Olivia," he said softly.

Still, Livvie couldn't speak. Instead, she forced her breathing to become even. Hopefully, he'd think she'd fallen fast asleep, and he'd fall asleep with her. Tomorrow, she'd have to deal with the fact she'd begged a man to have sex with her—a man who didn't want to commit. *Way to go, Livvie.* But at least she had tonight.

21

THE NEXT MORNING, Livvie awoke alone again. A sense of dread consumed her like never before. She looked at her night table to see if he had left a note as he had yesterday, but there wasn't one. Then she heard him speaking on his cell in the kitchen, and she sighed with relief. She didn't know what she would do if he decided to leave her today. After she had told him about her past, it felt as if the walls around her heart had melted. She needed a day or so to build those walls back up.

She got out of bed, brushed her teeth, ran a comb through her hair, and threw on a long pink sweatshirt that fell to the middle of her thighs. She was so excited to see Drake, she practically ran to him. And then she stopped. He was speaking on his cellphone in her kitchen, fully dressed, his suitcase sitting on the floor beside him. *Wow*, she must have slept soundly not to have heard him packing. And then her heart clenched. Her intuition had been right. Something was wrong.

When Drake saw her, he immediately ended the call and walked toward her. She looked into his eyes, searching for answers. All she saw was regret.

"Hey, beautiful." Drake kissed her on the cheek, which was all the confirmation she needed.

"What's going on, Drake?"

He smiled softly, but the smile didn't reach his eyes. "Mr. Birkshire called and said I'm needed at the vineyard."

"Of course," Livvie whispered.

"Don't look so sad, my little raffle winner." Drake grabbed a bottle of water from her fridge.

Livvie stood there trying to find the protective walls to place around her heart again, but she couldn't. She wasn't the same naïve girl who had found Liam cheating, nor was she the lost woman she had been with Zach. She was a survivor. Now she had to figure out how to survive without Drake Morganthal.

"Is that the real reason you're leaving?"

Drake rolled his suitcase into her living room and turned back to her, his eyes changing from warm to cold and distant.

"I'm not Liam or Zach, but I will be if I stay here any longer."

"What do you mean?" She needed him to spell it out.

He sighed and ran his hands through his hair. "I don't want a long-term relationship, and this has already become more complicated than anything I've had in the past." He was shutting her out. She could feel it.

"Please don't leave." Her voice grew louder.

"I have a vineyard to run." Drake groaned and then came over to her. He grabbed her shoulders and then dropped his hands. Remaining silent, he studied her…although it felt as if he was memorizing her. And then he bent down and kissed her on the forehead. "You deserve a man who wants to give you a real relationship. Our intimacy last night made me realize I'm no better than Liam or Zach. By staying, I'm leading you on, knowing full well I can't give you what you want."

Drake looked her straight in the eye, and she let him. She wanted him to see how much his leaving was affecting her. He was going to leave, anyway, so there was no need to hide the new scars that had formed. She never should have slept with him last night, but it didn't matter. He would have left her, eventually. It was probably better that her actions pushed things along.

"Olivia, all I'm giving you is that look in your eye. The one my mom had. And I swore to never do that to a woman, but I'm doing it to you now — to the only woman I've ever cared about. I accused Zach of giving you the same look. That doesn't feel good to me. I'm not your hero, Olivia. Next time you find a man, make sure he treats you like a queen. Never settle for less." Drake walked back to his suitcase and rolled it to the front door, which was already open.

His words had hurt her deeply, and she chose not to respond. She could see a limo waiting out front. If she hadn't woken up in time and run into the kitchen, would he have even said goodbye? But she chose not to ask that question because it didn't matter. He had made up his mind, and he was leaving…for good this time. She had no choice but to let him go.

"Goodbye, Drake. Take care of yourself." She swallowed hard.

Drake had one foot out the door, and then he paused. He acknowledged her by nodding, but he never turned around. She wished she could see his face one more time. She watched Mr. Birkshire help him into the limo. Drake closed the car door without even glancing her way. But as Mr. Birkshire opened the trunk to throw in the luggage, he did. And she could see the look of compassion all the way from here. She waved to him and then watched the limo drive away. Then she slid down her door, and when she reached the floor, she sobbed, not caring if the whole world saw.

Drake was wrong. He was worse than Liam and Zach combined. He was a coward.

Minutes later, Livvie crawled to her living room and closed her front door with her foot. Her cellphone was ringing like crazy. With trembling fingers, she grabbed it from the coffee table. Her heart sank when she saw it wasn't Carly. Livvie needed her friend right now more than ever. She knew there was no way it would be Drake. Instead, she saw a number she didn't recognize. Maybe it was for a new job? She forced herself to answer even though she felt like crap.

"This is Livvie."

There was a pause.

"Hello?" She was about to hang up until she heard a male's voice.

"Hi, Livvie. It's Stephan Brenson, from lunch at Morganthal Winery."

Livvie didn't want to deal with another man right now, but she couldn't be rude. "Hi, Stephan. Of course I remember you."

"Is this a bad time?" Stephan asked.

Yes, it's a really bad time. "No, it's a perfect time. How are you?"

"I'm great. Hey, I just wanted to know what the status is with you and Drake. I don't mean to pry, but I've been in LA for a super early meeting. I have about an hour to kill before I leave for the airport, so I wanted to know if I could stop by your house, or if you want to meet me somewhere?"

Livvie inhaled. "Okay."

Stephan laughed. "Okay to seeing me, or is that the status between you and Drake? I don't want to come see you if you're with him. I hope you understand."

He was a good guy. How could she turn down one of those when they were so rare?

"I'm not with Drake." Livvie paused. Did she want to meet Stephan somewhere in public or have him come here? Then she sighed. She was in no condition to drive. "Why don't you come to my house?"

"Great. Text me your address, and I'll be there as soon as I can. Does that sound okay?"

Livvie looked down at her pink sweatshirt. She needed to get dressed, but it wouldn't take her long.

"Perfect. See you soon."

They hung up, and she texted him her address. She quickly threw on black skinny jeans and a loose black tank top. It was the best she could do. She put on a lot of under-eye concealer, as her eyes were a mess from crying.

Minutes later, Stephan arrived in a limo, just as Drake had done.

"Hey, Stephan." She forced herself to smile and give him a hug. It wasn't easy.

He hugged her back tightly. But these weren't Drake's arms. "Hi, beautiful."

He waved at the limo driver and then walked past her into her living room. Livvie closed the door.

"Do you want a drink?"

"No. Sorry, I only have ten minutes. I found out I have another quick meeting before I get on my plane."

Livvie was so relieved even though she shouldn't be feeling this way. Stephan was the real deal, and Drake had proven he wasn't. This time her smile was genuine.

"No problem at all. Sit." She motioned for him to sit on the couch, and she sat on the chair.

"Since I don't have a lot of time, I'll cut to the chase." Stephan took a deep breath.

Uh-oh, thought Livvie. There was no way she could handle a serious conversation right now. She'd lose it. She gripped the arms of the chair for support. Why did her life always feel as if she was on a rollercoaster?

"When we met, I felt a connection between us. I'd like to pursue that connection," Stephan continued.

Livvie's heartbeat went wild. She wasn't ready for this. "But you live so far away."

"But you come to New York sometimes to visit your family, right? I figured you can write your novel from anywhere, and I could fly you on my private plane whenever you want. We can figure out a way to make this work."

She felt as if she was being strangled. Instead of answering him right away, she asked a different question. "How did you get my number?"

"I asked Mr. Birkshire for it before I left Drake's house. So what do you say?"

Livvie inhaled deeply, needing some air. Her adrenaline was pumping. She had to be honest with him. There was a reason she had refused to take Stephan's number to begin with.

"I'm not *with* Drake, Stephan." She paused to calm her nerves. "But my heart is."

Stephan's face fell, and she hated herself for feeling as if she was forced to tell him all of this.

"Well then forget it. Or forget it for now. Thank you for your honesty. I appreciate it." Stephan ran his hands through his hair. "I want you, but I want all of you. You're all I've been thinking about since I met you. Your face, your smile, your beautiful body." Stephan exhaled loudly. "You're the type of woman I could imagine spending the rest of my life with. And I'm telling you all of this, even though you're in love with Drake. I saw the two of you together. I saw your connection, but I also saw that we had one too. Just different." He slapped his hands against his knees. "When your heart is free again, I'd like to explore that."

"I'd like that, too," Livvie said. "Please, don't forget me."

Stephan stood up to leave, so she stood, too.

"You turned me down that day after lunch, but I thought I'd try again. I have to go, but call me when or if you're ever over Drake Morganthal." Stephan walked away from her and opened the door. Before he left he turned around and looked at her.

"And Livvie, I believe Drake has real feelings for you, too. So don't just stand there. Fight for him. Like I tried to do with you, but, unfortunately, you don't feel for me yet what I feel for you. Your heart is preoccupied. I understand. But if he consumes your thoughts as you consume mine, then, please, do yourself a favor. Fight for him."

"I've done that, Stephan. I've pretty much begged him." Livvie hated telling Stephan the truth.

Stephan looked at her for a brief moment before responding. "When I met you at Drake's lunch, I was attracted to you because I saw a woman who was being treated poorly and yet held her head up high. You were warm at that lunch. You spoke to everyone. You laughed when you wanted to cry, and you handled yourself with class and dignity. Most of all, I was drawn to your strength," Stephan said. "If you truly begged Drake to be with you, then you just lost yourself for a moment. Find your strength again. Figure out where you got lost, and then fight for him. At that lunch, Drake wanted the same woman I wanted. Don't allow Drake to take your power, especially since he hasn't earned it. Once you have your power back, fight for him. You'll have a much better chance at winning." He didn't say anything more. He looked at her for one more second and then turned back around and closed the door.

Stephan was right. Since Livvie came back from Napa, she hadn't found the time to ground herself. Aside from writing, she needed a yoga class. Mostly, she needed to figure out who she was without the job drama and the men drama. She needed her best friend.

Livvie picked up her cellphone and called Carly. It went to voicemail again. Sitting back in the chair, she closed her eyes. She needed time to think.

Hours later, what Stephan had said was still running through Livvie's mind. He thought she should fight for Drake once she was whole again.

With Liam, there'd been no point. He loved another woman. And with Zach, they wanted two different things. She wanted to be monogamous, and he didn't. To top it off, he wasn't in love with her. So no reason to fight there. But Drake had said he cared about her, and he had invested more in her than his other past relationships, although he refused to call it that. So it came down to whether or not she was willing to put her heart at risk and fight for him or not. Drake was wrong. She wasn't looking for a hero. She was looking for real love. Livvie would have preferred to ask Carly her opinion, but Livvie needed to make this decision for herself. She picked up her cellphone and called the one person she never thought she would call in her life.

"Hi, Veronica, it's Livvie. I need your help." And as she took her leap of faith, she hoped and prayed it would not lead to more heartbreak. But even if it did, she'd learned that she had survived before, so she'd survive again. Most importantly, she needed to work on herself, and become strong again. She needed to get back to Livvie.

22

AS IF NO time had passed, Livvie parked her rental car on the side of the road. This time, she'd chosen a black car, after mourning Drake for the last six weeks. She got out of the car, holding the door for emotional support, and gazed up at the castle that awaited her. Unlike the last time, she wasn't showing up as a lucky raffle winner, although, at the time, she'd felt anything but lucky. It was funny how life worked. Many times throughout her life, the universe brought her opportunities and situations she dreaded and had resented, but they had ended up being the best thing for her. Like what happened with Liam. Finally, she understood.

Today she wasn't a lucky raffle winner. Today she was a woman fighting to be with a man she could envision spending her life with. However realistic that was, she didn't know, but thanks to Veronica, Livvie was here to find out. At first, she thought Veronica would discourage her fight, but not only had she been encouraging, she'd thought of a brilliant plan to make it happen. Which was why Livvie was back in Napa six weeks later. Veronica had made it very clear that it took a man six to eight weeks to truly miss a woman. After that time, he would either realize she was the love of his life, or *she* would realize there was nothing left between them other than one blissful, beautiful week and two nights together. She'd also listened to Stephan and had used the six weeks to work on herself.

Taking a deep breath, Livvie got back into her car and made the left to take her up to Morganthal Winery. The drive felt surreal. While her heart was beating like mad, a feeling of numbness washed over her. She wasn't surprised. Numbing out her life was a survival tool she used when she felt scared.

And unlike last time, when she passed the security guard in front of his castle, she waved, and he let her pass without having her stop.

Her numbness dissolved the moment she pulled up before Drake's castle. Her heart beat louder. There it was, standing strong and proud, like the owner. She hoped the proud part wouldn't get in her way.

She didn't stop in front of the castle. Instead, she drove a little farther and then made the first right, which took her to one of Drake's guest cottages. Veronica had insisted Livvie stay in the castle, but she'd refused. She was courageous by coming here without his knowledge, but she didn't have enough courage to stay in his home. If it was up to her, she would stay at a nearby hotel, but Veronica wouldn't allow that. She had hired Livvie to write her memoirs, so Livvie didn't have a lot of room to argue. Plus, Veronica was paying Livvie. She would have written Veronica's memoirs for free, but Veronica said she'd always wanted to have them done, but she couldn't write. And Livvie was spending her savings quickly. She really needed the money. She charged Veronica enough to pay her bills and added in a little extra for food. Veronica agreed, although she had wanted to pay Livvie a lot more. In the end, they'd both settled on her staying in one of Drake's guest cottages. It would have felt too awkward if she stayed in his castle.

Maybe she shouldn't have involved Drake's mom at all, but she hadn't been able to think of any other way. She only hoped she wasn't making everything worse.

The road narrowed as soon as the guest cottages came into view. Veronica had warned her to be careful driving on it. The road became so narrow Livvie was lucky there was enough room for her rented SUV. But as she got a glimpse of the first cottage she smiled to herself. Between the narrow road and the fairytale-like cottages everything seemed so enchanting.

A white picket fence surrounded each little, white, thatched-roofed cottage. A cobblestone path led to the front door. She felt as if she was in Ireland. Between his castle, the cottages, the mountains, and the vineyard, this was the most beautiful place on Earth. And even though she'd stayed here for one week, she had only gotten a glimpse of these cottages from afar. She had never gotten this close to this area of the vineyard.

Veronica had told her to drive to the end of the road, and she would be staying at the last house on the right. Number 6. On the side of her house was a small driveway. When Livvie saw the cottage, tears welled up in her eyes, and she started to cry. It was so perfect. So what she needed. Since there was no cottage next to it, Drake's vines were leaning against it. All she could see from the side of the house was his gorgeous vineyard. This was the perfect writer's retreat.

Although she could barely see through her tears, she parked in the driveway and then grabbed her luggage from the trunk. As she rolled her luggage to the house, she noticed there were window boxes filled with different colored flowers. And then she stopped walking and stared. She hoped this would be her home for at least a few weeks, and if she was lucky, a month. Knowing Drake was nearby, she already felt safe and protected. As long as he didn't hate her, everything would be okay. And even if he did hate her, she would deal with it.

She opened the gate, walked through, and then her breath caught in her throat. The view from her cottage overlooked everything—the mountains, the vineyard, and Drake's castle. If she looked closely enough, she'd find his bedroom windows. Her heart felt as if it was melting.

Livvie found the key under the mat, exactly where Veronica said it would be. When she opened the door, she stood still. She had entered into a small, breathtaking living room. The wall opposite from her was all grey stone. And there was a spiral staircase protruding from the ceiling, which she felt would lead her to heaven. The terracotta floor and wood beam ceiling gave the cottage a homier feel. The couch was white with pink, purple, and green floral throw pillows. There was an area rug with a floral print that matched the pillows. And the wooden coffee table matched the wood in the ceiling. A fireplace sat perfectly inside the stone wall, and on the right was an enormous bay window, which overlooked lush greenery—Drake's vineyard to the left and the mountains that seemed to go on forever. But it wasn't the majestic feel of the mountains that held her gaze captive. It was the intimidating castle that loomed over her cottage.

Taking a much-needed deep breath, Livvie closed the wooden door and leaned against it. If she had her way, she would climb the spiral staircase and hopefully find a bed, where she could escape her problems and remain in her fairy tale. So that was exactly what she did.

She climbed the spiral staircase carefully. At the top she found a room the same size as the living room, except instead of a stone wall, there was one full wall of windows. In front of the clear-glass wall was a king-sized bed with a fluffy white comforter and a wooden headboard. Without thinking twice, Livvie lay down on the bed, but before she closed her eyes she looked out the window and once again saw the ominous castle that seemed to be watching every move she made. The feeling didn't scare her or make her feel uncomfortable. Instead, surprisingly, she felt at peace. She had no idea what the future held, but for the first time since she had left Morganthal Winery all those weeks ago, she felt as if she was home.

23

LIVVIE MUST HAVE fallen asleep, because sometime later, she woke up to the sound of her cellphone ringing. With her eyes still closed she searched the bed for her purse, which she had tossed down on the mattress when she had collapsed on it.

"Hello?"

"Thank God you're okay. I was getting worried about you."

Livvie winced. She had promised to call Veronica the minute she arrived, but her heart had felt so heavy that the only thing she could think to do was to fall asleep. "I'm sorry. I dozed off." She ran her free hand through her hair. "Thank you so much for inviting me to stay here. The place is beautiful."

"I knew you'd love it. When Drake's castle was under construction, I stayed there. It felt magical. It's my favorite of all of his guest cottages," Veronica said.

"Thank you. It's lovely. I don't feel like I'm in Napa." Livvie sighed, needing to release the constant pressure on her heart. The sadness was overwhelming.

"It's Drake's version of Napa. Do you know he designed each cottage himself? But this particular one reminded me of you." Veronica paused. "It's beautiful and special. Drake normally goes for models and actresses. You're different than they are because you're more beautiful and you belong with Drake."

"If only he believed that."

"Oh, he does. That's why he ran away from you. You scare him, Livvie."

She glanced out the window. With the sun setting behind Drake's castle it appeared to have a pink hue glistening over it, as if a love angel was casting a spell. How she wished that was true.

"Veronica, does he even know that I'm here?"

"No, not yet, but the plan is in effect, and he'll know any minute now."

"What's your plan?" Maybe this was a bad idea. Maybe she should have stayed home. Veronica thought this was a game, and to a certain degree, it was. But it was also Livvie's life.

"Stop worrying, sweetie. All I did was leave your signed contract on the table in the entranceway."

"Won't Mr. Birkshire see it and give it to you?"

"No, I told him not to."

Livvie heard someone on the phone yelling in the background. "Veronica, are you okay?"

"Motherrrrrrrrrrr!"

"Yes, Drake found the contract. I have to go."

Veronica hung up. Livvie began to shake. She had never heard anyone yell so loudly in her entire life. Maybe she should pack her bags now. No, she had been hired to write a book, and even if Drake hated her, she would write it. Unless Veronica had made up the entire book idea. If that was the case, then Livvie was being played as much as Drake was. But right now she was too tired to care.

LIVVIE WOKE UP to the sound of a key jiggling in her door. She threw the blanket off and jumped out of bed. Luckily, she was somewhat decent. After her call with Veronica, she'd gotten out of bed and had thrown on her matching white silk tank top and shorts. Her mom had gotten Livvie the pajama set last year for Christmas. It wasn't the sexiest nightwear she owned, but it was still sexy. It hadn't surprised her to receive such a gift from her mom. She really wanted Livvie to find love.

Whoever was at her door was having a hard time getting the key to work, which gave her enough time to run to the bathroom, brush her teeth, and smooth her hands through her hair. Veronica must be having a hard time opening her door. Who else would it be? The only other person who would come in here without knocking would be Drake. She hoped it wasn't him. She wasn't ready to see him yet.

When the jangling of the key continued, Livvie reached her limit. She ran downstairs and opened the door at the same time as the person finally got the door open. She collided with him. Drake Morganthal. If he hadn't caught her, she would have fallen forward on her face. *Classy, really classy.* Although she loved the feeling of being held by him again, it was wrong. But instead of releasing him like she should, she grabbed onto the back of his neck and squeezed him even harder, not caring that she could barely breathe. She hadn't been breathing for the last six weeks. Why start now? They had been the longest six weeks of her entire life. Sure, she had gotten a lot of writing done, and she did fun activities to make herself happy, but she missed him. He wasn't hugging her back, though. Feeling silly, she slowly stepped out of his embrace.

The look in his eye confirmed that she'd done the right thing. Just three weeks ago, she had seen him on some magazine cover with a beautiful woman, but Veronica swore he wasn't with anyone. At least the woman hadn't been Kayla Brenson.

Drake stood there smirking. She needed to say something. Anything.

"Hi, Drake."

"Hello, Olivia." He was still smirking and obviously not making this easy for her.

"I'm sorry. I was napping, and then all of a sudden, I heard someone trying to open my door, and it freaked me out."

"I understand, especially after what Zach pulled."

"Yes." She nodded.

"How have you been?" Drake grabbed on to the doorknob behind him, but he didn't close the door.

"I'm good. Would you like to come in?"

"No."

Butterflies were going wild in her stomach. She hadn't seen him in so long. All she wanted to do was run back into his arms and hold him forever. He looked beautiful in his faded jeans and white polo shirt. He had been working...creating the wines he loved. But she didn't tell him all that because she couldn't read the look in his eyes. He didn't seem to hate her, but he didn't seem happy to see her, either. He seemed indifferent, which was worse than anything.

So she asked, "How have *you* been?"

Drake was staring at her intensely. Too intensely. "I've been great. Thank you."

Livvie's heart clenched. "I'm glad to hear it." She wasn't.

"Congratulations on getting a writing job."

Livvie inhaled. He was angry. If only he'd just yell and get it over with. Anything but acting cold and distant.

"Thank you." She tried to smile, but she couldn't.

"And free room and board was included, I see."

Livvie looked down at her bare feet. She wished she had thrown on a robe or something.

"Do you want me to leave?"

Drake chuckled, and it wasn't a pleasant sound. "Why would I want you to leave? You struck a lucrative deal with my mother. I think it's great."

He was lying. She could see him clenching his jaw.

"Look, I'm sorry. As you already know, her house is being renovated. So since she's staying here..." Livvie cut herself off. What else could she say? After all, she was lying, too.

"Since she's staying here, she thought it'd be a perfect time to write her memoirs. So she contacted you, the only talented writer she knows in the entire world, to write her book. Does that sound right?"

Livvie swallowed. "If you don't want me on your property, just tell me. I can wait until she's back in her house."

"No. You can't. Because the scheme my mother and you came up with was to stay at *my* house."

"But I'm staying in your *guest*house."

Drake clapped his hands once, causing her to jump. "Right, I'm sorry. I meant *my* property."

Livvie sighed. "If you don't want me here, then say it." She was already mentally repacking her bags.

Drake slammed the door closed, forcing Livvie to take a step back. She'd been a lot happier when it was open. Before, there'd been the illusion of an escape. Now she felt trapped with a very angry man.

"How dare you come here after our expiration date," Drake said through grinded teeth.

"I thought you said we were friends."

Steam was practically coming out of his ears. "*Friends*, as in call a few times a year. Not *friends* that manipulate my mother into figuring out a way to stay on my property."

Livvie stood up straighter. Without him realizing it, he had given her the answer she needed. All she had left was her pride. "I didn't manipulate your mother at all, Drake. You're wrong." And that was the truth.

"Then why are you here, Olivia? Please, enlighten me."

Livvie exhaled. She had nothing to lose. "I wanted to see you. I needed to see you."

Drake's eyes widened, and the coldness was replaced by panic. "Why? Did Zach try to harm you again?"

"No," she whispered.

Drake's shoulders fell, and he sighed with relief. "I didn't think so. I paid someone to watch your house at night."

Livvie rolled her eyes, but inside, a sliver of hope ignited. If he had paid someone to watch her house, then he had to still feel something.

He began pacing back and forth in the living room. He stopped a foot away from her. "Olivia?" He grabbed her shoulders.

"Yes?"

"Did you run out of money? Was coming here your last resort?"

"No," she said, feeling more confused than ever.

Drake released her, stepped away, and stared at her for a few minutes before the anger returned to his eyes.

"Then my first instinct was right. You schemed and manipulated my mother into helping you come here and got her to pay you for it at the same time."

"I didn't," she said defensively.

Drake stepped toward her again. "Why, Olivia?" He took another step. "Why?"

He was inches away from her face, and she couldn't take it anymore. "Because I missed you. Because the last six weeks have been hard." Livvie paused and took a deep breath. "And you obviously didn't miss me, so I'll go." She sniffled back tears. "I swear I'll go."

Drake grabbed her shoulders again and squeezed them hard. He looked her up and down, and then his eyes became even darker. His teeth clenched, and he seemed to be contemplating something. Livvie was afraid to find out what it was. And then he told her.

"Prove to me that you deserve to stay here."

For a second, Livvie was confused, and then she understood. If she decided to do what he wanted, a little piece of her soul that had healed since he left her house would die. In the last six weeks, she wrote, slept, ate healthy again, went to yoga, and meditated daily. She worked on herself, and she didn't want to throw all that away. Not that there was anything wrong with giving a blowjob. She liked giving them. It was the way Drake was treating her that felt wrong.

But at the same time, she had come here to fight for the two of them. And he wanted her to prove how hard she would fight.

"I'm not giving you a blowjob like this," she said. Her tone was quiet but deadly serious. "I love submitting to you, but not when you're being mean. Maybe I shouldn't have come here, but I don't deserve this. I deserve better."

If sparks could fly out of Drake's eyes, they would. "I'm fucking angry, Olivia. I feel manipulated and blindsided," he said. "But that doesn't mean it hasn't been a long six-weeks for me either. Fuck. I've thought about you every damn day." He stepped even closer to her, grabbed the back of her head, and smashed his lips against hers.

He was being rough because of his anger, but she didn't mind. If anything, it brought out the passion she had stuffed down all these weeks without him.

He moved his lips aggressively. She couldn't tell who was hungrier—him or her. All she knew was how badly she wanted him. And now that he was finally touching her, she craved him more. As she kissed him back, she ran her hands through his hair, pulling it hard.

He pulled her silk pajama tank top up, forcing her to stop pulling his hair and to lift her arms above her head. They stopped kissing long enough for the tank top to fall onto the floor. Then he took both her breasts in his hands and pinched her nipples hard.

"Is this what you missed?" he asked.

"Yes," she whispered.

As he continued pinching her nipples, he looked at her breasts.

"God, I've missed these," he said softly, almost to himself, but Livvie heard. He kneeled down, so his mouth was eye level with her chest, and he sucked her nipple hard, exactly how she liked it.

She kneeled down with him and put her arms around his neck. Unsure of how he'd respond, she gently kissed him. In response, he bit her bottom lip and then slipped his tongue inside until their tongues were once again dancing.

While continuing to kiss her, he moved her silk pajama shorts aside and touched her inner folds.

"You're still so fucking wet for me," he said, breaking the kiss.

Livvie moaned as he circled her clit, but not in a way that would make her come. Then he pulled away and stood. She stood with him.

He pulled down her shorts then stepped back and got a good look at her fully naked while he was still dressed.

"Drake," she whispered, as he stared at every inch of her body.

"You may stay in my cottage," he said, his eyes cold and detached again. Then he turned around, walked out, and slammed the door behind him.

Livvie pulled up her pajama shorts and crossed her arms over her breasts. *What just happened?* One minute she refused to give him a blowjob, and in the next moment they were making out. And then he just left. A tear had slid down Livvie's cheek, and she brushed it away. She'd willingly come here, knowing he could hurt her. She had to stop getting upset over his actions.

A few minutes later, there was a knock on her door again.

This time, Livvie yelled, "Coming." And then she ran upstairs, threw on a pair of jeans and a navy-blue, V-neck t-shirt. She was feeling so vulnerable on the inside, so on the outside she needed to be fully clothed.

When she opened the door, she sighed with relief. Veronica and Mr. Birkshire had arrived with a huge tray of food.

"Hey, Veronica. Hi, Mr. Birkshire." She smiled as he stepped inside.

"Welcome back," Mr. Birkshire said. "Here's your favorite. Lobster tails and mashed potatoes. I'll leave a tray for you every morning and every evening."

"Thank you so much."

His kindness touched her so deeply; she feared she might start balling. Mr. Birkshire didn't seem to notice. He continued to walk into her kitchen.

"Enough talk of food." Veronica stepped into the house next and raised her chin. "My son made you cry."

Livvie cleared her throat. "No, I made myself cry. Please, Veronica, come in."

Livvie moved away from the door, and Veronica walked right past her and sat down on the couch. Livvie was glad to see her but wasn't in the mood for another interrogation.

"If you want to get out of writing my book, I understand, but if not, I brought additions to the contract you already signed. Drake hasn't seen this one. I decided to give you not only a large advance but royalties once the book sells."

Livvie closed the door, but her hand remained on the doorknob. "Veronica, you don't have to do this. No matter what happens with Drake, I promised you I'd write your book, and I will."

"So now you're looking at this like a charity case?"

She's good, thought Livvie. *Just like her son.* "No, that's not it at all. I do want to write it. In fact, I'm looking forward to writing it, but we decided on an amount already. You don't have to pay me royalties."

Veronica smiled warmly in the same way as Drake used to. "Good. I'm glad you're still writing it. I wouldn't want my son or any man to stop you from doing what you're meant to do in life."

Livvie smiled back and sat down in the chair across from her. "I realized that," she whispered. "I have to admit it took me a moment, but I did realize."

"Good. We women have to stay strong." Veronica paused. "But if it makes you feel any better, my son is miserable. After he saw the contract, he shouted orders at Mr. Birkshire and stormed into his vineyard like he always does when he needs to hide."

Livvie crossed her legs and sat farther back in the chair. *And then he came here,* she thought. "Why does he need to hide? He didn't do anything wrong. He just doesn't want to be in a committed relationship. That's not against the law."

Veronica smiled, but her eyes looked tired. "My son always hid from the world when life became too emotional for him, when he was forced to feel. He's brilliant at business, and as a child he was brilliant at school, but when one of his friends said something to hurt him or a high school girlfriend crushed his heart, he would hide in his room and shut off from the rest of the world. Especially when he saw how sad I was," she added.

"Why?" Livvie asked softly.

"I think it's my fault. I used to see him withdraw when I was down, but I was too depressed to do anything about it." Veronica's eyes glazed over and filled with regret. "Oh, well, I can't change what happened then, but I can help him be with the woman he loves now."

Livvie almost laughed. "I don't think he loves me." Although she hoped it was true.

"He does," Veronica said.

Another thought occurred to Livvie. "Is that why you want me to write your story? You think it'll help him to heal?"

Veronica smiled. "That's exactly why, and I've wanted to write it for a long time. I've watched my son get close to women and then pull away when there's a chance of happiness."

Hearing that he could have been happy with other women hurt Livvie's heart. She hated being jealous, but she couldn't help it. Veronica grabbed Livvie's hand and squeezed.

"I've never seen my son as happy as he was around you. And I don't want him to lose you, but he will if he doesn't give you what you need."

"How do you know?"

Veronica smiled again. "Because you're a strong woman who has been hurt by men before. If Drake continues to hurt you and doesn't fulfill your needs, you won't put up with his crap. You've learned your lessons, my dear, and you've turned a corner."

Livvie swallowed hard. Veronica was right. She was through putting up with crap. "Thank you for recognizing that, Veronica."

Veronica squeezed her hand once more and then stood. "Sign the contract, my dear, and when you're done, drop it off at the castle."

Livvie panicked. "How can I go up there? Drake hasn't invited me. He will flip."

Veronica put her hand on her hip and raised an eyebrow, reminding Livvie so much of Drake.

"So he'll flip. It won't kill him."

Livvie didn't respond. It may not kill Drake, but it may kill her. As Veronica turned to leave she stopped and turned toward Livvie.

"Don't worry so much. I have a good feeling about this." Veronica winked.

Livvie smiled. "Thank you, Veronica." She ran up to her and gave her a huge hug.

Veronica hugged her back, but it felt more like a pat on the back. *Intimacy issues*, thought Livvie.

"Mr. Birkshire, I'm leaving," Veronica shouted.

Livvie had forgotten he was still in her house.

"I'm coming." He walked into the living room, nodded at Livvie, and then resumed walking out the door.

Veronica rolled her eyes and then followed him. Once they had both gone, Livvie closed the door, leaned against it, and burst out laughing. What a couple of characters. But she loved them both and truly hoped that if she lost Drake, she wouldn't lose them, also. Carly had once told her to never get too attached to the family of the man she was dating. She was not dating Drake, but Carly had never been so right.

25

THE NEXT DAY, Livvie sat with Veronica for six hours and the day after that for ten. She had signed the contract Veronica left for her to read, but she wouldn't accept it unless Livvie personally delivered it to her at the castle. So far, Livvie hadn't found the courage. In the early mornings, she'd wake up and take a walk in the vineyard, but she tried to walk in areas where Drake wouldn't be. And it had worked out pretty well, so far. She hadn't seen him. In fact, except for the first day, he hadn't even come to her cottage to see her. Veronica said he was stubborn and not to give up hope. But that was the reason she had come here in the first place, to see if the hope she stored in her heart was real or just an illusion. But at least he hadn't kicked her out.

She loved working on Veronica's book. As Veronica gave details about her life as a young wife and mother, Livvie formed a better understanding of why Drake was the way he was. His mom had gone through some really dark days. Being married to a workaholic and living so far from her family had been rough on her and therefore, rough on Drake. And then once she'd returned to the United States, she had to reinvent herself. Being a single mother hadn't been easy. Even though her family was happy to see her, they judged her for getting divorced. And that was a struggle for her, too. But Livvie loved the way Veronica told her stories. They laughed and drank tea. If Livvie and Drake didn't get together, she would really miss his mother.

Last night when Veronica left, Livvie had sat on her bed, took out her laptop, and had written the first three chapters. She had been jotting down notes the last few days, but she hadn't started to write until last night.

Staying up all night writing had been exhausting but also exhilarating. Writing was her passion, her true love. No matter what happened with Drake, the completeness she felt all night from writing was a reminder that she was alive and satisfied in a different way. And she was grateful that she was being paid for doing what she loved. She also couldn't wait to show the chapters to Veronica. When Livvie had tried Veronica's cellphone earlier, she didn't answer. An hour later, Livvie still couldn't get in touch with her. She really wanted Veronica to see them.

And that's when a thought occurred to Livvie. The time had come.

Feeling courageous once again, she showered and put on a sundress that showed a good amount of cleavage. The dress was all white and came together slightly at the waist, making her chest look bigger. It fell to above her knees, and there were small pink bows along the bottom, which made her feel pretty and feminine.

If Veronica weren't coming today, then Livvie would have no choice but to go to her. And if she happened to see Drake, then so be it. His mom was paying her good money to write her book, and it was her job to deliver.

As she walked up to Drake's house, she felt different than she had when she'd stayed here as the raffle winner. Before, she'd been an unemployed television writer, but now she was an employed novel writer, and it felt incredible. She was living her dream, and she owed it all to Carly. If Carly hadn't forced Livvie to go to the black-tie charity event, she never would have won that raffle ticket. And therefore, she never would have met Veronica. Carly believed there were no coincidences in life, and there was a reason for everything. Maybe she was right. And if Livvie had never won that raffle ticket, Carly never would have met Mitch. Carly had finally confessed to fucking him that night. But Livvie practically had to drag the information out of her, and being so closed-mouthed about her sexual escapades really wasn't like Carly. She had been acting so weird since that night. In fact, Livvie had barely seen her friend. And when she asked about Mitch, Carly stopped speaking.

Livvie had felt as if she had to do life on her own since Drake had left. And she missed her best friend. She would never tell Drake about them, though. He had threatened to never hire Mitch again. But knowing Drake, he probably already knew.

When she reached the back door, an intense feeling of fear washed over her. She wasn't sure if she was feeling impending doom or if the butterflies causing havoc in her stomach were because she may see Drake. Whatever it was, she couldn't turn back now. Holding the chapters and the contract closer to her heart, she opened the door.

The second she walked into the house, Mr. Birkshire was there to greet her. How had he known she was here? And then she remembered. Drake had installed security cameras all around the place. Did that mean Drake had seen her, too?

"Ms. Collins, it's wonderful to see you here. I see that your baggage is gone." He winked at her but still without a smile.

She didn't care. She understood what he meant, and she was elated that he saw the difference in her.

She smiled wide. "Thank you. I tried."

"And you succeeded. Now how can I help you?"

"Is Veronica here?" Maybe Mr. Birkshire would get Veronica for Livvie, and she could leave without seeing Drake. But was that what she really wanted?

Mr. Birkshire nodded. "Come, follow me. I'll tell her that you're here."

Livvie followed him to the entrance hall and then froze when she heard a man's voice—the deep, dark voice she longed to hear day and night. Swallowing hard, she looked up at the top of the stairs, where the voice was coming from.

"Did you not hear me?" Drake yelled.

She'd heard him ranting and raving, but she wasn't sure what he had said.

"Excuse me?" Livvie asked with as much courage as she could muster.

"*What are you doing here?*" He emphasized each word as if she was an idiot.

Mr. Birkshire nodded at her and then left her alone without any protective shield. And she needed one. The last time she'd seen Drake, he'd left her standing alone naked.

"I'm here for Veronica. I have some pages of her book that I want her to see."

"And you couldn't email them to her?" Drake said as he walked down the stairs toward where she stood trembling.

She wished she didn't always feel so on edge around him.

"No, she likes to physically have the pages in her hands, so she can write notes on them. And these are the first three chapters."

"I see," was all he said, standing only a few feet away from her.

"You do?" she asked.

"Yes, you needed a reason to see me." Drake raised an eyebrow, daring her to challenge him.

"You're wrong. I came here to see Veronica."

Drake smirked. "Oh, I think that's part of it. But it's not your style to admit you came here because you've been craving me day and night since I saw you at my cottage. Especially since I left you wet and aroused."

Trying to remain calm, Livvie looked down at the pages, but Drake wouldn't have it. He yanked the pages out of her hand.

"Drake. Give those back!"

"Not until you answer my question."

Livvie's heartbeat was thudding while she waited to hear what he wanted to know. "What's your question?" The faster she got the pages back the faster she could return to the cottage.

"Were you more turned on when I was staring at you naked or afterward, remembering it?"

Livvie gasped. "Drake," she said. "Why are you acting like an asshole? And why did you have to bring that up, especially in the entrance hall where anyone could hear?"

"Answer me, or you don't get these pages back." He held the pages in his hands as if he was going to rip them apart.

She didn't think he would really do that, but she also didn't want him to read them. That wasn't fair to Veronica. She also didn't want him to read her contract. "After," she answered softly.

"And later that night when you were in bed, were you remembering and touching yourself?"

"Yes," she said a little stronger. She watched Drake's eyes turn a darker shade of green.

"And did you change the scenario and add me throwing you down and licking you afterward?"

Livvie groaned. "No." She was using her full voice now.

"No?"

"No, I was imagining us doing other things."

"Say it," he demanded.

Livvie shook her head. There was no way she would tell him what she had imagined when she'd masturbated. She wouldn't give him the satisfaction. If he ripped up the pages, then so be it. She refused to tell him intimate details when he was acting like a dick.

Drake's eyes became more intense. More dangerous. "Olivia, you had the courage to come up here yet you don't have the courage to tell me how you touched yourself?"

Livvie's heartbeat sped up even more.

He stepped closer to her and gently touched her hair and then her cheek.

Livvie stood completely still. "Because you're acting like an asshole," she whispered.

"Am I?"

Gracefully, his hand slid down her body, and Livvie remained immobilized.

"What are you so afraid of?" he whispered as he slid his hand under her dress and moved her panties aside.

"I'm not afraid. I'm mad at you."

Drake chuckled, while moving his finger inside her vagina. Her body couldn't resist him. All of her most intimate, sensitive spots were craving his attention. She was soaking wet. She knew it, and now, so did he. Her secret was out of the bag.

When Drake removed his fingers, he didn't say anything. Without words, he placed his fingers that had been deep inside her into his mouth and sinfully licked and sucked them clean.

Livvie clenched her vagina. She felt exposed, too exposed, and at the same time, she was more frustrated than ever. "Drake."

He smirked. "Yes, princess?"

She felt so on edge that she couldn't speak. Why did this man have to drive her so crazy? She hated that she couldn't get him out of her system. And she hated that she wanted him so much, and she didn't know how to tell him without making her look like one of his floozy women. Maybe she hadn't learned her lesson yet.

"Why are you so afraid to tell me what you want? What you need, like a drug?"

Drake knew what she needed. But as much as she wanted him, this felt wrong. She wasn't feeling any love from him. When he came to the cottage, he had admitted he missed her. But she wanted more. She would always want more from this stubborn, infuriating man.

"I'm surprised that such a talented writer is having trouble putting words together," Drake said with a twinkle in his eye.

"I can speak," she said quietly.

"I know you can speak, but instead of telling me what you want right this minute, you're choosing to hide your words."

"It doesn't matter how I feel," Livvie said. Her body was still pulsing, but she had to get herself together and be in control again.

"Look at you. Your eyes are dilated. Your body is trembling. Your heartbeat is so loud that I'm sure everyone in my castle can hear it. Your skin is flushed. Your nipples are hard. And I'm sure your pussy is still dripping wet. Yet you can't, or rather you won't, tell me how badly you want me." Drake paused. "But I can tell you. I want you all day and all night. I think about your sinful lips, those same sinful lips that sucked my cock so beautifully. I think about your delicious pussy that tastes better than anything my cook and baker combined can make. I think about your breathtaking blue eyes looking at me as if I'm the most incredible man in the world. I think about caressing your long, dark hair and pulling it hard, causing you to moan, which is the most intoxicating sound I've ever heard. But that's not all I think about. I think about your laugh that makes me want to laugh. I think about your smile that lights up the room. I think about all of our conversations we've ever had, especially out in my vineyard and on the rooftop. I think about how I like to give you orders, and how much I love watching you obey them. But mainly, I think about how extraordinary you are, and I question if I have it in me to love such an extraordinary woman." Drake stared at her for a moment and then handed her back the pages.

Livvie stood there, still speechless. This was what she had wanted to hear. This was what she'd been dying to hear. Almost. He still hadn't told her he loved her.

From the look in his eyes, he was waiting for her to respond, but she had no idea what to say.

Drake stared at her for a moment, nodded, and then walked away.

"Drake!" she yelled.

He didn't say he loved her, but he still used the word. That had to mean something. Drake turned around and looked at her with those beautiful eyes.

"Am I a challenge to you, Olivia?"

"What? No," she whispered. "Why would you think that?"

"Because of your past," he said. "Every night for the last six weeks, I'd lie in bed, wondering why you want to be with me. I've never promised you anything. I've never offered you the life you want. And then it hit me. I'm a challenge to you."

"Drake, that's not true."

"Isn't it? Your two biggest relationships ended because they had cheated. I think you want me because the others have left you."

"That's not why I want you." Livvie had no idea where this was coming from.

"Hear me out. Liam and Zach taught you not to trust men. Therefore, you don't trust me."

"You haven't given me any reason to," she cried.

"Haven't I? When you stayed here that week, I didn't make love to you until you wanted it. I flew down to Los Angeles when I thought Zach was harming you. I got the pictures and video of us off the Internet. I did that for you, Olivia. I was there for you when you spoke about Liam," he continued. "If you trusted me, you would have had the decency to call me and tell me you were writing my mother's book. And if you asked me if you could stay here, of course, I would have said yes."

"You don't want to commit to me. You left me in Los Angeles." A tear slid down Livvie's face.

Drake sighed. "I wanted to stay. You have no idea how hard that was for me. Every single night since I left I imagined another man touching you. A man who wasn't me. Do you know how crazy that's made me? I left you because my vineyard needed me more than you did. I was giving you time to heal, but not only from me. Zach said some pretty harsh words to you. I thought I'd give you space to write and get back to yourself. I planned on seeing you again, but not like this. I'm afraid to commit, but you want a guarantee. You want me to take a leap of faith and then you want to lock me into a future."

Livvie threw her hands up in the air. "What do you want me to do? What do you want from me?"

"I *wanted* you to let me know you were coming here," he said. "What do I want from you now? I want you to trust me as a friend and as a lover. Only then would I consider taking a leap of faith with you." Drake didn't say any more. He turned and walked out of the entrance hall.

Livvie stood there alone again. She didn't trust him, because he wouldn't commit to her. But what if Drake was right? What if she couldn't trust any man? If she started dating someone else, would she always worry he'd leave her? Probably. Maybe she was hopeless. Or maybe she should take baby steps. It sounded as if Drake had done just that. Maybe if she put his commitment issues aside and trusted him the way she trusted Carly or her parents, their future would work itself out its own. However it was meant to be. Or maybe she should have written Veronica's book somewhere else and never have come to Drake's home in the first place.

Livvie put the chapters and contract on the table. Then she walked out of Drake's house and back to the cottage. She had some serious soul-searching to do.

26

LIVVIE PACED BACK and forth in the small cottage. He hadn't given her any reason to trust him. She was attracted to him more than she had ever been attracted to any other man. He was hot, and she loved his dominating nature. She loved when he gave her orders and how his eyes changed according to his mood. She loved how intelligent he was and how he mentally stimulated her. She loved how she could talk about any subject with him, and he'd listen. But she didn't trust him. And why would she? He hadn't earned it. And both Liam and Zach had taught her that a man had to earn a woman's trust. She never should have trusted either of them. And how could she trust Drake if he never wanted anything real with her?

Livvie sighed. These were questions she should be asking him. And if he answered them the way she wanted, would she suddenly be able to trust him? She honestly wasn't sure. He never told her he'd commit to her. Every man was not Liam and Zach.

And it wasn't fair of her to put Drake in that category. Yes, he had his issues, but so did she. So did everyone.

Livvie stopped pacing like a maniac and sat in the comfy chair. She grabbed her cellphone and debated if she should text Drake and ask him the question that had been looming in her mind for a few weeks now, or if she should ask him in person. But every time she physically saw him, all she could think about was sex. Texting was the way to go.

Hi, Drake. It's me.

She waited, practically begging the phone for Drake to respond. After the way he had left her standing in the entrance hall, she wasn't sure he would answer. But then she saw the three dots, which implied he was typing. She sighed with relief.

Yes?? He responded.

Well, he wasn't being warm and fuzzy, but at least he wasn't ignoring her. Her fingers trembled while touching the keys. She had to ask him. It was crucial. She took a deep breath and then typed.

I saw you on the cover of a magazine with some blonde. Have you been with a woman since our expiration date?

There, she had sent it. It was a stupid question, since they weren't sleeping together then, but it would make a difference. It would mean he was over her, and everything he had said today was a lie. When she saw the dots on her phone again, she froze, awaiting his answer.

Her name is Brittany. She's been my go-to fuck for the last few years. But I didn't fuck her. I tried, but I couldn't.

What did he mean by that?

Because of me?

She immediately got a response.

Yes.

Livvie kept her fingers on the phone. She wanted to ask him more, but texting was the easy way out. She really wanted to tell him she was willing to trust him. So when she saw Drake was typing, the nerves in her stomach were going crazy.

Anything else? I can feel your mind thinking.

Livvie laughed. *No. I'm good. Thank you.*

She put down the phone and stared at her hands. Maybe coming here wasn't such a good idea. Maybe she could never trust him, and he would never want a real relationship. Livvie looked at the beautiful cottage she was staying in. She wanted to trust him. She really did. And he hadn't been with Brittany. *Because of me...*

Livvie sighed. Maybe she should go back to Los Angeles and write Veronica's story from there. She picked up the phone to call her, but it went to voicemail. Why wasn't she answering? Livvie groaned out of frustration. She was too stuck in her head, analyzing her life, and it was driving her crazy. With Veronica not answering her phone, there was only one thing left to do to calm herself down and think more clearly.

So she ran upstairs and opened her night table drawer. She pulled out her journal—the one with the story she was writing about Blake and Haley. Just one more scene to write. How should they end? Happy ever after or break up forever?

She sat on the bed and leaned against the headboard. Grabbing the pen Drake had given her, she started to write her idea of the perfect ending.

Haley had her bags packed, and she was rolling them out of the cabin.

"So that's it? You're leaving without saying goodbye?" Blake was walking up from the lake when he saw her. His expression was grim.

She'd hurt him. She could see it in his beautiful eyes, but she was hurting, too.

"You said we'd be together for the week, and then that's it. We were through. Done."

Blake ran his hands through his hair. "But that was before I fell in love with you."

A tear slid down Haley's face. "You're leaving, too, Blake. You have a full life in Raleigh, and I have a full life in New York. How are we ever going to work?"

Blake ran up to her and grabbed her shoulders. She could feel her entire body heat up from his touch. She wanted him, and she was about to leave. It didn't make sense. None of this made sense.

"Do you trust me?" he asked.

Haley looked deep into his eyes. He had told her that after this week, they wouldn't be together, and now he seemed to have changed his mind.

"Do you want us to be together still? Have a long-distance relationship?" she asked him.

Another tear slid down her cheek, and Blake caught it with his thumb and placed it in his mouth, which was almost as intimate as when they made love.

"You didn't answer me. Do you trust me?"

She didn't even have to think a minute before she answered. "I trust you with my life," she said softly.

Blake grabbed her and held her as if their lives depended on it. She didn't want to lose him. She loved him so much.

"Then we will make this work." He kissed her head and held her tighter.

"How?" she whispered. Long-distance relationships worked at the beginning, but in her experience, as time went on, it became more difficult.

He stopped hugging her but grabbed her hands instead. "Marry me."

"Marry you?"

"Marry me. Move to Raleigh. I have plenty of money to support us."

"Why won't you move to New York?"

His eyes became more intense as he looked at her.

"If you want to stay in New York, I will. Just marry me, and I'll move tomorrow."

"You will?" she whispered again.

"Yes, I love you."

Haley thought about it. She hated New York. Living in Manhattan wasn't easy, and the winters were awful. And she had loved this week at the cabin with open spaces and clean air. But most of all, she loved Blake.

"I'd rather move to North Carolina. So yes, I'll marry you."

She watched the tension leave Blake's face but not completely.

"But do you trust me? Do you trust that I'll always be there for you, no matter what? Do you trust how much I love you? I promise you I'll do my best to never hurt you. At times I will, unintentionally, but if we communicate with each other, we'll always work through it."

Haley grabbed the sides of his face and gave him a kiss.

"Yes, Blake. I trust you with my life."

Blake looked at her with intense love. Then he picked her up and kissed her with passion, and most of all with love. Nothing in life was ever a guarantee, but Haley was convinced that their love could survive anything.

Livvie put down the pen as tears flowed down her cheeks. She wanted to have the courage Haley had. And she wanted Drake to be like Blake and do whatever it took to be with her.

Exhausted, Livvie leaned back and closed her eyes. Maybe she would get her happy ending, too. But before she succumbed to sleep, she opened her eyes and looked at Drake's bedroom window in his castle.

"I love you, Drake. I really do." She closed her eyes again and heard her journal fall onto the floor. She would pick it up later, and maybe then she'd put her fears behind her and tell Drake that if he took a leap of faith, she would trust him.

27

WHEN LIVVIE HEARD the key jiggling in the lock on her front door this time, not only was she prepared, but she also knew who it was. She quickly got out of bed, opened her dresser drawer, and changed into her favorite navy-blue silk tank top, and grabbed her favorite skinny jeans. Then she heard Drake scream her name.

"*Olivia*, I know you're here. If you don't come down in one second, I'm coming up." Drake continued to yell.

"Coming," she shouted back. Livvie inhaled and closed her eyes. Whatever he was about to say, she needed to be prepared. She only hoped that once he left, her heart wouldn't have another scar on it, even deeper and darker than the others.

"*Olivia!*"

Livvie's eyes shot open, and she cleared her throat. She started walking toward the steps when she noticed she was barefoot. Oh well, she liked being barefoot. It made her feel more grounded.

"I'm coming, asshole," Livvie said somewhat under her breath.

But when she reached the bottom step, she stood staring at the most beautiful man she'd ever seen. He was wearing jeans and a dark-green polo shirt, which made his olive complexion stand out more. His stomach was flat, but his muscles seemed to have gotten bigger. And his eyes were intoxicating as he stared at her as if she was the sexiest woman in the world.

If he was going to throw her out, she hoped she could tell him how she felt first. As she walked down the last step and moved toward him she felt as if she was facing a demon and an angel wrapped into one. Both of them combined were going to make her confess her deepest and darkest sins.

"I'm here," she said softly.

Without missing a beat, he spoke in that dark tone she had become addicted to.

"Did you just call me an asshole?"

"Yes." Livvie had to bite her bottom lip to stop from laughing.

"Why?" Drake honestly looked surprised.

"Why what?"

"Why did you call me an asshole?"

"Because you are." The tension in the room rose. Livvie regretted saying that. He was arrogant, but he was never an asshole to her.

Drake ran his hands through his hair and walked away from her. He paced around her living room and stopped when he reached the empty fireplace. Then he leaned against the stone wall, crossed his arms, and looked at her.

"Do you really believe that?" His tone and demeanor had changed. His body was tense, even though he tried to appear casual, and his tone was warm, even though he looked as if she had hurt him.

She took a deep breath. "No. Sometimes your words hurt me though."

He nodded as if he understood. "Or maybe my words, which I speak from a place of truth, aren't the words you want to hear."

Livvie swallowed hard. "You're right."

Drake nodded. "And maybe the words I've spoken don't fulfill your needs."

"They don't," Livvie instantly said.

"Then maybe I'm not the right man for you."

Livvie chest tightened. "There are so many reasons you're not and so many reasons you are."

Drake continued to stare at her with no expression. Livvie wished she could read his mind.

"Obviously," Drake said while continuing to stare at her.

"What does that mean?" Livvie asked. She hated standing there with nothing to do with her hands and her feet, but she didn't feel comfortable enough to sit.

"You want it all, and I've never given my all."

Livvie blinked, unsure of where he was heading. "But it seemed from what you said earlier that there's a chance for us."

"Have you thought about what I told you?"

"I'm still processing." Livvie's heart beat wildly.

Drake nodded. "So do you trust me, Olivia?"

"I want to try," she whispered. It was funny that earlier Blake had asked Haley the same thing.

Drake smirked. "There's no trying. You either trust me or you don't."

Livvie wanted to cry, but she couldn't. At this point in her Blake and Haley story, he had proposed marriage to her. Drake wasn't even close. Still, she had a battle to fight. "But you need to earn it, Drake. You can't expect me to trust you if I'm constantly thinking you're going to leave me."

"I'm not Liam or Zach." Drake's eyes remained fixed on hers.

Tears welled up in her eyes, but she blinked them away. She had to stay strong.

"And I'm not one of your famous actresses or models."

Drake's eyebrow rose.

Livvie swallowed. "Why are you here, Drake?"

Without blinking an eye, he responded. "Because of the texts you sent me earlier. You were in your head. And knowing you the way that I do, I know that's a dangerous place for you to be."

She looked down her hands. "I only asked you about the woman I saw on the magazine cover."

Drake smiled softly. "But you wanted to ask me so much more, and you didn't."

Livvie nodded, but she felt as if he wasn't telling her the whole truth.

"Why else are you here?"

"To negotiate with you."

"Why? I thought you didn't negotiate. I thought you always got what you wanted."

Drake nodded and then smirked. "I want you, but you have trust issues."

"And I want you, but you're not willing to have a real relationship with me."

"Which is why we're negotiating."

She bit her bottom lip. "How?"

Drake paused, and his eyes darkened "Come here." With the crook of his finger he motioned for her to come.

Livvie anxiously walked toward him. She was clenching and unclenching her hands unconsciously, and only noticed when her nails dug into her palm too deeply.

When she stood a foot away from him, she stopped. Drake had other plans because he grabbed her, picked her up, and pushed her against the stone wall. It hurt her bare arms, but she didn't care. Her body was pulsing so strongly that she could barely feel the pain. She wrapped her legs around him, and he pushed into her even closer.

"I want you, Olivia. I want you so fucking much. You're the hottest fucking woman I've ever seen." He pressed his lips against hers and seductively moved them. But the moment the kiss intensified, he pulled back and looked her straight in the eye.

"So you see, we have a problem. And I've figured out a solution."

Livvie smiled. She couldn't help herself. "What happened to us negotiating?"

Drake's answer was to move his hand under her tank top until he found her hard nipple. He moved her bra up, so he could get better access, and then he pulled her nipple and circled it in between his fingers. It felt so good that Livvie moaned.

"So this is what I'm thinking." He continued the torture on her nipple and then moved to her other one. "You stay here, in my cottage, for the remainder of the time it takes to finish writing my mother's book, which I assume will be at least a month. And we will fuck. In your bedroom. In mine. In the vineyard. Wherever I fucking want. And if you don't want to stay in my guest cottage, you can have the room next to mine, the room you stayed in when you came for the week." He moved away from her nipples and began to unzip her jeans.

Livvie's vagina clenched. She had to think clearly, but she didn't want Drake to stop.

"Drake, that's not really negotiating. You're giving us an expiration date."

Drake moved his hand inside her jeans and pressed firmly against her wet crotch, leaving her panties as the only barrier of protection.

"You're wrong." He pressed his hand even firmer.

She grabbed his shoulders and pulled her chest back, trying to create a little distance between them.

"I'm right. After I'm done writing the book, we'll be finished, too."

"We can see what happens after that. See what the universe has in store for us."

Livvie dropped her legs and pushed him away, forcing his hand to leave her pussy. And then she stepped away from him. Not far but enough so she could think.

"How can you expect me to trust you if we're going to wait and 'see what happens'?"

She tried to say the last part in his dominating tone.

Drake ran his hands through his hair. "I can't promise you anything."

"But you'll try," she said in a lot stronger voice than she felt.

He nodded. "Yes, I'll try. But you're trying to lock me into a future."

"I see." Livvie paused. "Then how is that any different from me trying to trust you?"

"Because we'll be making each other feel good. I'll make you come more than you could ever have imagined."

Livvie rolled her eyes. "That's exactly what a normal man would say. And yet I thought you were extraordinary. I thought you were the one man I could learn to trust, and that the love I feel for you was returned." She blurted the words without really thinking, but she did love him. He was offering her nothing but fucking without a real relationship, and she wanted everything. They both couldn't try. They had to be all in for this to work.

Drake stormed to her door. Livvie stood there dumbfounded. She had just told him she loved him, and he wanted to leave her like this.

"What happened to our negotiations?" she said with a desperate tone as his hand was on the doorknob. *Please don't leave. Please don't leave,* she repeated over and over in her head.

He opened the door but he stopped before he walked out without even turning around to look at her.

"They stopped the minute you said you loved me."

And then he walked out and slammed the door behind him. Livvie stood there stunned. What was she supposed to do now? She ran to her door and opened it, but he was long gone. He wanted her, but he wasn't willing to love her. And that was the answer she had been looking for when she came here. Unfortunately, it wasn't the one she wanted, nor was it her idea of the perfect ending.

28

HOURS LATER, LIVVIE knew what she needed to do. She wasn't happy about it, but what choice did she have? Once again she was at a crossroads. Either road she took would lead to heartbreak.

She could sleep with Drake for the next month. She may even be able to stretch it out a little longer, but then what would happen? They would try the long-distance thing. But if no commitment were made, they would soon die out. What was the use in trusting him if he wasn't going to be part of her life anyway? And God knew what he was thinking since she'd blurted out that she loved him.

Livvie sighed. Once again, she had to choose between Plan A or Plan B. Plan A had so many more possibilities. It wasn't as if she was expecting Drake to marry her, but if he would commit to making them work, she could move out of Los Angeles. She didn't need to be there to write novels. She could move to Napa, rent a small house, and not have a long-distance relationship with him at all. The possibilities were endless.

Instead, Livvie stared at her phone sitting on the coffee table. It wouldn't be fair to call Veronica. She had been so supportive and kind. Livvie needed to tell her in person. And if that meant having to go up to the castle again, she would.

With her decision made, she ran to the castle, holding her head up high.

But this time when she entered, Mr. Birkshire wasn't there to greet her. The energy in the castle felt different. Less warm. More intimidating. She had felt safe for the week she had stayed here, and now she felt the complete opposite.

"You're only here for one of two reasons. You either want to clobber my son, or you want to tell me you're leaving."

Livvie opened her mouth and then closed it. Veronica sighed dramatically.

"Come, my dear. Let's sit on the couch and talk."

Livvie followed her to the living room, and they sat on opposite ends of the large, brown leather couch.

"Okay, out with it." Veronica scooted closer to Livvie and grabbed her hand.

Livvie was thinking of a way to tell Veronica that she had to leave without insulting her son.

"I think I should finish your book at my house in Los Angeles. I think it'll be easier." There, she'd said it.

Veronica smiled. "Of course it would be *easier*, Livvie."

Livvie swallowed. "So...you're okay with it?"

Veronica laughed. "It's not for me to be okay with or not to be okay with. It's up to you." Veronica paused and squeezed Livvie's hand. "But in my opinion, brilliant women like us should never do what's easier. We should fight for what's rightfully ours."

Livvie looked down at their joined hands. Veronica was not letting her off the hook as Livvie had hoped.

"Drake wants to be with me, but he gave us another expiration date."

Veronica laughed again. "Of course he did, my dear. Because that's what's easier for him." She gently brushed Livvie's hair away from her eye. "Let me tell you something. Love isn't easy. I've learned that lesson. But if you love someone, you have to choose not what is best for you, but what's best for the both of you."

"I understand, but he's asking me to give him my heart and soul for as long as I'm writing your book, and he said that at that point, we'll see what happens."

Veronica nodded. "And how do you think he'll be at the end of the month, after the two of you have had the chance to bond more? Do you think he'll be able to let you go?"

"He did last time."

She squeezed her hand again. "I disagree. When he thought Zach was stalking you and giving you a hard time, he left his precious vineyard and flew down to rescue you."

"But then he left," Livvie chimed in.

"But he wasn't actually done with you like he said he would be at the end of the week."

Livvie thought about that. "No, he wasn't."

"So how do you think he'll be at the end of the month or at the end of three months, even? A lot has happened in my life, Livvie, and, frankly, I don't think one month will be enough."

Livvie exhaled. "So what are you saying?"

"I'm saying that if I were you, I wouldn't take the easy way out. If you truly love my son, I suggest you fight for him. I wouldn't be a coward and leave if I were you."

"He wants me to trust him."

"Then trust him."

"But I'm scared," Livvie blurted out.

"Of course you are. But are you going to allow fear to dictate your life? Are you going to allow Zach and Liam to ruin your love life?"

Livvie had never thought about it that way, but Veronica was right. Zach and Liam were both in her past. Livvie deserved to have a fresh start. She inhaled deeply and leaped into Veronica's arms, giving her a huge hug.

"Thank you, Veronica." Because of her, Livvie was choosing Plan A. And wasn't that what her heart had wanted all along?

Veronica hugged Livvie back and then left her on the couch to contemplate her next move. But before Livvie told Drake she would accept his so-called negotiations that were hopefully still on the table, there was a certain room in his house she needed to see.

Walking up the grand staircase felt surreal. It was amazing to think that two months ago she had walked up these steps, pretending this was her home. At the time, she knew it was an illusion but a beautiful one.

As she walked down the hallway leading to her old room, she stared straight ahead at Drake's bedroom door. She walked extra quietly in case he was inside. It would feel extremely awkward if he happened to come out of his bedroom. She wasn't sure why she felt the need to see where she had stayed that week. She simply knew she had to. So she decided to trust her intuition.

When she reached the closed door, she gently turned the knob to see if it was locked. She assumed it would be, but the knob turned. Her heart beat wildly as she slowly opened the door.

"I was wondering when you'd make it up here."

On hearing Drake's voice, Livvie jumped and gasped at the same time.

"Drake, you scared me half to death."

"I can see that."

Drake was standing by the window, facing her and looking as gorgeous as ever. He had changed into a black polo shirt and a pair of darker jeans. His arm muscles looked so good she wanted to bite them. But then she remembered she was technically trespassing on private property.

"I'm sorry. I'll leave."

Drake took a step toward her. Luckily, there was still plenty of room between them. She couldn't think when he was near. She couldn't breathe, either. Maybe she shouldn't have trusted her intuition after all.

"Please, you don't have to leave on my account."

Livvie nodded. "Okay, I'll stay then." She agreed only because if she left, she'd look like a coward. And those days were gone.

Drake turned away and looked back out of the window, which overlooked his magnificent vineyard.

"Is there a reason you're here?" he asked, still not looking at her.

"I missed this room, I guess. And I felt an incredible need to see it."

"For one last time?"

He still wasn't facing her, which made her feel uneasy. At least if he faced her, she could see his eyes and gage what he was thinking.

"No, Drake. Not for one last time." She inhaled deeply and closed her eyes briefly. When she opened them again, she spoke. "I want to accept your offer, if it's still on the table."

Drake turned around so quickly her breath caught in her throat. She stared into his hypnotic eyes, hoping for some answers, but the intensity she saw was too much for her to take in. A feeling of emotional exhaustion consumed her. The feeling was so strong that she walked over to the lavender and white bed she'd slept in two months ago and sat down on the edge of it.

"Why?" Drake asked.

Livvie took a deep breath. His power, which radiated off of him in waves, surrounded her and engulfed her, trapping her. She gripped onto the edge of the bed, hoping it would help keep her steady and emotionally balanced. Who was she kidding? Feeling steady and balanced in a room with

Drake Morganthal wasn't an option. He had asked her a question, and he expected an answer. No, he had demanded one.

Livvie inhaled. "Because I love you."

Drake exhaled. "And you believe love is enough to sustain a relationship?"

Livvie ran her hands through her hair and turned her head away from him, looking anywhere in the room but at him. He was right. Her love wasn't enough because he didn't love her back. It hurt when Zach had told her he didn't love her, but Drake not loving her back put hurt into a different category altogether.

"I wouldn't know." Livvie swallowed hard and turned her head back in his direction. "I've only felt this way with you. And it feels enough to me."

Drake raised his eyebrow.

"What about Liam and Zach? You loved them, too."

So he was jealous. And that alone was the confirmation she needed to take this risk.

"I did, but not to the degree I feel for you." Speaking her truth was harder than she thought, and she had only scratched the surface.

"Then why are you stooping so low as to sleep with me for a minimum of a month when I'm not guaranteeing you a future?" Drake asked.

Livvie clasped her hands in her lap and began telling her story of what she'd been through without him for the last six weeks. This was the best way to answer his questions.

"When you left my house six weeks ago, not even an hour later, I received a visit from Stephan

Brenson." Livvie watched Drake clench his jaw as anger filled his dark-green eyes.

"I'll kill him," he said.

Livvie smiled. "You'll do no such thing. Nothing happened. He wanted to start something with me, but I told him my heart was still with you."

"Good," Drake said in the dominant tone she loved.

"He told me I should fight for you."

Drake raised his eyebrow. "And then you called my mother."

Livvie looked down at her clasped hands. "I called your mom, yes, but it wasn't like that. She'd always wanted help writing her memoirs, and I wanted you. She told me to give it six weeks and then call her back. I used that time to find happiness within myself again, but that's not the story I'm trying to tell you." If Drake were going to act self-righteous and arrogant, what she was trying to get across to him wouldn't work.

Drake nodded. "Go on."

"I missed you terribly." Livvie inhaled deeply. It wasn't easy, feeling raw and vulnerable in front of another human being, especially with a man she didn't want to lose.

"Olivia, if you're trying to legitimately fight for us, you have to tell me what's going on in your mind." He uncrossed and then crossed his arms again.

"Can you at least sit down?" She needed him to be at her level, and right now she didn't think she could stand.

"No."

And with that one word, Livvie understood what was going on in his mind. He didn't want to go down to her level. He wanted her to meet him at his. Even though what Drake had negotiated with her earlier was far from a guarantee, he wasn't giving them an expiration date like the last time. For him, that was a huge step. And now it was her turn.

"My novel is about a woman named Haley, from New York, who rented a cabin in the woods for a week. When she arrived at the cabin, she found that the travel agent had double booked the cabin. A man named Blake was staying there. Since they were both supposed to stay for the week and neither of them wanted to leave, they agreed to stay together."

"They stayed together for one week? Sounds familiar," Drake chimed in.

Livvie continued to tell the story as if he hadn't interrupted her. She had to get it all out before she lost her courage. "At the beginning, they fought a lot, but then they fell in love." Livvie paused and looked Drake straight in the eye. "I wrote the first fifty pages or so the week I stayed here. I wrote it in the journal you gave me. Once I was back in Los Angeles and thought you were out of my life for good, I switched to a journal I already had. I wanted a fresh start without a man. You saw that journal. Remember?"

Drake nodded. Then she continued.

"When you left me at my house in LA, I continued to write in my old journal. At this point, Haley and Blake were falling in love. But once they fell in love, I could no longer get the chapters to flow. No matter how hard I tried, something wasn't working. And then I picked up the journal you gave me, and my writing changed, and the novel became better. Their intimacy felt real. That's when I knew what I felt for you was stronger than anything I've felt before. Like the characters in my novel, my love for you was real. It felt right. And it terrified me, because you left me and didn't return my feelings. At the same time, I refused to give up on us." Livvie stopped talking. She was having a hard time reading Drake, and she felt foolish having revealed her heart to him. Her heart had bled in front of his eyes, and he was taking his time responding.

"How did the story end?" he finally asked.

Livvie exhaled. "Their week was over, and Haley was packing up her rental car. Blake had returned from a swim and saw her about to leave. He asked her why she was leaving, and she told him their week was up." Livvie paused as she swallowed back the tears. "Then he asked her if she trusted him."

"What did she tell him?"

Drake uncrossed his arms and put his hands in his pockets. He wanted to appear casual. Livvie knew better.

"She told him she did."

"Of course she did," Drake said a little too arrogantly.

"But then he said he'd do anything to make them work. She could move to Raleigh, where he lived, or he would move to New York where she lived. And then he proposed."

Drake cleared his throat. "Did he agree to move to New York?"

Livvie shook her head. "No, she wanted to move to him. But my point is, he was willing to do whatever it took to be with her."

"And I'm not," Drake interrupted.

"That's not what I'm saying. I'm trying to explain what has been going on in my head since you left me in Los Angeles." Livvie felt her cheeks flush and not from blushing. She loved Drake even when he was infuriating. "I've heard that writers write from their subconscious mind. I think I'm both Blake and Haley."

"Then who am I?" Drake interrupted again.

Livvie groaned. "You're the asshole I'm telling the story to."

Drake didn't respond. Instead, he smirked, which irritated her more than she let on. She couldn't let his reaction to her story stop her from getting her point across.

"I want to trust you, Drake, and I want to do whatever it takes to make us work. You may not love me the way Blake loves Haley, but something about us feels right, like writing in the journal you got me." Livvie blinked back tears, hoping it would stop them from spilling.

Drake stood up straighter and glared down at her. Livvie gripped the sides of the bed again, preparing herself for the worst.

"I never said I didn't love you, Olivia. The problem is I love you too much." Without waiting for her to respond, Drake stormed out of the bedroom.

That was okay. She couldn't think of a brilliant response. Because no matter how hard she gripped the bed, nothing could have prepared her for Drake finally admitting he loved her. Nothing at all.

Until what he said sank in.

Livvie took a deep breath and then stormed out of the room after him. She heard his footsteps walking down the stairs. Livvie ran until she was standing on the landing while he was already downstairs with his hand on the knob of the front door.

"Is that the best you could do?" Livvie said loud enough for him to hear even as she was trying to catch her breath.

Drake turned around. "You want me to be Blake." His tone was stern, dark, and unnecessarily accusatory.

"I don't want you to be Blake. I told you *I'm* Blake. I want you to be yourself," she said through clenched teeth.

Drake ran his hands through his hair. "Well, I want to be Blake."

It took a moment for Livvie to register what he was saying. "So be Blake." Livvie slowly walked down the stairs. She kept eye contact with Drake until she was a few feet away from him. Then it became too hard. So instead she looked past him, out the front window.

"I won't accept what we negotiated," he said.

Livvie panicked and brought her attention right back to him. Her heart felt as if someone had punched it.

"Why?" she whispered.

She watched Drake clench his jaw.

"Because I hated the deal I came up with."

"I don't understand," she whispered.

His eyes became a shade darker. "Do you trust me?"

Livvie trembled. She didn't know what he was getting at, but like Haley, her answer was important. "I trust our connection. I trust what we have, and I trust that I love you. Everything else will fall into place."

"But you're scared I'll hurt you."

That wasn't what she'd have Blake say, but she still had to speak her truth.

"Yes." Even though he'd said it as a statement she answered him anyway.

"Then can't you see that what I negotiated with you can't work? You're scared I'll hurt you, and I'm terrified of seeing the same look in your eyes that I always saw in my mother's."

Livvie prayed she wouldn't have a panic attack.

"So you'd rather not have anything with me then?"

Drake fisted his hands. "No, I'm saying we need to renegotiate."

Livvie could handle that. "Okay."

Drake stared at her for what seemed like forever before he finally spoke. "But not now."

Livvie's heart sank. "Why?"

Drake placed his hand on the doorknob and opened the door.

"Because I need to put myself in Blake's shoes."

Technically, he was in Blake's shoes, but Livvie didn't want to stress that point. Before he walked outside, she grabbed his arm.

"But I told you, I'm Blake." She sounded desperate, and she was.

Drake looked at her hard as he removed her hand from his arm.

"A part of you may be Blake, but another part of you wants a man to step up and be like him."

"But I wrote him," she said.

Drake opened the door a little more and smiled softly at her. "Then you should have also written his evil twin."

Livvie wrinkled her forehead. "I don't like books about evil twins."

"But then I'd have had a character that would be easy to emulate. You raised the bar high by creating Blake."

"Drake," Livvie pleaded. "You're not Blake."

Drake chuckled. "I want to be. Please, Olivia, let me be him. Blake doesn't have the issues I have. And maybe knowing that makes what I'm about to do easier." Drake turned around to leave.

"What are you going to do?" Livvie asked before he stepped out.

Drake responded but kept his back toward her.

"Something I should have done six weeks ago." Drake walked out the door. Then he turned back to her. "Wait in the living room for me, Olivia. Please don't go back to the cottage and pack your things."

"Haley would have left."

"But Blake stopped her, and I'm stopping you now. Wait for me in the living room, and then we'll renegotiate."

Drake turned and resumed walking. It looked as if he was heading to the garage. In his tone, he wasn't asking her to stay. He was demanding she stay. Livvie would wait, regardless. She was trembling so hard she didn't think she could walk all the way back to her cottage anyway. So instead, she closed the door and walked into the living room. She lay down on the couch and closed her eyes, not caring if anyone came into the room to see her like this. Haley would have waited for Blake like this. In her story, she may have been packing to leave, but she saw him step out of the lake and walk toward her. Blake was worth it, and Livvie knew without a doubt that Drake was worth waiting for, too.

Haley would have been much more patient than Livvie. She'd dozed off on the couch for the first hour or so, but now she was pacing back and forth like a crazy person. What was taking Drake so long? If she were writing the scene, she would have had Blake return a long time ago. Mr. Birkshire had stopped in a half hour ago, looked at her expression, and had walked back out. Smart man. She'd seen him walk upstairs. He'd probably gone to tell Veronica to stay away.

After another fifteen minutes had passed, Livvie was about to do the one thing Drake had asked her not to do—walk back to her cottage and pack. But then, finally, the front door opened, and Drake stepped inside and walked into the living room.

"Finally," she said, stomping her foot.

Drake smirked. "When I worked on Wall Street and I was negotiating with another party, if one party wasn't happy with the terms, we'd renegotiate. And during that time, new paperwork was drawn up. We could wait days if not weeks for the paperwork to be done. You only had to wait two hours and seventeen minutes. You have no idea how lucky you are."

Livvie placed her hands on her hip. "Are you serious?"

Drake threw his keys on the glass coffee table and sat in the large, brown leather chair next to the couch.

"Yes. I am. Sit." Drake nodded toward the couch.

"Sit?" she asked.

Drake clenched his jaw. "Olivia, if we're going to start the negotiations with you repeating everything I say, we're not going to get anywhere. And we're not leaving this room until we've signed off on a deal."

That she could live with. Livvie sat in the middle of the couch. Not too close to him, but not too far away, either.

"Okay." Drake cleared his throat. "So here's what I came up with. Are you ready?"

Livvie nodded. It was either now or never. Drake leaned forward in the chair with his elbows leaning against his thighs and his fingertips touching like a steeple in a church.

"Good. I'm going to start by going over specific bullet points. Bullet point one: I'd like you to stay here while you're writing my mother's book. Do you agree?"

Livvie swallowed. "Yes, I agree."

Drake nodded. "Bullet point two: Instead of you sleeping in my guest cottage, I'd like you to sleep here in my bedroom with me. Do you agree?"

Livvie's heartbeat sped up. She put her hair behind her ear and sat up straighter.

"Yes, I agree."

"Bullet point three: Once the book is finished, I'd like you to move up here permanently."

Livvie inhaled loudly, and Drake continued.

"Hear me out, Olivia. Your dream is to write novels, and you don't need to stay in Los Angeles to do that. And it's not that I'm unwilling to move there, but my vineyard is here." Drake paused. "Do you agree?"

Tears were blurring her eyes, but she couldn't help bursting out into a smile. "Yes, I agree. I love your vineyard, and I can't imagine living anywhere else with you."

"If you stay with me forever, the vineyard will be yours, too."

Livvie's heart stopped ferociously beating. She unconsciously rubbed her hands up and down her jeans and then wiped the one and only tear that had fallen.

"What are you saying?" she whispered.

Drake stood and pushed the heavy leather chair back. Then he did the one thing Livvie never thought he'd do. He got down on one knee and took out a black box from his pocket. He opened the box, revealing the most beautiful diamond ring she had ever seen.

"Marry me, Olivia. I love you, and the negotiations I came to you with earlier were garbage. Not meant for a beautiful, intelligent, kind, loving woman like you. You deserved so much more than what I was offering you. And it took what you told me about your character Blake for me to realize it'd be foolish to lose the woman I love when there were ways to stop that from happening." Drake paused. "I want to be your Blake, Olivia. I want to give you the world. Besides, you were right. How could you trust me if I didn't earn it? And I can't imagine my life without you. I lived it for six weeks, and I was miserable. Just ask Mr. Birkshire."

Livvie laughed softly. "You don't have to marry me for me to trust you, Drake. I'm willing to agree to your terms and see what happens."

He shook his head. "But I want to marry you. And if you have my mother's look in your eyes from time to time, then we'll talk about it. I realized I didn't want you to see me as Liam or Zach, yet I was seeing you the way I saw my mother when I was growing up. And that wasn't fair."

"You're right," she said quietly.

"So then I thought that in business I'm either all in or I'm nothing. With you I'm choosing to be all in."

"But, Drake, you haven't known me very long. What if you fall out of love with me?"

"Trust me, I won't. I fell in love with you the moment I saw you in my entrance hall, looking all flustered. No, even before that...when my camera caught you on the bottom of my hill, looking up at my castle. You're real, Olivia. You're a gift. You wear your emotions on your sleeve. And you're also beautiful and as sexy as hell." He looked at her deeply. "Will you be all in with me? Will you marry me?"

Livvie didn't need a second to answer. She kneeled down with him and threw herself into his arms. Then she grabbed his face, kissed him on the lips, and looked into his mesmerizing eyes.

"Yes, Drake Morganthal. I agree to your terms."

Drake grabbed her by the back of her head and kissed her hard. But when they heard the sound of clapping, they literally jumped.

"You haven't placed the ring on her finger, darling."

Veronica and Mr. Birkshire were standing by the entrance, both of them beaming. Livvie had to take a second look because Mr. Birkshire was smiling. *Miracles do happen.*

"Mother, how long have you been standing there?" Drake said with a twinkle in his eye.

"Long enough, dear. Now place the ring on her finger."

Drake rolled his eyes, and Livvie laughed. Then he took her hand and placed the beautiful diamond ring on her finger. Finally, it sank in. She was engaged to Drake.

"It's beautiful." She kissed him again. And then she stood and grabbed Drake. She turned toward Mr. Birkshire and Veronica and became serious again. She had no choice. It felt imperative that they hear her out. "Let's keep this between us, if that's okay."

"What do you mean? I want to tell the world," Drake said.

"Well, I'd like to tell my parents and Carly, of course. But I want the next six months to be just about us. The minute this gets out, the media will go nuts."

"She's right, dear," Veronica said.

"I'd have to agree, too. Look at what happened with the pictures and videos from the club," Mr. Birkshire added.

"I don't give a damn about that," Drake yelled.

Livvie blushed. "But I do. I want the world to know you're a trustworthy and decent man. The way the media portrayed you for all of these years was wrong and unfair."

"Olivia, I was a playboy who didn't treat women well."

Livvie hugged him tighter. "But those days are gone."

"You might as well listen to her and get used to it, dear," Veronica chimed in.

Drake exhaled dramatically. "Okay, fine. But six months from today, the word gets out that we're engaged, and three months after that, we get married. Here, at my vineyard. Unless you don't want to."

Livvie laughed. "I'll marry you anywhere." She looked down at her ring, and then she looked into Drake's eyes. But she had one more question.

"Drake, I have a serious question for you, and if you don't answer, I won't marry you." She saw the look in everyone's eyes; they were filled with dread, especially Drake's.

"Ask me anything. I'm an open book with you."

Livvie smiled. "What's Mr. Birkshire's first name?"

She looked at Drake and then at Mr. Birkshire. He was laughing, and so was Veronica, but Drake looked relieved. He glanced at Mr. Birkshire, who nodded.

"Mr. Birkshire's real name is Paul Galliger. But when he gave me this place and came to work for me, he said he wanted to change his name, just as he was changing his life. So he came up with Mr. Birkshire."

"I thought the name sounded snooty and ridiculous enough. It was perfect," Mr. Birkshire said.

Livvie was beaming. "You're all perfect." She hugged Drake and then hugged all of them. This was her idea of a perfect ending, even though her and Drake's story was only just beginning.

Between living her dream as a writer and finding the love of her life, she truly had it all. And all because of a winning raffle ticket. Life was about choices and taking chances. For the first time in Livvie's life, she had succeeded at both. And now, since she thought about it, so had Drake.

Epilogue

AS LIVVIE HELD her three-month-old baby girl in her arms, she smiled. One day, when Haley was older, Livvie would tell her daughter the story about how she met her dad. She hoped Haley would find it as romantic as Livvie did. As she was rocking the sleeping baby in her arms, she looked around at the renovations she'd done to their bedroom. The night they'd agreed to the new terms in their relationship, Drake had demanded that she move in. And she had wanted the same. He'd ordered a moving truck to pack all her things at her house in LA and drive them all here. The room needed more of a feminine feel, so Drake had allowed her to add her special touches. She remembered feeling so nervous, as if it was a test to see if the new terms in their relationship would work. She'd changed all the bedding, and she'd ordered a different dresser. And to her surprise, Drake had loved it. He said that now when he looked around the room, he wouldn't have to remember the lonely times.

They'd waited six months before they told the world they were engaged, which was the right decision. Livvie had made sure in those six months that his PR team put out articles about him being a good guy and not a guy who hurt famous women. Drake didn't care, but Livvie did.

And Drake used those six months to strengthen his security team, which was smart. From the moment the news spread, which was exactly at the six-month mark, there'd been a media frenzy. They parked on the bottom of the hill, and helicopters flew overhead. When they saw all of this, Drake had kissed the top of her head and thanked her. He'd said he was glad they had waited the six months in order to prepare better for this moment. And Livvie understood the need for a bodyguard. They'd received a few letters from people wanting to kidnap her for money. But she felt safe...*Drake* made her feel safe. And when they fought, it wasn't a big deal, because they were both in it for the long haul.

"Hi, beautiful." Drake walked into the bedroom and gently closed the door. He walked over to Livvie and kissed her on the forehead. "My angel is sleeping?"

Livvie smiled. "For now," she said softly.

"Are your parents still coming tomorrow? I think the airports have reopened."

It was snowing hard in New York. Her parents were supposed to have arrived a few days ago, but a blizzard had hit New York. She hoped they would move here. At the wedding, Drake had pulled them aside and had promised to build them a house on his property. There was so much empty land. And the moment her parents met him, they had adored him, but her mom thought it would be smart if she and Livvie's father stayed in New York for the first few years of Livvie's marriage, so she could enjoy her husband without her parents around. Even Veronica stayed away, although Livvie had a feeling she was seeing a new man. In the end, Veronica had decided she didn't want a book to be written about her, as she was afraid of how the media would interpret Drake's childhood. Livvie agreed with her.

Drake began caressing Livvie's hair, which jarred her out of her thoughts.

"Yes, the airport has just opened up, and they're flying out first thing tomorrow."

"Then we'll be able to give them the good news in person."

Livvie looked into Drake's magnificent green eyes. She would never tire of that. "What is it?"

He stopped caressing her hair and took a newspaper out of his back pocket to show it to her.

When she saw the article, she whispered and yelled at the same time.

"Oh, my God." Tears welled up in her eyes when she read that her story of Blake and Haley had made it to the *New York Times* bestsellers list. She'd named her daughter Haley, too, because if it weren't for Drake, the character of Haley never would have been written. And if it weren't for Drake, Haley would never have been born.

Drake bent down to meet her at eye level. He kissed her gently on the lips and then kissed his baby girl, who had the same color green eyes as her daddy did.

"Congratulations, beautiful," he said while kissing Livvie again.

"Thank you so much," she whispered, feeling elated.

Drake's eyes darkened and filled with unmistakable desire.

"Why don't you put our sleepy little girl in her crib, and we can celebrate properly?"

"Naked?" Livvie said innocently.

"Always," Drake said as he gently lifted Haley from Livvie's lap. As he placed her in the crib by their bed, Livvie felt as if she was the luckiest woman in the world. A fact that had been confirmed the day she won the raffle ticket.

Once the baby was sleeping soundly, Drake turned toward her. "Now take off your clothes quickly. I'm going to make you come so hard and so many times that you'll barely remember your name."

Livvie smiled as she drew her tank top over her head. She would always remember her name: Olivia Morganthal.

As Drake became impatient, he pulled up her skirt and ripped off her panties, and she became even luckier.

Get More Romance in Your Inbox

Sign up for Rochelle's newsletter to stay tuned on her latest releases and updates:

www.RochelleKatzman.com/free

AUTHOR'S NOTE

Dear Reader,

Thank you so much for reading about Livvie and Drake. I absolutely loved writing about them.

When I started writing about Livvie, I was remembering all the unavailable men I had dated, even though the male characters are nothing like the men I had been with. And then I thought of my friends who have also dated unavailable men. It's so easy to find them and so challenging to release them. I'm sure most women can relate!

I feel I healed as Livvie healed, so I'd like to thank her for helping me. Hopefully, if you're a woman dating a commitment-phobe, this book has helped you, too.

I would love to hear if Livvie's journey has helped you or if you were able to heal from a past relationship through reading this book! Please, send me an email, and let me know!

My website is:

www.RochelleKatzman.com

Twitter:

twitter.com/RochelleKatzman

Facebook:

www.facebook.com/

RochelleKatzmanAuthor

I can't wait to hear from you!

ACKNOWLEDGEMENTS

WRITING A ROMANCE novel is a huge dream of mine. I'd like to thank the following people who have helped me make it happen. First, I'd like to thank my family for their amazing support, and my mom who listened to me obsess about all the changes I made a week before the book was due in to the publisher. I'd like to thank Jody for reading each chapter and her invaluable critique. Thank you to Keidi Keating, for giving me the confidence to believe in my writing. To Jill N. Noble-Shearer, who is teaching me the craft of writing, to Tom Corson-Knowles, founder of TCK Publishing, who has taken a chance on me. And thank you to my dog, Henry, who has kept me company while I write.

Thank you for making my dream come true!

ABOUT THE AUTHOR

ROCHELLE KATZMAN SPENT her childhood penning stories, and at the age of six, she won two creative writing awards. When she was twenty-two years old, she received her Bachelor of Fine Arts

(BFA) in musical theatre from Syracuse University. Rochelle is also an international yoga instructor and a life coach.

When she's not traveling the world teaching workshops or helping women to achieve their dreams, she's at home writing books. She currently lives in New York, but she'd love to move to a beautiful land filled with ethereal fairies and magical castles. Rochelle enjoys spending time with her dog, Henry, when he's not eating her favorite shoes.

She'd love to hear from her readers!

Here's where you can find her:

www.RochelleKatzman.com

Twitter:

twitter.com/RochelleKatzman

Facebook:

**www.facebook.com/
RochelleKatzmanAuthor**

Get Special Deals on More Best Selling Books

Get discounts and special deals on our best
selling books at
www.tckpublishing.com/bookdeals